THE ART OF SEEING

A NOVEL

CAMMIE MCGOVERN

SCRIBNER

NEW YORK LONDON TORONTO SYDNEY SINGAPORE

SCRIBNER
1230 Avenue of the Americas
New York, NY 10020

SCRIBNER and design are trademarks of
Macmillan Library Reference USA, Inc., used under license
by Simon & Schuster, the publisher of this work.

For information about special discounts for bulk purchases,
please contact Simon & Schuster Special Sales:
1-800-456-6798 or business@simonandschuster.com

Designed by Kyoko Watanabe

Text set in Berthold Garamond

Manufactured in the United States of America

1   3   5   7   9   10   8   6   4   2

Library of Congress Cataloging-in-Publication Data is available.

ISBN 0-7432-2835-9

To my family

"The oldest hath borne most: we that are young,
Shall never see so much, nor live so long."

—William Shakespeare, *King Lear*

PART ONE

WHEN YOU ARE A YOUNGER SISTER, you are born with an eye not on the horizon, but on the hem of a shirt just ahead, the flash of a ponytail whipping side to side. You learn to hold still and trace the movement of another up the street, into a tree, onto a branch that will—you can see it before it happens—give way to a fall that will break her arm so seriously there will be talk of amputation. "They almost chopped it off, and then they didn't," she will say, hacking a line on her cast, triumphantly, already just a little theatrically.

She's good at telling stories, drawing a crowd of neighborhood kids and moving through them, reenacting the fall as if it were all a comedy act. Only you understand how bad it might have been—that an arm is a thing one doesn't easily live without—that you have to be careful, you have to be *still*. You can't just run after some line in the distance and not expect sooner or later to get hit by something: a Mack truck, a tornado, boys playing hockey where they shouldn't.

Your stillness, you believe, holds her back, just enough to keep her alive. There is an invisible cord between you that will break if you do not watch her carefully because you *do* have an effect. Your eyes can stop her, on a street corner, in conversation, in the nick of time. To everyone else you look like the quiet one, but only you know— even in your silence and your stair-sitting ways—you have all the power.

Or you did.

Jemma, 1975

By the second week of kindergarten everyone has adjusted but me. The three girls with the prettiest names—Hayley, Stephanie, and Claire—and the longest, straightest hair have formed a friendship that I watch alone, from the outside. They share secrets and jacks and make rules that everyone else obeys. "No drinking from that water fountain in the morning. No drinking from that fountain ever."

Though I try to be invisible, a complicated process that involves walking without letting my toes touch the inside of my shoes, it is hard. Sometimes, they notice me, even so. Once they announce that because I have worn a purple shirt that day, no one is allowed to talk to me. Usually no one *does* talk to me, but this sounds so final that a wave of terror washes through me and I wet my pants on the spot.

Only I know it has happened because I am sitting in a wooden chair hollowed out for fannies. For the next hour and fifteen minutes, I neither speak nor move. Finally, when a teacher asks if everything is all right, I ask if she could please get my sister. Something in my voice must communicate the urgency because, a few minutes later, Rozzie is standing in front of me, delighted to have been called out from her class. In this room, everyone is younger and watches her and she knows it.

She bends down in front of me, as if she were the mother and has to accommodate an enormous height difference. "What is it?" she says, and I know she is drawing even more attention to herself, that her voice is louder than it needs to be if I am the only person meant to hear. Still, it doesn't matter. I am so grateful to see her, it is all I can do not to cry on the spot and compound my problem.

"I wet my pants," I whisper.

She seems neither put off nor particularly surprised. "Why?" she asks, as if I might have done this for a reason.

"They said my shirt was purple."

"Your shirt *is* purple."

"I didn't know, though. Now no one can talk to me."

She does what I have been waiting for her to do because she is brave like this: she turns around and stares at the group. "Who said that?" she asks. I point to the triumvirate of girls who are in the corner, trading barrettes. She walks over to them. "Did you tell my sister there's something wrong with her shirt?"

They blink up at her, frightened. She is only two years older, but it seems much more. In this moment, she appears capable of doing anything a teacher might do: delivering a lecture, a warning, a time-out. Instead, she stands in front of them, her hands on her hips. "That's pathetic," she says, using a word I know but have never said out loud. "Making something up just to make someone else feel bad is mean and pathetic."

They are more contrite than any punishment would have made them. All three look down. One—Stephanie—starts to cry. In that instant, I love Rozzie more than I have ever loved anyone else my whole life, including my mother. Maybe it will be all right, I think, my stomach loosening, my heart lifting. Rozzie is here.

Later, Rozzie goes out of the room, takes off her own tights, and comes back in. She hands them to me in a tight ball in her fist. As she does this, she leans into my ear. She smells like her shampoo, Clairol Herbal Essence, the way I imagine a jungle must smell.

"Clean the chair with your skirt when you stand up," she whispers. This time no one can see her lips move. I do as she tells me, powerless to her spell. And it works. No one sits in the damp chair and figures out the truth. I've miraculously gotten away with a transgression I was sure I'd be paying for the rest of my life.

After Rozzie's visit, I am transformed, no longer invisible. Other kids make overtures with their paste brushes. ("You need this?" they ask. "Okay," I say.) People share their crayons, pinwheels, toilet paper under stall doors. One girl lets me wear her yarn wig for twenty minutes.

And then one day one of the triumvirate invites me to join their jacks circle at recess. It's Hayley, the same one Rozzie yelled at, and I know it isn't me she wants, but my sister. The scorn has sat with her, festered into a clawing ache, a dark need. I am a pathway to my sister's approval. All I need to do is accept this role, as easy as breathing, forever and ever, amen. And I do.

"Okay," I say, taking the smooth rubber ball in my hand, the spiny metal jacks. I am not good at jacks, but this time is different, I am not myself, not the crybaby who gets homesick an hour into school. I am a bridge—a tangible connection between these girls and Rozzie. As such, I make it, no problem, to foursies. I hand the jacks away. Everything is going to be all right.

Then I look up and see Rozzie on the far side of the playground, flying around on the rings. She is good at this and can make it around five times without stopping. The other girls look up and see this, too. They draw a line with their eyes, so that it's not invisible anymore, this force that connects us. Others see it, too, and in that instant, I believe I can travel back and forth, switch bodies on the spot and be her for a while, feel what it's like to move unafraid, to fly in a circle, my dress hiked up, my underwear showing. To be watched all the time and want that.

I also know how dangerous this is. That underwear, like belly buttons and family secrets, shouldn't show.

There will be a price to pay for joining this jacks circle, turning my caution watch into a ticket for popularity. It means no one is watching either one of us. It means anyone, at any minute, could fall.

Jemma, present

At the hospital the only difference between night and day is the number of nurses on duty. Night shift loses three, half the floor staff. So the ones on are thinner and move faster; they are also quirkier— women who've made the choice to be awake while everyone else sleeps. Though they have more to do, they sometimes talk longer; occasionally I will hear a whole life story: "Married one man I didn't love, another that I did. You want to know the difference in the end? Not much. Swear to God, not much."

One woman tells me, "I have a sister, too." For a long time she doesn't say any more, as if she is trying to decide which part to tell me. Finally she goes on, "Older, too. Like yours."

My sister lies between us, asleep finally, her face mostly obscured by bandages.

"Beautiful like her."

I smile and think: *Don't start, please. Tell me anything else, just don't tell me this.* And my face must show my inability to hear about other people's sisters because she stops and, for a long time, says nothing. Then she chooses the obvious, the standard: "My brother loves her. Has for years," nodding at Rozzie, changing whatever bag is dangling in the darkness above her.

*　　*　　*

"You want to know what your problem is?" Rozzie says to me, as if, lying here in this hospital room, she has no problems herself. She is eating her lunch, struggling with some applesauce, which she keeps missing as if the spoon has a mind of its own.

"Not really," I say. "But go ahead and tell me."

"Your problem is you don't know how to talk about yourself. You always deflect conversation away to other things."

I smile. "I don't want to talk about that."

I've gotten to know one nurse more than the others. Her name is Paula; she is tall, with short hair and big arms and, in the dark, can look like a man. She is the only one who can take Rozzie's vitals at night without waking her. Often she'll write the stats she gets— temperature, blood pressure—on the back of her hand. "Forgot my damn sheets," she'll say.

Once I ask, "Do you have to keep track of all this?"

Even in the dark, I can see her roll her eyes. "Oh yeah. Everything that goes in, everything that comes out. We got a whole file of this crap back there."

Later that night I run into her off duty by the vending machines. She has a cup of coffee in one hand and a pack of cigarettes in the other.

"That's a surprise," I say, pointing to the cigarettes.

"Oh, please."

I ask her if I can have one and she looks pleased, shakes two loose, and holds out the pack. I appreciate Paula because I've never once seen her hover with a piteous expression on her face, never felt her eyes on me in search of clues. She must not realize who Rozzie is, must think of her only as another patient on a floor of many. To Paula we're paperwork, vital stats to lose track of, nothing more. To the rest, we're a story they're telling at home—not an unkind one, but weighted just the same. *She's so nice,* I can hear them tell their families. *You wouldn't believe how sweet she is.*

Paula doesn't care one way or another. She lights my cigarette and then looks around for something to talk about. She points to a *Time* magazine with a cover story on children shooting their classmates: "Can you believe that shit?"

Sitting beside her reminds me we are still a part of the world at large, that we should read these stories and have opinions on them. Many people have written to Rozzie or sent care packages—boxes of food I open and, for the most part, eat myself—giving me the impression that we are the only people in the news, which of course isn't true.

Halfway through our cigarettes, Paula asks how long we've lived in Minnesota.

"We don't live here. We just came for the treatment."

"No kidding." Paula seems shocked. "But you've got the accent."

I wonder if this is true. We have always sounded like one another, our voices indistinguishable on the phone. Are we both, in an effort to blend, starting to sound like the nurses around us?

At night my parents and I take turns staying in her room until Rozzie falls asleep. She is scared of sleeping, understandably, and we don't want exhaustion to add to her problems, and so when she says softly, "Can you just talk until I fall asleep?" I do. I try to tell her small things, thoughts I've had, observations from the day to keep her company and walk her up to sleep. I talk about the nurses and describe what they look like. If anyone else were around, I wouldn't make it so obvious she's never seen them. In the daytime, when visitors come in and out, or fans who've heard that she's here stop by, we have a little trick we do, though we've never discussed it. I walk behind whoever's come in and from over their shoulder say, "Look, Rozzie, it's Vanessa." Rozzie smiles and points her face in our direction. As long as the person doesn't move, I don't move either and we're fine. I'm not sure why we go through all this when Rozzie's obviously blind, with two large bandages over her eyes. She talks about not seeing and still we do this.

At night, we drop the facade. I tell her who was here, who was fat, and who was not. I bore her to sleep with what she's missed, hoping it will seem like not that much. "Miriam had on the *oddest* shoes today," I'll say.

Because we are in Minnesota, some people have assumed we are at the Mayo Clinic and Rozzie has cancer. Yesterday in the mail, a bulky envelope arrived full of pot, sent anonymously.

"Is there a return address?" Rozzie asks.

I turn the envelope over. "No. Just a Post-it saying, 'In case you need this.' "

Rozzie laughs. *"In case?"*

Every morning I expect to walk into her room and find her crying, but one day melts into another and she may be quiet or introspective, but then there'll be a joke, or a laugh so sincere I'll think, *My God, maybe I am the only one with problems.*

I need to understand why it is so hard for me to talk about my own life. Every question Rozzie asks, I want to fire back at her. "Did you ever want to be a teacher like Mom?" she asks one day. I want to say, I'm not sure. Did you? I always want to hear what she'd say first. Not because I would repeat her answer, but because her answer would shape my own.

I remember when we were children and my mother told me it was important to think for myself.

*   *   *

Paula and I start smoking together in a tiny, uncarpeted smoking lounge furnished with all-plastic chairs. I buy a pack of her brand and ask her to keep it so my parents won't find it. They have probably smelled it—I know Rozzie has—but in our family we let much pass unmentioned, especially if we don't see the evidence.

"Very mature," Paula says, pocketing the pack.

One afternoon she settles beside me on the far side of the ashtray, hands me a cigarette, and I can see something is different. Someone has told her. "So I never knew what your sister did." She lights her cigarette, then mine. "Movies, huh?"

I nod.

"Freaky."

I nod again.

"I don't see many. What is she, pretty famous?"

"I don't know. There's a lot of people more famous than she is." Usually I have set answers to the questions people standardly ask: *What's it like? Do you ever get jealous?* This time I don't.

"So this eye thing is an even bigger drag. Not too many blind movie actresses, I guess."

"Right," I say.

"Though of course almost any job you had, going blind would"— she rolls her hand, in search of the right word—"suck."

I nod. Sure, I shrug.

"So how's she holding up?"

For a while we smoke in silence and I can feel a tickle in my eyes. I know there's a danger I will cry in front of this woman, who doesn't want to see my tears, who's trying just to get through a cigarette and feels obliged to talk to me.

"Okay," I say in a small voice.

"And what about you?"

I say nothing. If I speak, I'll cry, so I nod my head. Rozzie has been in the hospital for two weeks, and though our parents are here, they have jobs that obligate them to leave for an hour, or a morning here and there. They are not the ubiquitous presence that I am, refilling water pitchers, answering the telephone, negotiating visitors. By all evidence, I must seem to these nurses to have no life beyond this one of servitude to my sister. Which isn't true. I have a life I am running away from. And in recent months I have spent an equal amount of time hurting my sister as helping her. So every impression I give is false.

Paula looks at me sideways, asks with her expression why am I here, sneaking cigarettes, acting like a child. If I could do it without crying, I'd go over it all, as I've been doing in my mind, trying to understand so many things: where this business with her eyes began, when I started not seeing what was obvious.

I wonder if I have stood too close or too far. Sometimes I think to explain it all I'd have to go way back, which is what I've been doing. My memory begins with the memory of watching her, studying her movement from my shaded spot on the porch, the leaves that rustled and parted as she moved through the tree, higher and farther, onto the branch, in search of the bird's nest she thought she'd seen. It's as if my life began in the terrible moment when my sister fell and I understood, in that instant, I would forever be responsible for her.

I still am. I know that.

But it's complicated. I try to leave the past behind with a sense of pride, as if doing this were a sign of getting closer to the future. Recently I have been going home for shorter visits, deciding about Christmas at the last minute. Many people are surprised by my age when I tell them. They thought I was older, which I take to mean I seem like a person who has put distance between herself and her childhood. I don't seem like a daughter first, the way some young women do, threading a mother through so many of their stories.

Or a sister, I think, and then I wonder.

Maybe *not* talking about her, as I have been doing for the last eight months, is as obvious as the way I used to work her into every conversation. For years this was my forte, my hostess gift to any dinner party. "Oh, tell about the time you were on the set in Italy," someone would say, and I'd wait just long enough for people to quiet, for one guest to tell another with her eyes, *Listen,* and then I'd begin with a tale about one of my real or fabricated encounters with celebrities, and I'd imagine a web in the room tightening around us all, everyone connected.

Now I see I was really cutting myself off. Anecdotes about the rich and famous make people cough into their fist or refold a napkin, staring into their lap. For a while I couldn't figure out why; I thought maybe my stories weren't good enough and tried exaggerating. I put myself at dinner parties with shockingly famous people, but the effect was no different, so I stopped cold turkey.

I pretended to know no one, including my own sister.

I shrugged when anyone asked if I'd seen a good movie.

Rozzie, present

She collects secrets, and hordes them.

With no other work, this has become her job: seeming one thing, improvising hourly. She once wanted to be many things in addition to an actress: a painter, an activist. Now she wants only to disappear, to do whatever is required to ensure that she will never be truly seen again. So everything is a lie.

For now, it means appearing fine to her family, making no requests.

She wonders if she's depressed, but she's been depressed before and knows what that feels like—the flat, tasteless landscape of days— and this is different. This is even exciting sometimes, how she sees certain things, like the clarity of death and the release it would be.

She doesn't want to die, but she wants to do something close to it. She imagines falling into this darkness and embracing it, living in it forever. If she could, she would stop up her ears, too, and let nothing in. She'd sit alone in a room full of books she couldn't read, but could imagine, the ones she hasn't gotten to yet, but are on her shelf. She would press her face into the pages, find the words with her one eye, letter by letter: *Anna Karenina, Madame Bovary.* She'd fill her mind with the sad stories of women more victimized than she, and she'd take comfort in that, find solace in characters she will never play. Here, she would think, is a worse life than my own. And here.

Other times, she does want to die.

She sees it as a quiet, understandable sleep. Who would blame her? she thinks. There are so many others who've died from diseases not technically fatal.

Sometimes she even composes the note, addressed to her family, assuring them it isn't their fault. In the end, it isn't fear that stops her, it's something else. Curiosity, she thinks, for lack of a better word, because something is happening. It starts on the edges though she's wearing bandages that block all light. It's a flickering of color, first red, then shades of red, crimson, fuchsia.

She's sure it is a memory of some kind and tells no one. What's there to say, anyway? Yesterday I saw some red? Where does that get her? What might it be?

Jemma, 1976

In the middle of the night, we wake to the sound of sirens shrieking up our otherwise perpetually quiet street. I get out of bed and go to Rozzie's side of the room. She is lying still, with her eyes open. "Did you do something?" she says, as if we're both going to get in trouble for this.

"No," I say, pretty sure, though the power of Rozzie's implication is mighty. I am six and she is eight. *Maybe I did do something,* I think. *Maybe I got up in my sleep and set a fire.*

We know it's a fire because it's so close we can smell the smoke. Right next door, as it turns out, in the house of our friends, the Cantalonis, the other sister pair on our block, Wendy and Jane. We go to the window and see first the fire trucks and then the fire, reaching out of the upstairs window. It looks like the red arms of an angel.

"That's Jane's room," Rozzie says, even as I am thinking: *No, it can't be.*

It's a long time before our parents finally burst in and pull us away from what we shouldn't see: their mother on the street screaming, nightgown open, the firemen pulling Jane out, the dramatic rescue of a girl who will later turn out to be already dead.

A week afterward, we are told the mother blames the father. Too cheap to hire a proper electrician, he installed wiring himself that eventually smoldered into the fire that asphyxiated his daughter. Our mother tells us not to listen, that Jane is in heaven now and is happy there. As she says this, though, she cries, putting some doubt in our minds.

I picture the fire, reaching up to the sky, Jane's soul borne in it. I believe this is possible, just as I still believe if I pray at night, God listens to what I say. A week after the funeral, the family distributes Jane's toys to her neighborhood friends; Wendy, her sister, stops by to give Rozzie and me a ceramic-angel music box. "Here," she says, handing it to me. "My mom wants you to have this." She doesn't look at us. How can she possibly? We are still a pair; she is only herself now with parents who, everyone says, would rather get divorced than try for another.

Then Wendy says something softly. She is seven, with short hair that often gets her mistaken for a boy. When people did this, Jane corrected them. I never heard Wendy tell anyone herself that she wasn't a boy. "Jane isn't dead, though," she whispers. "She lives in the woods now, at the end of the street."

Rozzie and I are old enough to know this isn't right. Our parents have been to the funeral; they brought home a program with her picture on the front.

"I bring her food," Wendy keeps going. "Anything good I can find. Candy, spaghetti, stuff she'd like."

I look at Rozzie. *What should we do?* I say with my eyes, and Rozzie answers me by answering her. "What's she doing there?"

Wendy shrugs. "She wanted to get away from Mom and Dad fighting. I said it was fine."

"Is she going to come home?"

"Probably not. She hasn't decided yet."

Rozzie hesitates. "Is she happy?"

Of this Wendy is sure. "Oh, yeah."

Though her parents stay together, and Wendy lives on our street for the next ten years, I never again hear her mention Jane's life in the woods. I never hear her say Jane's name until many years later, in high school, when it's safe and clear again. We're going to Jane's grave; today would have been Jane's birthday.

I wonder how long she believed her sister was alive and needed food, how long she believed she was still in some fundamental sense the sister she had always been. I worry about this periodically over the years—that at any time the same thing could happen to us.

Christmas two years later, the fire still haunts us. There are lights on our house, but not next door. We have heard Wendy's mother no longer trusts electricity, that if at all possible, she sits in the dark.

Rozzie and I are finished opening presents, sitting in our room, surrounded by our haul. It isn't even lunchtime yet so this is the longest it can possibly be until Christmas comes again. I tell Rozzie this—we still share a room and most of our thoughts, but recently she has gotten quieter, more distracted. I'll say something and see she isn't listening, she's staring down at her tights drawer or tracing the lines on the palm of her hand. Now she doesn't say anything because she is studying the present that has most captured her fancy, an album called *Mud Slide Slim* by James Taylor. Until now, the record we listen to the most is Peter, Paul, and Mary's *Ten Years Together,* and our favorite song is "Leaving on a Jet Plane." Clearly this is different. On the front is his picture. He has long hair and a mustache and his thumbs are hooked into two suspenders he seems about to take off. She is reading the lyrics on the back.

Secretly my favorite present is from our aunt, my mother's sister, Emily, who is supposed to be sad because she's twice been divorced, but I always think of her as pretty and fun. I am a little too old for the lunch-bag decorating kit, but still I study all the contents: rubber stamps, glitter pens, corrugated scissors. I want to get started right away, only I won't waste my time on lunch bags. I have in mind something like the poster collage my friend Mary did of photographed lips. I want to do the same thing, only not lips, eyes maybe, and make it more abstract with these pens and stamps.

"Listen to this," Rozzie says.

I listen. She reads, " 'Mud Slide Slim and the Blue Horizon. Whoa, Mud Slide. I'm dependent upon you.' "

I look up at her. She smiles. "Do you get it?"

"Get what?"

"It's drugs."

"What is?"

"Mud Slide."

Mud slide means "drugs"? I know so little, only what I've heard and read in Rozzie's copy of *Go Ask Alice,* where people put drugs in Coke cans at parties, and once is enough to get addicted. Instantly I am scared. Why did Rozzie ask for this record? Why did our mother buy it for her? I want her to look over at my box and see these glue sticks and want what I want: to spend the day cutting up magazines and making a collage. She won't, though. It's Christmas and I'm scared she won't want to spend it with me, that she'll call her friend Carol and start reading these lyrics with her. Carol will understand what means drugs and what means sex.

For a long time I lie on the floor between our beds and feel sadder than I've ever been over something that hasn't happened yet. This is the way these days, though I don't have any words to explain this feeling or to stop it from crowding over me. I think about poor Wendy, who has no sister at all.

Then I hear Rozzie say, "You know what I want to do?"

I look up, but she's got the record out of the sleeve, is holding it by the edges, studying the grooves as if this will help her understand the meaning of the lyrics. I wonder if I imagined her saying some-thing. I don't speak.

She puts the record back into its sleeve and into the jacket. "I feel like making cookies."

I am so surprised I don't say anything. I watch her stand up, walk to the door. "You want to come?"

"Sure." And then it's as if I'd been holding my breath for a long time and now it's okay. Everything's all right. We stand up and go into the kitchen, where I won't remember what happens next but I can guess. These are still the days when we eat the same things, when we are composed of more or less the same material, the same urges. We will both eat enough cookie dough to feel sick, so I won't remem-ber that part; I'll only remember the earlier one—the part that keeps happening over and over, so much that it will become our whole relationship, our whole life, I sometimes think—this feeling that I am about to lose her and then, at the last minute, I don't.

Jemma, 1983

"Jemma, please," Rozzie says, her voice weary. These days, she isn't much interested in her role as older sister, but if we are alone in the backseat of the car, or walking home from school, she will still take the time to explain the world to me, to pass along her pearls of wisdom. "Only snobs worry about matching their socks and their turtlenecks."

I am thirteen, Rozzie is fifteen, and we are both painful to look at for different reasons. Rozzie is growing her blond hair, which is so pale and thin, it seems some days to disappear into the pattern of her shirt. Though barrettes are big, she owns none; she has never cut feathers, never done anything with a curling iron. I am doughy in strange places—under my chin, the back of my arms—but I have skinny legs. Though I wear a bra, there isn't much point. When I take it off, my breasts released look more or less like the folds in a fat boy's chest. I already know my hair is my strength, thick and curly, much darker than Rozzie's. Sometimes it is too curly, but people have said, "I would kill for your hair." I also know my weaknesses: My teeth have gaps between them, one wide enough to stick in a ruler. My eyebrows, if I'm not careful, can go thick like two rectangles hovering above my eyes.

I have my own set of problems, but they aren't my sister's. In a year and a half, she has grown six painful inches. At night, she tells me, she can feel herself grow. "It hurts," she says, pushing up her glasses, which no longer fit her face and will not stay up her nose. Sometimes, at dinner, they drop onto her plate. "See?" she will say when this happens. "See what I have to put up with?"

She has gone from being the joyful center of attention in our neighborhood crowd of twelve kids to being a sort of shadow figure, a girl who holds grudges forever, against our parents primarily, but also against her clothes, her friends, her body that is changing in ways that horrify her. Everything is painful; every night a battle. In the dark drama that has become her life, I no longer play even a speaking role. I am part of the house she is obliged to live in, as significant as, say, a picture on the wall or a lamp, maybe. Some dinners she will tell story after story, not looking, even once, at me.

Even in the face of this kind of rejection, I still study everything she does. Strangely, I don't even resent her apathy. Her life is harder than mine—anyone can see that. I don't know what it's like to lie in bed at night and feel my feet grow away from me. There is nothing I can do for her except go back to watching her carefully (now spying because she doesn't want to be seen) through a trick of our windows— our house bends in an L; my window looks into hers, though she doesn't, amazingly, seem to know this. At night, I watch her study herself in one of the four mirrors she's planted around her room.

It's not the horizon she's running toward now, it's something in these mirrors only she sees. Some glimpse of the future. She is not putting on makeup or trimming her eyebrows as I have learned to do, combing them up, cutting along the line. Nor is she experimenting with home perms and do-it-yourself highlighting kits as I have also done on the sly and turned my hair into frizzy, orange stripes I claimed were natural. She is staring into the void, making assessments (I imagine) but taking no action.

I have read *I Never Promised You a Rose Garden*. I have also read

David and Lisa. I am fascinated by crazy young people and I know staring in mirrors for hours at a time is not a good sign. My sister feels too much. She is too intense. I want to dilute her problems by mixing them with mine, but she won't let me. She loves her troubles. She hordes them, clings to them as if they are badges of some kind of honor. "You don't have to wear glasses," she says, not like I am lucky, but like I've missed out. She relishes her suffering and her loneliness and keeps it all private—as if sharing it would be the same thing as giving it away.

And so I watch her burn putrid-smelling sticks of lavender incense, alone in her room, with all the lights off. I watch her light fifteen candles in saucers around the room, cue up Joni Mitchell's *Blue* album, and sit in the trembling darkness. I have read the books; I know all of these things are signs of disturbance and perhaps drugs.

She has become such a mystery, any of this is possible.

Even as I watch her, alone in my room, I worry that she has equated me with our parents. I am too young not to be lumped in with them, too earnest, too much a do-gooder. I can't help myself; I still eat dinner with them every night as I am expected to, though she has announced she is too busy to be home every single night. She has said this as if it were a preposterous expectation. I also help with dishes; I stand in the kitchen and talk to our mother, who sometimes looks in the direction of Rozzie's room and stops what she is doing to concentrate on not crying. Sometimes, I admit, I get a small thrill out of so easily being my parents' favorite these days. It takes next to nothing, so why not do it?

The thing is, I would trade it all in, in a heartbeat, in a second, if Rozzie would say to me, once, *Come here, come in my room. Smell this incense. Listen to this song. I have this problem. Help me.*

Even the things I am most worried about—drugs, secrets, sex with boys she barely knows—would seem like nothing in the face of a little inclusion. If she asked me to smoke pot, I would. If she asked me to help her shoplift, I would. I can't think of anything I wouldn't do.

One Saturday, Rozzie uncharacteristically agrees to go on a family hike, and we are all so excited, we talk too much in the car, too quickly, as if we expect her at any moment to change her mind and tell our father to turn around. The distance she has kept from us recently has made her that much bigger in our minds, already something like a celebrity. Then, when we get to the parking lot, she climbs out of the car, walks over to the view, and—in a single horrible instant—her glasses drop off and flutter down into the ravine. She screams and then begins to cry uncontrollably. No one can console her. With the eyes of other hikers on us, we get back into the car after five minutes and leave.

Later that week, she sits in the TV room with me. She has refused to get new glasses or accept the contacts our mother has offered to buy her because somewhere she has read that nearsightedness, uncorrected, makes eyes look bigger.

This, too, seems crazy to me. She can hardly see far enough to point her face toward the person she is talking to, which, oddly enough, at this moment is me. "Here's what I'm thinking," she says. She is three inches from the set, blocking my view, but it is so rare that she will watch with me that I say nothing. Behind her, the Partridge family climbs onto their bus.

"Do you want to hear what I'm thinking?" she repeats, impatient now. I forgot that she can't read my face, my expression that says, *I am listening, I am listening.*

"Yeah," I say. The trick to getting her to talk, I know, is not sounding too eager.

"I think I'm going to try out for the school play."

I nod. For some reason I expected much worse. *Here's what I'm thinking: I hate you and Mom and Dad.* This seems perfectly innocuous, even thrilling when she asks me to read a few lines of a scene with her. "It's called *The Children's Hour*," she tells me, handing me the play. "It's about two teachers at a girls' boarding school who are accused of being lesbians."

She says *lesbian* as if it is a perfectly ordinary word, one she has used many times. We start to read. She tells me she is trying out for the role of the sympathetic teacher, played by Audrey Hepburn in the movie. The other is Shirley MacLaine. This surprises me because it seems to be the same thing as saying, *I'm trying out for the pretty one.*

I'm certainly not going to be the one who tells her, *You're not.* But anyone can see she might once have been pretty, might one day be pretty again, but for now, she is painfully, sadly not. The journey of my looks has been less marked by peaks and valleys—I was never that great to begin with and am not so bad now. Some might even say what with my hair, I'm doing well. Still, I have enough self-knowledge to know you don't go for Audrey Hepburn or nothing. You aim lower, for Shirley MacLaine; you let your personality fill in the gaps. You imply that if you really tried hard, you'd look better, but you don't, so it's fine. This way, you'll never be like the sad girls who sit with lipstick on their teeth in the first seat on the bus, looking up hopefully at everyone who walks on.

The night before the audition we go over the scene again and she tells me she thinks she is going to get it. "I'm good," she explains, which terrifies me. She has never acted before, so no one has ever told her this. I worry that the disappointment will be too much—that if losing her glasses produced a scene, losing this part will be much worse. Then she does her monologue for me and I forget all that. She *is* good, it seems, and she even knows how to cry real tears on command. Maybe she will get it, I think. And then she does.

Overnight, she changes.

She gets contact lenses so she can see what she's doing in rehearsal. She memorizes her own lines in three days and everyone else's in a week. She knows the play inside out and talks about it constantly. She no longer calls her character Audrey, she calls her by her name, Karen. "The great part is, they *were* in love. Or Martha was certainly in love with Karen. The little girl has accused them of the one sin they're guilty of. Except of course it's just sexual feelings. They've never done anything."

Is Rozzie a lesbian? I wonder.

This is the longest she's talked to me in ages, and yet I don't understand what she's trying to say. I don't know how to talk about sex without feeling humiliated. The sexiest thing I have ever done was go skinny-dipping last summer with my friend Sally. After we had slipped out of our clothes and bright white bras into the freezing water of the lake that took our breath and then gave it back, we swam away from each other, into the darkness, scissoring our legs, letting the water touch us with its cold hands. I think about that now and wonder if maybe I am a lesbian.

"This play is really about how poisonous repression is."

"What do you mean?" I ask.

"People should be more honest than they are. I'm just sick and tired of all this duplicity."

I say nothing because I don't know what *duplicity* means. I assume it has to do with sexual repression, which I must have because I get so embarrassed so easily. I don't even tell people when I have my period. Rozzie, on the other hand, says things like "Don't talk to me today, I'm bleeding like a stuck pig." The truth is, though I am embarrassed about sex, I think about it often and I wonder if Rozzie does, too. I can't ask her questions because she might either laugh or tell me I'm the one with problems. What if this is true?

As rehearsals progress, Rozzie becomes more and more involved. One night she announces that the people from the play are now her best friends: "They understand me. Better than anyone I've ever known. They also care about things that matter." By this, she means politics, current events. In addition to her own problems, Rozzie likes to take on world problems, as well: animal rights, global hunger. A few years ago, she talked about going to Africa to work with chimpanzees, like Jane Goodall, or gorillas, like Dian Fossey. Recently Rozzie has started working the Oxfam lunch fast table, getting people to sign a pledge that says they'll only eat rice and vegetables for the day, which everyone signs, but no one does, except Rozzie, who eats her lunch with big wooden chopsticks.

I don't do any of these things. I say to myself, they are symbolic acts, gestures at best. Better to do something real and immediate, such as be nice to the girl who has no friends. So I try in that way. But maybe that's just symbolic, too. It's hard for me to say.

One afternoon I sneak into rehearsal to watch, and almost instantly, I regret coming. Rozzie is so serious about her role, she seems unable to contain herself onstage. With every line, she brandishes her arms to include the wall, the sofa, the ceiling, in her torrent. "You!" she screams. "You have ruined me. Don't you see! You are a wicked, wicked girl."

Her voice bounces off the rafters and echoes into the back. She looks and sounds nothing like Audrey, and I am so scared for what is going to happen when people see this play that I can scarcely breathe. My fears run all over: she will seem like a lesbian, like she is overacting, like someone with emotional problems. When we were little, everyone used to watch her with awe and admiration. She drew and held a crowd with a charm that now seems to me to have turned in on itself. Instead of masking her weaknesses, it is drawing attention to them—*Here, I am vulnerable. And here. And here.*

After half an hour, I can't watch any more and I walk home, going over in my mind what I will say.

These last few weeks, Rozzie has seemed to want my company, and she even, occasionally, solicits my opinion. What will I tell her? What if she makes another pitch for honesty?

Then, unexpectedly, she doesn't ask. Maybe she doesn't know I came to watch. I let it go. It's her life, not mine. I need to find other subjects to wrap my thoughts around. Sometimes I make up whole stories in my head that aren't about good things happening to me but good things happening to Rozzie. Boys falling in love with her. Teachers looking up, eyes wide with surprise. If I keep hovering like this, inches from her intensity and unhappiness, it will swallow me up, take me into the mental institution with her.

And so I devise a plan: I won't go to her play. I'll fake sick and will stay home all three nights. Opening night, I do my own raspy performance. I have had strep throat enough times to know what it sounds like. Rozzie stops by my room, as if she is genuinely upset that I won't be there. Does she really care? I assume not, but I can't tell. "I wish you could come," she says.

"So do I," I rasp, adding guiltily, "Maybe I'll be better by tomorrow," even though I know I won't be because I never want to see this play, never want to have to tell Rozzie how scared I am for her. That she is becoming different not only from me, but from the rest of the world, too. After this play is over, I fear she will begin to live on an island of her own construction, and the only bridge across will be me, explaining to people, over and over, that really, she's fine.

After the first night, even though my parents say it's really good, that she's wonderful, I keep up my own show and never see the play. On the night of the third and final performance, she comes into my room and says, "You don't want to see it, do you?"

"Of course I do. My God, Roz."

She stares at me. "If you wanted to see it, you'd come see it."

"I can't, Rozzie," I rasp with no voice now. "I'm sick. I have a *fever.*"

"Yeah, right."

Only when I'm back at school do I understand what really happened. She was better than good. People can't stop telling me their mother cried, they went and saw it twice, she was that good. I hear the word *good* so many times it loses meaning. There is an acting award given out at the end of the year, and already there's talk that she'll get it. I am relieved, of course. A storm has passed. No one is saying the bad things I expected.

Only at the end of the day do I realize I haven't seen Rozzie once—not in the cafeteria or the hallways. It is a small school; if I need to find her, it takes a few minutes of looking between classes. But today she hasn't been in any of her usual places.

After school, when she's not on the bus, I get off and look around. Did she walk home early? On a hunch, I go over to the theater auditorium and find her there, sitting alone in the dark, staring up at the bare stage. Besides the yellow electrical tape on the floor, there is no evidence that yesterday a show was going on. She is sitting as someone might sit in church, leaning on the chair-back in front of her, staring ahead, hands clasped, as if she might go down on her knees to pray.

"Rozzie? Are you all right?"

She turns around and I see the tears in her eyes in the dim light. "I'm just thinking about it all." She turns back. This is too much. If people saw this, they might hold back their praise, nervous of its effect. "My best night was the second. I was the most on. The most connected to Karen."

What am I supposed to say? "Good," I try.

"The worst was the last. I didn't want it to be over. I wanted to stay onstage forever. I wish there was some way to make these things last. When you really love something, it seems like it always has to be temporary."

"Everyone says you were so good, Roz. All day people have been telling me that."

"I *was* good. But I keep thinking whatever else happens, even if I act for the rest of my life, you'll never have seen me in *this* part. It's gone forever."

It's hard to understand. I have grown so sure I don't matter to her, and now here she is, crying as if I do. She turns around again and for the first time I see it: In the dim, eggshell gray light, she looks beautiful. Really beautiful. With her new contacts, and the glint of tears in her eyes, there is something almost ethereal about her face. I am filled with a surprising lightness, even hope: *Maybe this will save her,* I think. *Maybe it will be all right.*

Rozzie, 1984

The first time it happens, she is in eleventh grade, in French class, where she sits, by assignment, in the back of the room. Having recently lost her glasses again, she is wearing old ones, tilted at an angle to see better. She looks peculiar, she knows, like an old lady, but she doesn't care so much what these people think of her anymore. She already has a life she is leading in her head, far from here and from these people. In her mind she is in New York, working as a waitress so that during the day she can go to classes taught by Uta Hagen. *Respect for Acting* is her favorite book, and every time she reads a new chapter, she pictures herself in such a class, stripping down emotionally, for audiences full of people she has never met.

For now she is able to shut out the French lesson and the thirty students around her passing notes and planning weekends to hear the monologue she is delivering in her head. She has been doing this for weeks now—visualizing one life, passing through another.

Then, quite suddenly, the world cracks before her eyes. She thinks her glasses must have shattered, but when she reaches up to touch them, they are perfectly whole, tilted and smooth on the tip of her nose. There are patches of shapeless color and stripes of clarity—as if she is looking out through a badly washed windshield. She moves her head around to find an eye, a shirt collar, and the teacher's mouth. It continues this way for a minute, then two. She looks down at her own hand and can see only one finger at a time clearly. She is both panicked and fascinated.

Within a few minutes, it passes. Apparently, she is not dying or going blind, as she assumed. Over the next six months, it periodically happens again. Sometimes she is fine for a month, then it will happen three times in a week. She thinks of it as a bodily quirk, not so unusual; something explainable, though she never attempts to have it explained. She never mentions it, because—what can she say? It's nothing, she tells herself, though from here on out, she will keep track, in her head, of famous blind people. When she hears of a new one, it's like an electrical current going through her body. "By the end, Melville was virtually blind," her English teacher says. The word itself—*blind*—sticks in her head.

In a bookstore once, she sees a display for a book called *Natural Eyesight Healing*. The introduction proposes that eyes, like muscles, must be exercised. If exercises are done consistently, myopia can be averted, glasses thrown away. She opens to a chapter about the Chinese approach: nationalized eye care. Workers are given ten minutes a day to do eye exercises—cranial massages, focusing instructions. The program is illustrated with a picture of a Chinese man pinching his nose. She laughs but later remembers every exercise described. She reads quickly through the rest, looking for testimony that might sound familiar—someone who sees fine one minute and in soapy triangles the next.

She doesn't find any.

One night, she begins doing the eye exercises she has read about in the book. She closes her eyes, imagines a room full of Chinese workers, pinching their noses, finding their eyeballs below their lids and pressing with their thumbs, so the eyes disappear and reemerge like spring-loaded mechanisms. She loves exploring her body in a way that only she and a million Chinese people have done. She imagines standing before them, leading the exercise, saying, "Now, okay, watch me."

There hasn't yet been any pain, no headaches that splinter from her temples backward and down. Nothing is really scary so far.

It's just different.

As she has always felt. Sometimes, in an argument with her mother, she'll scream, "You have *no* idea what my life is like. You don't understand what it's like to be me."

And really she doesn't. No one does.

Jemma, 1985

I take up photography the second semester of tenth grade, almost by accident. I am sick the first day of class registration, and journalism is the only sixth-period elective open by the time I sign up. On the first day, I tell them I will take pictures because that appeals to me more than writing articles. I have fiddled around with my father's Nikon, taken some pictures that people tell me are good, though I have never shot black-and-white and have never covered an event. Within three weeks, though, I love it so much I spend all my money on a used Pentax with a telephoto lens that's so big, it's impossible to wear without someone making a phallic-symbol joke. I love the weight of this equipment hanging around my neck, and the excuse it gives me to go everywhere and stand on the sidelines of football games, dances, Martin Luther King Day activities.

Quickly, I'm a ubiquitous figure, known by many as the girl with the big camera. I talk with the people I shoot—about my lens, or getting them copies of the pictures I've taken. It doesn't make me friends with the popular crowd, but it gives me a way to watch their life and understand it better.

So far, I have never been particularly ambitious in school. At night I read chapters I cannot recall the next day in English class. Even plot eludes me, so when called on to analyze a passage, I take wild, desperate stabs: "Man versus nature?" I try. Everything I say has a question mark at the end. But photography is different. In this class, I learn fast and am told by the editor, a month after I start, that I am the best events photographer he has. It's possible he means I am the only one who consistently shows up to the events I am assigned, but I take the compliment and roll it around in my head for days afterward.

I sign up for a photography class after school at the local community college, and once, for a portrait assignment, I ask Rozzie to pose, though I'm not sure ahead of time what she will say. Recently, she has grown so unpredictable our father has begun calling her Our Lady of the Perpetual Mood Swing. One day she'll find me in the kitchen and put her arms around me, the next she'll scream that if I ever so much as touch her turtleneck again, she'll kill me. Last week she asked if I wanted to go shopping; this week she told me my problem was how much I depend on conventional morality.

I am nervous about shooting her because lately she is suffering more acutely than usual. It is the spring-musical time, and because she can't carry a tune, she is participating as assistant director, a title that seems pretty good to me, but has left her unfocused and mercurial. She will spend hours in the bathroom, doing nothing as far as I can tell but brooding over her reflection. I see the potential she has for great beauty, but she must not. I want to say something to her, but don't know what. She is pretty in a way high school will never appreciate or understand. She will never be elected to a prom court she claims to care nothing about, even though when the names are announced, I find the list, crumpled on her bedroom floor. I want my pictures to make her see, as I do, how beautiful she is, that her face is extraordinary.

We start off in the living room, every lampshade off, some of the lamps moved, stretched as far as their cords will go. She settles onto the sofa and gets ready.

I don't expect her to be as serious as she is, as willing to follow every direction I give her: *Look up. Now out the window. Push your hair back. Smile. Don't smile.* In less than half an hour, I've finished a roll, thirty-six exposures of her.

As I rewind it, she says, "Should we try outside?" I can't believe she wants to keep going. I find more film and we take two with our dog, one with our cat, a whole set under a birch tree. "We'll call this girl and tree," she says, and rests her forehead meaningfully against the trunk. Halfway through this roll, she asks about props. "What if I got a few things from my closet? Like Granny's shawl or that Japanese fan. That could be good." She comes back with a cardboard box filled with artifacts dredged up from her closet. She has become so private these days I can't believe she's brought these outside for me to look at: a peacock feather, a strand of fake pearls, platform shoes she spent thirty-five dollars on and has never, to my knowledge, worn. She puts one on and I take a picture of her feet wearing two different shoes.

"That'll be a good one," she says.

Next she's threading the pearl necklace through her hair, playing peekaboo over a fan. I laugh, and then, when she doesn't, I stop. She isn't joking. She's acting as if I were a real photographer and she were a real model.

When I develop the pictures, I can't believe how good they are; the indoor ones are dramatic, high-contrast silhouettes, like Barbra Streisand's album cover of *A Star Is Born*. The light fans out and flares in such unexpected ways, I almost start laughing in the darkroom, watching the picture come up in the developer bath. The outdoor ones are softer, truer portraits, and interesting in different ways. Rozzie's face is complicated; her expressions have a depth. In one she is smiling, but she also looks lonely, as if the peacock feather in her hand is reminding her of some other, much better time in her life.

When I get home, I show her the pictures in careful order, best first, and it is clear, quickly, she doesn't like them. "Why is this so fuzzy?" she says, talking about the one that I love with the refracted light. I say nothing. *It's not* sticks in my throat. She looks at another. "My cheeks look so fat," she says softly. She flips through two more. I want to grab the rest, tear them up. *Forget it,* I want to scream. *Never mind.* She points to a dark outline that falls on her face in one: "What's that?"

It's my shadow—a beginner's mistake, or one could say an interesting accident—because once you look closer, you know it's a perfect outline, me on her face. "Whoops," she says. When she hands them back, she tells me it's okay, they're good pictures: "I just hate looking at myself."

I take them back and don't point out that, these days, this is nearly all she does.

Jemma, 1985

The summer before her senior year, Rozzie leaves for six weeks to attend a theater acting workshop held in Los Angeles, which is, if I am honest, a bit of a relief. In the last few months, life has gotten easier for Rozzie and harder for me. She is so obsessed by acting that she thinks of little else. If something bad happens, she uses it as a tool—closes her eyes and breathes with her diaphragm. Sometimes on the school bus, I watch her do vocal exercises and stretch her mouth in disturbing ways, even if people she hardly knows are sitting beside her. She both lives for an audience and seems not to care what anyone thinks. She dresses in leotards and skirts that look like wraparound tapestry bedspreads. She wears earth shoes and Birkenstocks and doesn't shave her armpits. While I can see the relief in caring as little as she seems to, I can't bring myself to do this. I worry about everything—if my barrettes match, if my hair is curling under, if my pants are too short.

Rozzie gets away with doing nothing because she is pretty now, tall and thin from eating health foods no one else will touch in the fridge. Every night she eats vegetables flavored with No Salt and I Can't Believe It's Not Butter. She no longer likes sweets and doesn't touch chocolate. Once, someone gives her a Reese's that sits by her bed for five days until, finally, I go into her room and eat it. I expect her to yell at me but apparently she never notices.

I want to be like her—eat nothing but broccoli and grapefruit and sometimes a dinner roll, but I don't have the willpower. I go jogging for twenty minutes, then sit in front of the TV eating striped shortbread cookies. I make jokes about my thighs and then go into my room and measure them with a string. Being around Rozzie too much makes me nervous and underscores my weak points. I'm not ambitious, not clear in my goals; sometimes at night, I unwrap Hershey's Kisses, lie in bed, and let them melt in my mouth.

The first week she is away, she writes home twice, once to say she is miserable, once to say she's started classes and is happier than she's ever been. Our mother seemed to think this was terribly significant and pointed out to our father that she has never said this before. I wanted to say, "That's because we haven't *done* anything. We're in high school. What are we supposed to love—football games?" I didn't because my mother thinks I've recently grown needlessly sarcastic. She looks at me sometimes the way she used to look at Rozzie. Not often, but sometimes.

This summer I have just turned sixteen and am working for the first time, as a cashier in a supermarket where I wear an orange polyester smock I have never once washed. I tried to get a job in the camera store where I buy all my supplies, but when I asked, the boy working behind the counter said, "Usually the owner likes to hire guys."

"Oh, okay," I said amenably, as if it meant nothing, but for weeks I've thought about it. Is there such a thing as a camera that's heavy to lift? Or f-stops a woman couldn't understand? Instead I check out groceries and am considered the rocket scientist of the group because I can remember the price of a tomato paste from one day to the next. Other cashiers will hold up a roll of paper towels and say, "Jemma?" I'll look up and guess, "Fifty-nine cents?" Nine times out of ten, I turn out to be right. I don't know why my head can hold these figures but not material I need for class, but so be it. For the summer, I am considered a genius, and early in the morning, when we have no customers, Theo, the head bagger, will stand in an aisle and call out products. "Rice Krispies, forty-six-ounce."

"A dollar ten," I'll say.

A whistle will come back. "This woman is incredible."

Obviously I hope this talent will have no bearing on my future, but then what am I doing now that will? I wonder. These days feel like a holding pattern, a long, long wait for the good part to begin.

When I complain about this job, Theo tells me not to be dramatic. "We're in high school. We're supposed to have retarded jobs. That's the idea. Then you get to look back and say, 'Thank God I'm not doing *that* anymore.'" Theo is my best friend at work. He claims to love me and has several times asked me to marry him; I usually tell him I think we should go on a date first.

"See, that's the problem. I don't have a car and I'm too embarrassed to take you on a bus date." Theo has a big, jokey personality even though he has mild cerebral palsy and walks with a slight limp and keeps one hand curled, like a squirrel's, at his hip. If people don't know him, that hand makes them nervous, as if he's going for his fly or covering a wet spot. It makes them doubly nervous because Theo is good-looking. If you take away the smock and the hair his mother still cuts even though he's seventeen, the limp, the hand, the polyblend shirts that he sometimes wears inside out—which is a little bit like saying if you take away everything except his face—he'd be beautiful, which is true. He has green-yellow eyes with long, girlish lashes. Every once in a while I picture saying, "Yes, Theo, I'll marry you," or, "Let's really go on a date," but our jokes aren't like that. I'm not meant to take him seriously. His love for me is like everything else in my life right now—a way to pass time.

*   *   *

One night, Rozzie calls to tell us her teacher is sending five people from her class to audition for a movie.

"What kind of movie?" our mother asks nervously.

"A dirty movie, Mother, come on. I don't know what kind of movie, but it's all for the experience."

The next day, sweeping a pile of spilled cereal into Theo's dustpan, I tell him, "My sister is auditioning for a movie."

"What kind of movie?"

"A dirty movie. Come on, Theo, what difference does it make?"

"Do you know who's in it?"

"I don't know anything else about it."

"Interesting." He nods. "Very interesting. This time next year, she may be a star."

"Oh, please." This hardly seems likely. But suddenly I worry: What if she is? I am no longer afraid of Rozzie failing or going crazy or looking stupid in the eyes of the rest of the world. Instead, I worry about me getting left behind. If Rozzie got a part in a bona fide movie, where would that leave me? Alone with this job, with my paltry high school friends, who are already fixated on college and who is going to apply where, two years before the fact.

Some days I wish I had done something more adventurous this summer, gone somewhere like Rozzie, have something to show for myself. One break I tell Theo this.

"If you could be doing any job at all right now, what would it be?" he asks.

"I'd like to be a professional photographer working on assignment." I've never said such a thing out loud before. It makes me nervous.

"A photographer." He nods. "I can see that."

It's sweet of him to say even if it's also ridiculous—he's never seen one of my pictures. I wish I could explain this restlessness. It's as if even working in a grocery store stocked with food that I help myself to constantly, I'm always hungry.

Theo loves movies and sees everything that's out. This summer, he has seen *Mad Max Beyond Thunderdome* three times, though he tells me not to take that the wrong way. "I'm not into Tina Turner. What I like is the story." He'll then take three full-basket customers to tell me the whole elaborate plot of the movie. Usually, I'll let him get all the way to the end, then turn around and say, "Wait. *What* happened?" This is our shtick. That and the price-checking game.

One day he tells me I have to see this movie, *Feathers of Hope*.

"Why?"

"Well, a lot of reasons. It's good for one thing."

It is morning, slow enough for me to have a magazine open on my register and some Good & Plenty in my open coupon drawer. When I think no one's looking, I eat a handful and turn a page.

"Uh-huh."

"Well, I probably shouldn't say it."

"Say what?"

"It has this *scene*," he whispers.

I look up at him. I know it must be about sex because he's turned bright red, but I can't help it, I want to egg him on. "What scene? Tell me."

"Well, the guy is in a wheelchair so—whatever—not everything works, I guess." Now Theo is looking at me, making sure I understand. "But he still wants to do it."

I smile. "Do what?"

Theo blushes crimson. "Guess."

"Play basketball?"

"Have sex, Jemma. Obviously. Are you intentionally being dim?"

He stares at me, and for a second I stare back. "So what happens?"

It's too late. He's mad at me and I've blown it in some way. "Let's just say they manage," he says, and walks away.

That afternoon, before I get off, Theo asks if I want to go to a movie with him Friday night. We are alone by the punch clock and he isn't joking. He doesn't seem optimistic about my answer, though. He asks quickly, without his usual fanfare and charm, as if he'd decided days ago to do this, and now he has to. I stare at the clock and try to think of something to say. I like Theo, but he embodies everything that's sad about this summer. I have so many limitations. I want to be the sort of person who could go out with a boy who has a pronounced limp and a hand that rests motionless over his crotch and not worry about the people we might see, what people might think, but I'm not.

"I can't," I say. "I have this thing with my grandparents I have to do."

He must know it's a lie, must see what a small, putrid person I am because he doesn't suggest an alternative night, doesn't even say, *Another time, maybe.* He only says, "I understand," and walks away.

The next week Rozzie tells us she's been called back. "The director told me I'm good, that I have a natural quality. But he's concerned about my lack of experience." I picture her sitting in a room, across from a man old enough to be our father. "I need to ask a favor. They want a picture of me as soon as possible. Could I get one of those head shots you took?" My heart wakes up for the first time in months. She needs one of my pictures? I remember her initial reaction, which she has apparently forgotten entirely. Suddenly they're good enough?

The only prints I have are matted with my project. I'll need to make new ones and will have to find a darkroom to use because the school one is locked up for the summer. No matter. I imagine the director holding a photograph I've taken in his hands, turning it over, looking closer. Suddenly my summer has taken a different shape. I'm not just passing time, I *am* a photographer on assignment.

I find a darkroom three towns away that will rent me space by the hour. The next day, I call in sick and get my mother to drive me—an hour each way. I can tell my mother thinks I've made too big a deal out of this. "I don't want you spending too much of your own money," she says, staring down at the new box of paper that cost me a week's paycheck from the grocery store.

"I won't," I say, though of course it's too late. I hardly slept the last night thinking about all this—printing these pictures, Rozzie getting this part.

"It's just a small part. She probably won't get it, and even if she did, it's not going to change her life." My mother wants to believe this, though I'm not sure she really does. She is famous in her own way, as a special-ed teacher who works primarily with autistic kids. Three years ago she was voted Teacher of the Year in Massachusetts and filmed in her classroom for a PBS special called "The Unreachable Child." Rozzie and I stayed up late to watch, thrilled by the sight of her familiar yellow pantsuit on national TV while she sat behind us, counting her mistakes. "I shouldn't have had my hand on his," she said, as if anyone cared. Afterward, my mother believed the attention she got set her work back. For months she spent her time away from the classroom, on the telephone, answering letters. "Never again," she used to say, which she must be thinking about now.

I want to tell her to quit being so negative; this isn't just about Rozzie, it's about me, too, and this chance for my pictures to be seen by people who matter in Hollywood. "It's not small, Mom. The director wouldn't be talking to her if it was a small part." I don't know this, of course. I have told myself this just as I have told myself a story in which the director looks at my picture and says—to the air, to his secretary—*Who took this picture?*

I use up half a box of paper and still can't decide on the best one, so I send her three and we wait every night for a week for her to call. I start talking at work as if it were almost a sure thing. "There's one other girl in the running and she's supposedly too old for the part," I tell Theo as we sweep. "So I'd say there's a seventy percent chance she'll get it."

Theo shakes his head. "Wow," he says, and walks away.

After four days I want this to happen so desperately I'll be miserable if it doesn't. This is my dream, too, not just hers. We wait for her to call. Every night at dinner we stop talking when the phone rings, sit silently, and listen as my mother says, "Hello?"

Finally it's Rozzie. "It's *her*," our mother mouths to us. She listens for a minute, then screams, "She got it!" The house echoes with her jubilant voice, even though, in theory, she's opposed to all this. My father and I fan out around the house, get on separate extensions. Rozzie is in the middle of her story when I pick up. "What else? He said that I was talented, I guess. And now I have an agent. A pretty big one."

She sounds far away and distracted, as if she hasn't registered the news she is telling us. I know Rozzie's moods—that this probably means nothing, but our mother gets worried—"Are you all right? Is there something you're not telling us?"

"No, no. I'm fine."

"You don't *have* to do this."

"I want to," Rozzie says, her voice airy, almost absent.

"Why don't you come home and we'll talk about it?"

"I can't."

"Of course you can. We'll find the money somewhere."

"It's not that. I have a wardrobe fitting on Saturday. I can't go anywhere." Rozzie tells us more in the same glassy voice: She has meetings and rehearsals the following week. They will film in September and schedule her scenes so she misses as little of school as possible. They will put her up in a hotel, give her a tutor for the time she's supposed to be in school. I listen as she says all this to our parents, who are, above all, obsessed with college.

"What about your applications?" our mother says. "Can the tutor help with your essay?"

"I'll get it done. Don't worry."

I know Rozzie is just saying this—that our parents can't see what I so easily can: College is beside the point now. When you have been tapped like this, you don't stop everything and go to college the way people with no other choices do. Even over the telephone, I know she's twisting the cord around her finger, waiting to get off. At the end, as my parents say good-bye, she says softly, "Is Jem still on?"

"Yeah?"

My parents hang up so it's just us, alone on the line. Suddenly she sounds lonely. "Thanks for sending the pictures. They were great."

"Oh, sure. Did you use them?"

"I guess. I gave them to the secretary. I don't know what she did with them."

That's okay, I tell myself. *It doesn't matter.*

"It's weird. They want me to stay here till filming starts. They don't want me to go home at all. They're not going to schedule around school, I just said that so Mom and Dad wouldn't freak out."

"Oh." My heart has begun to race.

"It's a pretty big part."

"How big?"

"I might not be back until October."

"Wow."

"I wish I could come home."

I don't know how to answer. "It's okay. Mom and Dad will get over it."

A week before school starts, I quit working, hand in my orange smock and get my cash drawer counted for the last time. When Mr. English, the day manager, tells me I'm $4.72 short, I lean into the barred window he stands behind and say, "Whoops." Usually we're meant to offer explanations. If it's over ten dollars, we get it taken out of our paycheck.

From the corner of my eye, I see Theo standing in the doorway of the employee smoking lounge, talking to Theresa, a pretty Hispanic girl who wears a gold crucifix. Since the time he asked me out, we have been cordial with one another, but distant. Now I want to go over and say good-bye, tell him the news about Rozzie, thank him for helping me make it through this summer. I feel bad that I haven't made more of an effort and handled things better.

"So, Theo," I say. "This is it. My last day." I expect his face to register this, for him to walk away from Theresa and say, *Your last day, I didn't realize.* I half expect him to ask me out to lunch. Instead he holds up a hand: "Bye," he says, and turns back to Theresa.

Like the pictures, I tell myself, *It's okay. It doesn't matter.* I focus all my attention on going back to school, carrying my news of Rozzie's triumph. When I get there, it takes a day for the news to travel far enough so that, at three o'clock, the drama teacher, Mr. Wilkenson, finds me in the hallway and asks if it's true.

"Yes," I say.

He is an old man—or at least forty, anyway—with a wife who is beautiful and rumored to be agoraphobic, a recluse who dances and writes poetry behind curtained windows. There are other rumors about him, that he used to live in New York, that once he was an understudy for *Hair* on Broadway. We think of him as being bigger and better than this town we all live in. I know that Rozzie has, at times, had a crush on him, in spite of his wife and his head of thick gray hair. When no one else is around, she calls him Daniel. In front of other people, Mr. Wilkenson. By *no one,* I mean me—she calls him Daniel to me. Despite his being a teacher, he seems nervous about approaching me. "May I hear how it happened?"

"Oh, sure." I tell him as much as I know.

Mr. Wilkenson listens and shakes his head. "I had a feeling something like this was going to happen. Right before she left."

He stares up the empty hall at nothing, as if he has more to say. Then he doesn't. I fill in nervously, "Supposedly she'll be back in October."

"Yes, that's right," he says, almost as if he already knew. I have to wonder, Did he talk to Rozzie? Did she tell him?

I wonder if there was a time before he got old and his hair turned gray that he thought he might be a real actor, too. I always assume our teachers have lives that don't extend beyond the classrooms where I know them. As a rule, they are a predictable bunch who dress badly and carry tote bags full of papers to correct. Now I look at this man and wonder what he is feeling. His expression is unreadable, but his eyes are shiny, as if he might cry.

On the phone Rozzie tells us that she has been moved from her dorm to a hotel called Montmartre on Sunset Boulevard where she is in the same room Marilyn Monroe once slept in.

"Oh, come on," I say.

"It's that kind of place. Very old Hollywood."

What does this mean? I have no idea.

"The truth is, it's strange. I can't describe it. I was going to ask Mom and Dad what they'd think of you coming out here."

"Really?"

"Do you think they'd let you?" Her voice is tiny and hopeful and hard for me to understand or believe. When she left three months ago, I was hardly worth the time it took to say good-bye. Now she wants me to come visit? "It'd be nice to have someone I know with me. The company will pay for it. You wouldn't believe the things they pay for."

"I'd like to," I whisper. For a while I was upset that nothing ever happened with my pictures. Now I think, *Maybe this is better.*

Our mother is opposed, of course. Even though I will only miss one week of school, she doesn't want me to go. She says she'd like at least one person around here to make school a priority. The trick to talking her into this, I know, is lying more. "I'll bring all my books. I'll get the assignments ahead of time. I'll make it all up." I stare at her. "Rozzie needs someone there. I think maybe she's having a hard time."

There isn't too much my mother can say to this. When the plane ticket arrives, special delivery, in a large cardboard envelope, we don't say anything. We take it out and look at it. FIRST CLASS, it says, in raised gold letters.

The day before I leave, I stop by the supermarket to buy some shampoo and look for Theo, who's in the back, doing inventory. "Hi!" I say. He's been on my mind lately. I want to talk to him about all this with Rozzie, tell him I'm sorry.

He looks up and smiles. "Well, look who's back."

"Just to visit. I wanted to talk to you, if that's okay." My heart is hammering; I wish I'd planned what to say.

"Sure." He sits down on a box. He pats a carton of cereal boxes next to him. "I mean, I'm supposed to be working, but what the hell."

I sit down next to him. "I wanted to say I'm sorry. This was a hard summer for me. I wasn't very happy and I think maybe I took it out on other people."

"Okay."

"That's why I said I couldn't go out with you."

He nods but doesn't say anything.

"Now I'm going to L.A. tomorrow to be with Rozzie, who's filming this movie."

"That's great." He hesitates. "Isn't it?"

"I don't know. I keep thinking people are going to ask me questions about what I did this summer."

"And you don't want to say you were a supermarket cashier?"

I smile. "I don't know why not."

"Tell them you're studying to be a photographer. Tell them you want to take their picture."

It's funny that he says this. It's what I want to do, pretend I'm older and serious about this, an artist, too. "Yeah, I should," I whisper.

For a while we don't say anything.

Finally, he claps his hands together and stands up. "Okay, so I should probably keep going here." He points to the boxes.

"Right. I know."

I look down at the ground. I don't know what else to say.

As it turns out, no one cares what I've been doing this summer. Everyone is friendly and happy to meet me, but no one cares much about my life at all. For instance, no one asks where we are from. Maybe they already know or maybe it doesn't matter. Filming has been going on for a week, and already Rozzie seems accustomed to the rhythm of rising at 5 A.M., being driven to a trailer where she sits for an hour while other people curl her hair and put on makeup. She closes her eyes and lets them touch every part of her face. Her eyelids don't jump when they put on liner.

After Rozzie leaves, escorted by a guy wearing a wraparound headset, I am left alone with Marcie, the makeup woman, who looks over at me and says, through a fan of eye-shadow wands she holds with her teeth, "She's beautiful, you know. Very special." She shakes her head to tell me this is good news and bad. "She may get very big very fast. I've seen it happen." The undercurrent to her voice is clear—*Watch out, help her.*

"I know," I say, though this sounds stupid. I don't know. After one day I can see the life I have given Rozzie in my mind isn't what's happening. I can't describe or explain what's happening because it's all stretched out in terms of the future. There are other jobs, it seems, though she doesn't mention them. Other people do.

"I don't think this town is going to *let* her go home," one woman says to me. She had introduced herself as Rozzie's manager, then added, "Well, not her manager yet. Just hoping. Fingers crossed."

When I ask my sister about her, Rozzie doesn't recognize the name or the shirt I describe her wearing. But this isn't unusual. Rozzie doesn't register much about the people who buzz around her all day. If I say, "Where's Marcie?" she'll say, "Who?"

"Your *makeup woman?*" I'll have to explain, though Rozzie has been sitting in a chair in front of this woman for two hours.

Rozzie hasn't talked about her summer, nor have I talked about mine. She hasn't asked once about anyone at school. All this seems to matter little here. At night we go back to the hotel, where we eat a dinner that is, for me, awkwardly silent. I go over potential conversation starters beforehand. Maybe I'll tell her about the play that has been scheduled for the fall: *Equus,* rumored to be about a boy having sex with horses. There is a storm of controversy about it, and some parents aren't letting their kids try out, afraid of their getting cast as the boy. Six months ago Rozzie would have had a lot to say about this. But I'm not sure anymore: maybe none of this matters in the face of making a movie.

After four days I wonder why she wanted me here. I don't do much except wander between her trailer and the craft services table, stocked constantly with a new and amazing variety of snacks. I have made a few friends—the guy who restocks the table (and asks what I'd like him to put out!), the makeup ladies, a costumer—but I don't seem to be making a dent or impression of any kind. I am invisible, in a way. Except for the food I eat, there isn't much trace that I have been here at all, especially on Rozzie, who will go three or four hours without saying anything. If we speak, it is usually the strained small talk of strangers; we point to magazines and articles, saying, *Did you see this about the earthquake in Mexico City?* I suspect Rozzie wants to seem like her old self, still interested in causes and current events, so I give her these openings, and she's always obliging. "It's *terrible,*" she'll say with great feeling that dissipates within a minute. I don't point to the articles I'm really reading, about using natural henna or the benefits of Jell-O for growing fingernails.

After five days, she and I have said so little of any substance, I begin to wonder if she's sorry I came.

Then one night in her hotel room, we are lying in bed side by side, listening to the hum of traffic that sounds exactly like an ocean, and out of nowhere she says, "I thought I was going crazy before you came. I really did. Now I'm better."

"Good," I say. And that's all. A few days later, I go home.

Jemma, present

After Rozzie has been a week at the hospital, I realize some people are confused: they think she's still missing. They call her agent and tell him they saw her in a grocery store in Topeka, Kansas, buying vitamins. Or on the side of a highway, selling vegetables. They write him letters telling him to leave her alone, let her live as she chooses. She's an adult now, not a child, they point out, obviously unaware of how patronizing this sounds. People presume an intimacy with actors and actresses because, to them, the star has become many things: ideal girlfriend, fantasy friend—some women even write Rozzie to say, *I wish you were my sister,* which makes me wonder, of course. Rozzie never reads these fan letters. In the beginning she did and found it too unsettling, too full of *I've been watching you* stuff.

So I read them instead. These days, all of them, and there are a lot. My favorites are the ones from abroad, written months ago, before she was in the news, on see-through airmail paper, in stilted English. "This is to say that long I have loved you," one German man writes. To me, the foreigners are especially appealing; they seem far away, innocent characters like Hans Brinker or the little boy who stuck his finger in the dike. They will never take shape off the page, never turn real or menacing in any way. Because the day is long and there is nothing else to do in the hospital except watch television, which she hates, Rozzie lets me read her snippets from some of these letters. "I have lived with my mother for ten years," I read. "Though I should say my mother lives with me."

Rozzie laughs. "Crucial difference." She affects a German accent. "I sleep with my mother, or should I say she sleeps with me."

We both laugh and I read some more: "My favorite of your movies is *Leopold the Handsome,* filmed on location near my hometown, Friedberg, Germany." Rozzie was not in this movie and has never been to Germany. In public she is often confused with other actresses, but usually not by someone who has taken the time to find her address and write her a letter. On the street, people will stop her to pin down where they've seen her. They'll think she's on a soap opera or they'll say, "Wait, don't tell me," and go on and on, guessing one movie after another. In this and other ways, being a celebrity can be horribly humiliating, being recognized a way of feeling erased.

But this letter is so odd, it's funny. Who's ever heard of *Leopold the Handsome?* "You were so touching, so poignant and vulnerable."

Rozzie smiles, as she does a lot these days, even with so little to smile about. "Yes, I was, wasn't I? I think I might move to Germany. That's where my talent is truly appreciated." She keeps saying things like this: *Maybe I'll live in Montana, maybe I'll become a veterinarian,* as if it might be possible. As if she could leave one life and start another—disappear, so to speak, as I am doing.

In my own way, I am missing, too.

No one from my real life knows where I am. Though surely they could guess, they have no phone number, no means or invitation to get in touch with me. Several times an hour, I pick up the ringing telephone and feel the briefest flutter of dread that it is one of my friends, worried about me, and then when it isn't, a combination of relief and sadness washes through me. *Thank God they haven't called,* I think, and then I wonder: *Why haven't they called?* The truth is, I have been a disappointment to people who love me for no other reason than that the weight of their love feels ominous; as if in a matter of time I'll be outside all that again, looking in.

About Rozzie's condition, we know this much: Her retina detached and has been operated on. Healing is slow and requires her to remain as still as possible. For three hours twice a day, she lies facedown on a stretcher to improve circulation to the retina and to prevent bedsores. Flipping her takes twenty minutes. They say this will continue for at least two weeks, though no one has offered anything more specific than this. Beyond meals, and the flipping, her day has no other structure. It is empty time she must wait out, and we are here to help her do it.

To fill the time, we talk a lot about numbers—there's a 30 percent chance Rozzie will regain 15 to 20 percent sight in the one eye she's had surgery on. There's less hope for the other eye, the one that went first, though we never knew about it; a year ago at least, it partially detached but went untreated. Now it has less than a 5 percent chance of any recovery. Rozzie doesn't dwell on these odds or play them over in her mind the way the rest of us do. Alone, we close one eye and narrow the other trying to approximate 20 percent vision. Sometimes we'll guess, *It's not that bad. You can see more than you think.* Supposedly it's enough to safely cross a street, negotiate a sidewalk, read a billboard. All this is speculation, though. Right now, we are waiting for the bandages to come off.

One morning I go in and Rozzie is lying on her side, on top of her covers. "I know what's going to happen," she says softly.

My heart stops. "What?"

"It won't be any different. It won't be worse, but it won't be better, either."

"How do you know?" I feel like crying.

She shakes her head as if to say, *It doesn't matter.* We are all awaiting this outcome, and out of nowhere, she's saying, *Don't hold your breath.*

"I had a dream."

A *dream?* Is she kidding? "What kind of dream?"

"I couldn't see much, but it was okay. I was very calm, and making dinner for someone, I'm not sure who. Maybe me. I was in New York, puttering around my kitchen, looking for some crackers, actually." She stops there, says no more.

I don't tell my parents what she's said. They are too focused on being optimistic, saying things like "When she's better . . ." or "When she's working again . . ." The irony, of course, is how nervous her work originally made them. Now they are practically sending out audition tapes. That night they bring food into her room, and because it's a novelty—Chinese and chopsticks—it feels like a party. They tell a story about a Chinese dinner they had when they were dating. Surprisingly, they can both tell the story, though we've never heard it before: Our father bit a chili pepper and tried for a few minutes not to let on. He sat there, talking, tears streaming down his face. It's a different sort of story from what they usually tell and we're all surprised by it—this reminder that they were once our age.

After we've finished dinner, our parents leave early, saying they're tired. I say I'll stay, there's a movie I want to watch that I can't get at the hotel. We make up these reasons for staying late, taking turns so Rozzie won't have to face sleep alone.

After they're gone, Rozzie asks what I think about their marriage. I say I don't think about it too much.

"To me it seems really strong. The only good one I can think of," Rozzie says.

Again, I wonder: *Is she serious?*

"They stand by each other. They're loyal."

Sure, I think, but what about the dinners they eat with two books open between them? What about the ludicrous arguments during which they disagree on facts and don't speak afterward? Dare I remind her what driving in the same car with the two of them is like?

She keeps going: "It's hard to find someone who will stand by you. I don't know if you've noticed or not."

I assume she must be referring to me; that she is angry and this is her way of telling me. Or maybe she's also trying to say, *In its own way, this is a marriage, too—you and I.* I'm not sure.

Later she asks, "Do you remember those camping trips Dad used to drag us on?" Sometimes our talk gets so nostalgic I worry we must sound much older than we are—like spinster sisters who've lived together for years. I worry and, of course, I also love it.

"Sure," I say. "That blue tent."

"You want to know where I really lost my virginity?"

"Oh, God. Where?"

She grins. "In the blue tent."

This is the new Rozzie. The old one would never have joked about this. I smile, too, and so she knows what I'm doing, I laugh. "With who?"

"Some guy. I think his name was Mitchell. It was that last summer when I was sixteen and Dad made us go to Joshua Tree and I didn't want to. Do you remember that?"

Of course I do. This is my life, too. I remember trying the whole time to make Rozzie happier. Eventually I gave up and joined Rozzie in bad-mouthing our parents every chance we could. I remember one morning, sitting outside our tent, Rozzie smoking a cigarette butt she'd found and saying, "I have to say, Mom and Dad are really *working* my nerves." I loved the way she said *working*, rolling it around in her mouth. At the time, I thought it was the funniest thing anyone had said in weeks.

"You think his name was Mitchell. That's nice. Very romantic."

"I didn't think sex was supposed to be about love. It was about being mad at Mom and Dad." She laughs and then thinks of something. "Why didn't you ever do stupid things like that?"

"Like what?"

"Sleep with dumb people?"

"I did. I have."

"What? *Once?*"

This is an irritating habit of hers, believing she is always the one in more trouble. Saying I haven't made any bad choices is like saying I haven't felt what she has, that I don't know her pain. "I've done things"—I hesitate here—"that I'm not proud of."

"Oh, yeah? Like what?"

I almost tell her. And then I don't, of course.

Not surprisingly, spending all this time together has left us working each other's nerves, too. A few days later she asks if I'm aware of the sounds I make when I eat.

"What sounds?"

"It's like a clicking."

"No, I don't," I say, worried.

"Oh, yes. Trust me."

"A clicking?" I swallow. I hear nothing. "There's a clicking?"

"You're not doing it now. You're too self-conscious."

I believe her and worry over this for the rest of the night. Maybe this is my problem, with my life, with my work. I'm doing something wrong and I don't even realize it—something I can't see. The next day

I tell her to go to hell; I asked our parents and it's not true. "There's no clicking. They listened for it all night."

"Of course there isn't," she says. "I'm pointing out how gullible you are."

"Shut up."

"I was trying to show how you listen when someone says something negative, but not when they say something positive."

I stare at her. "Doesn't everyone do that?"

"Not to the same extent. If someone says you're a good photographer, you always say, 'I got lucky.' If someone says something mean, you think it's true."

I hate that she is right about this, that one of the main reasons I am here has nothing to do with Rozzie and is much more about my work and the vortex of my own thoughts, which have lately turned to nothing but actual and imagined criticism. Recently, it has gotten so bad, I've stopped taking pictures. In the last two months I haven't taken out my camera once, the longest I've ever gone without using it. I know the hospital is rife with subject matter—people poised in crisis; on Rozzie's floor alone are seven people trying not to go blind. My old self would have seen this opportunity and seized it. At my best, I am a fearless photographer, which is what you have to be. "You must photograph what scares you," my best teacher used to say. "What you've been taught would be politer not to look at." This was the woman who shot cancer patients, whose book is so full of bald heads, you do what she wants, which is to stop noticing. You look at eyes, cheekbones, the fourteen-year-old hairless boy touching his nose ring.

Something has happened and I am afraid; fear has crawled under my skin and paralyzed me. Every morning I think about bringing my camera to the hospital, and suddenly it feels impossibly onerous, too heavy a burden. If I start taking pictures again, I'll start seeing everything that's wrong with my work.

*　　*　　*

Rozzie's condition—detached retinas—is more typically present in diabetics and premature infants suffering from retinopathy and is almost never seen in an otherwise healthy adult. But the damage level in her eyes suggests that her retinas have been loosening for years, since adolescence, or perhaps even earlier. This is one of the mysteries right now: How long was Rozzie not seeing well, and not saying anything? Even she isn't sure. "I never knew how other people saw," she says. Some days were fine. "I could see everything. Blades of grass, everything." Other days were harder. For years now, her retinas have been breaking free and reattaching, doubling her vision, then clearing it. I think about the mistakes we made—how we thought she was going crazy, not blind.

Now we wonder why she is so certain the operation didn't work. The bandages aren't off and the doctor thinks she should be more optimistic. "There's pretty good odds for success in her case," he says. "She's young and healthy. Her body has a better capacity for healing itself than most of the patients I have."

This doctor is also young and stops by more frequently than the others. He occasionally makes odd, non-sequitur remarks that we realize later were probably jokes. He may have a crush on her—his left hand is ringless—but Rozzie laughs if I suggest this. "Please," she says. "The man has fondled my retina."

The day she gets her bandages removed, two doctors are present, but the young one announces he'll do it, as if there has been some discussion of this and he has won. Before he starts, she tells him if this operation didn't work, she isn't interested in having any more.

"Of course you are," our father says, and turns to the doctor. "Of course she is."

Rozzie shakes her head, and because the moment is so awkward, nothing more is said. The doctor coughs and starts unwinding bandages so tenderly his hands are shaking. "Okay, Rozzie. You won't see much at first. It'll be my face, which isn't much."

He's probably planned this line, I think, and then feel embarrassed for him.

Her eyes, which we haven't seen in weeks, look damp and puffy; her lashes are bent. She blinks. She moves her head toward the window, then moves it again. *She's looking,* I think. *She sees.* The window, then the lamp. She's going from one light to another. "Nothing," she finally says. "Just gray."

The next day the doctor comes in and asks Rozzie what she sees. She waits a long time, then says, "Lemonade."

A silence falls over the room. She blinks twice slowly. "I feel like I'm looking through lemonade."

There should be more by now. Light and dark. Shapes. Some people can even recognize faces. She shouldn't be seeing lemonade. We all know this, even her.

The next day it's worse. Just gray—no light at all—though one nurse says this isn't uncommon, that retinal reattachments can worsen in the first few days and then improve. I try to take heart, but as I understand it, Rozzie should be seeing double, or a confusion of images, as the retinal muscles adjust to their new position. This gray isn't good.

Rozzie doesn't seem as worried as we are. We can't tell if she's acting or not. We try to play along and sound optimistic, sitting in a row of plastic visiting chairs by her bed. The nurse says there's still hope. She could wake up tomorrow and be reading.

"Maybe," Rozzie says, smiling in my general direction as if I'm the one who needs reassurance. She doesn't sound convinced or in need of convincing. Every time we leave and come back, she says, without emotion, even cheerfully sometimes, "About the same."

Finally I ask her, "Aren't you scared?"

She shakes her head and shrugs.

Later, I ask the doctor if it could be psychological, if she's willing herself not to see for some reason. "I don't think so," he says. "That would be a fairly extreme response." He considers this further. "No," he finally says, shaking his head.

Rozzie, present

When her eyes first started to go, she imagined her bad episodes had to do with being recognized, that being seen meant she could no longer see freely herself. Fame took away the luxury of staring at strangers on the street. To put this in perspective (surely she was wrong, she knew fame alone didn't turn storefronts into wave machines), she started reading books, anything where a famous person wrote about its effects.

But she wasn't *that* famous, just as she wasn't completely blind. She was *almost* all these things and none of them completely. Still, she had waited for buses standing in front of pictures of herself, had ridden above posters of her own face. *It must be surreal,* people said every time her face was plastered around town. And it was, unless they knew her trick: That long before she had lost any sight at all, she pretended not to see. As if she knew this was coming, or maybe willed it to happen.

Now, she can still see the red. Not all the time, not in conjunction with any object in her room. Occasionally she worries that she is seeing something within, a spray of blood, leaking capillaries, and then her vision will shift, go amber at the edges and yellow, and it will look, for an instant, less like blood than a seabreeze, the grapefruit-juice/cranberry cocktail their mother used to drink when they were children.

One night, she gets in a fight with her father. He tells her she is young, has a long life ahead of her, that she needs to work harder at recovering. He makes her so mad, she wants to tell him the truth, that her concentrated years have made her older than he could ever imagine, that she doesn't feel young at all, she feels at the end of a long life spotted with a few bright moments. If she could, she would tell him there are many things she would rather not see. But that's not exactly true either.

She is rarely alone with her mother, though it's hard for her to say if this is by design or by accident. She can tell her mother wants to talk, not about her eyes, but about everything else. Her mother wants to understand all that has happened, but knows her well enough not to push. Rozzie can feel this. Sometimes her mother's questions come out as a whisper, "Is water okay? Or something else?" She speaks so softly, it's impossible not to hear the frustration behind her words.

Still Rozzie doesn't tell her. She can't. She doesn't even know where she'd begin. With high school? With Daniel? Is that when this urge to separate first began? To be so secretive? Sometimes the impulse was so powerful she lied about things that didn't matter, told her mother she'd gone to the pool when really she'd gone to the lake. She wanted privacy, silence, the darkness of her room lit by candles. Maybe even then it had to do with her eyes.

*   *   *

Finally her father demands an explanation: "It's insanity to give up so quickly. You've never been a quitter before."

This is a ludicrous statement, evidence that he maintains a false illusion of her in his mind. As a child, she quit everything. Gymnastics, piano, horseback riding. Her mother would grow thin-lipped and impatient. "I just want you to finish what you start," her mother would say, and Rozzie would dig her heels in, fake sick, manufacture sprained ankles.

Later, she quit men. Always quickly, sometimes not knowing at the start of a night that she would end it before dinner was over.

"It's hardly insanity," she tells her father. "The odds of any success are less than thirty percent. I have nearly the same odds that the vision will improve doing nothing. Why don't I just stick with that? Why don't we just say if God wants me to see something, it will happen?"

Her father stopped going to church so long ago, she can't actually picture him in one. She is the only one who's stuck with it long enough to still justifiably use His name, which she only does occasionally, for moments like this, when she wants the power to silence someone else.

At least with Jemma, conversation is easier. Her sister has been around enough to expect less, sit in silence for a while, then speak distractedly of nothing much.

This is all she wants, all she can manage right now.

Being with her sister is as close to being alone as anyone will allow, so she asks her sister to stay behind, to hang out for dinner, watch a movie. Always, of course, Jemma says yes. This is the least they can do for each other. She can ask, Jemma can say yes. It's a small kindness, but it's something.

Jemma, 1986

After Rozzie is cast in her second movie, our mother develops a host of misplaced anxieties and irrational fears. She worries about crazy things: that Rozzie will undergo a metamorphosis, start buying expensive cars, convert to Scientology. "What is *that* all about? Why do all these movie stars belong?" she asks me one day.

"I'm not sure," I say.

"Do you think Roz would ever fall into something like that?"

Rozzie's new life may be a mystery to me, but I know she's in little danger of this. "Mom, please." My mother worries that being in movies will brainwash Rozzie, erase her past and imprint all new ideas: only looks matter; strive for fame; be thin. My mother is nervous about every new development in Rozzie's life: "I'm getting a manager," Rozzie will say, and my mother will gasp, "To manage *what?*" When we call and Rozzie says she's in the middle of a photo shoot, my mother asks what that means. "A photo shoot, Mom. They just take my picture wearing different dresses. It's nothing."

"Oh, dear God," my mother will say.

Our father's response is different. Though he rarely sees current movies and has never heard of most of the people Rozzie is acting with, he is tickled by the idea of acting for a living and confesses—out of nowhere—he once considered doing the same thing.

"Warren," my mother snaps. "You did not."

He is a math teacher at the local community college, and in truth it *is* hard to picture him acting at some point.

"Oh, sure. In high school. When I played Tybalt." My father has the sort of memory that allows him to deliver an entire speech of Tybalt's, then to keep going, doing the whole scene, everyone's lines.

"Oh, Warren, stop," my mother says, smiling.

One night while Rozzie is still away, he announces that he's thinking about starting a play-reading group. "We'll cast it ahead of time and do a staged reading. A few props, maybe, some costumes, whatever people feel like."

My mother stares at him. "I don't get it," she says.

"For fun."

For the first play, he chooses *King Lear* and casts himself as the lead. On a long-distance call from L.A., he offers the part of Cordelia to Rozzie. He seems to think she might fly home for the chance to participate. She says she'd like to but can't because she has to work. I am asked next and have no excuse. Two weeks later, a strange group of my parents' friends gather in the living room, all holding worn Penguin editions of the play on their laps. One or two have taken this as seriously as my father and have highlighted their lines in yellow pen. My father has constructed a crown for himself and a costume cape out of a plush magenta bath towel.

I am the youngest person in the room by twenty years and am so embarrassed by this whole endeavor I stare at the carpet on the floor and count brown flecks in the weave. As we begin reading, everyone else stays seated except for my father, who moves around, from sofa to sofa, making entrances and exits through imaginary doors, whipping his bath towel in people's faces.

In the beginning, people laugh, but then they stop, caught up in the story, goaded by his efforts into acting more also. Frieda, a coworker of my mother's whom I've always thought of as sadly reserved, a woman who has worn the same nonhairstyle—a thin ponytail—for fifteen years, jumps up to shout a Goneril speech at my father. He falls back onto the sofa beside me, one hand raised melodramatically to his throat. She hovers over him and continues shouting. It is all so unexpected, electricity fills the room; we dart glances at each other. Where is this going? everyone seems to wonder. Now that Frieda has shouted in public, she might do anything, we think: unloose her ponytail, take off her top.

Of course she doesn't. The moment passes; she returns to her seat, our father sits upright, then stands, straightening his towel over his shoulders, adjusting his crown. He doesn't look silly anymore. He looks like a king, confused and old, grasping for the power that his children now have.

After this evening, it's clear to me: What has happened to Rozzie, so far away, has changed all of us, even Frieda, who is the last out the door, carrying a plastic cup of water, a mustache of sweat on her upper lip. Everyone is touched in different ways by her fame.

I have started to believe some portion of the attention Rozzie is getting awaits me, too. At night, falling asleep, I imagine my photographs hanging in galleries, a horseshoe of people clustering around each one, pressing closer, squinting to see.

After the movie finishes filming and before the next one starts, Rozzie is allowed to come home for three weeks. "That's *all*?" our mother says. "What about school?" She can't let this go, even though bringing it up is ridiculous now.

"School will have to wait," Rozzie says, without wavering, amazingly sure of herself.

"That makes me very uncomfortable."

"I know, Mom. But if I say no, I won't get offered parts like this again."

Our father thinks it's fine for her to do it, that she'll go to college a few years later than everyone else. She has showed him her new contract; he knows what she will earn on her next movie. Apparently, he is not a man bothered by the prospect of a seventeen-year-old daughter earning more in a few months than he does in a year. On the contrary, at her first dinner home, segue from nothing, he starts to rattle off a list of large-ticket items he'd like for his birthday, coming up next month.

"Oh, honestly, Warren," my mother says, shaking her head.

"What?" he says, grinning.

The next day, Rozzie comes to school with me. The idea is that she will go to her classes and talk to her teachers. She will buy the books and use them with the set tutors she is required by law to have three hours a day. She tells her English and her history teachers she still wants to consider taking AP exams. Before all this happened, she had a chance to start college with enough credits for sophomore standing.

Now credits don't matter.

The books she takes, the syllabi, the paper assignments, are all symbolic. She can read whatever she wants and not read whatever she doesn't want. She will graduate regardless. Her connection to these teachers and this school is so gossamer a breeze could sever it, which everyone seems to sense. Her old friends come up and talk quickly; they complain about the play they're doing and then say, "This must all sound so stupid to you now."

"No, no," Rozzie says, but her expression is altered, even her voice different, and people seem frightened of talking too long. At lunch, she and I sit alone with our trays of food. Six months ago we hardly ever ate together. She had her friends, I had mine. Now she has no choice, apparently. "This is so strange," she whispers to me, picking turkey out of her sandwich, eating only that. She could rectify the situation by seeking people out and going up to them, seeming more like her old self, but oddly, she doesn't. She spends the day hovering near me, as if this is my school she's visiting, not her own.

The next morning she stays in her nightgown and we pretend that the plan all along was for her to go just the one day.

Her last day in town, our parents throw a party, mostly for their friends, the *King Lear* crowd, though Rozzie invites her old drama teacher, Mr. Wilkenson. The party is outside with paper plates and potato salad my mother has made using so much dill it looks as if someone has thrown lawn clippings in the bowl.

Frieda is there, standing where she usually does on these occasions—with a coworker she sees every day, talking about one of their difficult kids. This time, though, I watch her eyes follow Rozzie around the yard. Everyone looks at Rozzie differently now. She is not a star yet, but the potential blazes around her. They have wondered, *Why her?* and now they see, *Oh, yes. It's clear.*

For no fault of her own, Rozzie is hard to be around. Everyone is polite and demure. We eat potato salad and wipe dill off our teeth. Everyone is staid and slightly self-conscious. No one has as much fun as we did a few weeks ago, reading *King Lear*.

Rozzie can't help the effect she has on a room. Absent, her luck energizes people and fills them with hope; in the flesh it does something else entirely—it seems to point out the bleakness of their lives.

Rozzie, present

In the hospital, she reminds herself she still has secrets—things about her no one knows. Even if she told, they would never know how it felt to become a person she didn't recognize: to look in a mirror and not find herself.

In the beginning, it happened quickly, in makeup chairs, without her knowledge. Her eyebrows became foreign creatures on her face, two tiny, bent lines where real brows used to be. Once, it took her a day to realize her hair was a new color, that what she'd thought was a conditioning treatment must have been a henna pack or a cellophane because, when she lifted her hair, her roots didn't match.

Slowly, she has learned to separate herself from her body. Contractually, her surfaces belonged to whatever movie she was shooting. If they wanted her brunette, that was that. Expressing an opinion, she would feel the embarrassment of watching producers pretend to listen to her. It wasn't worth the effort, she'd found, and in the long run, it didn't matter. Once she thought she was in control; now she understood control was something only very young people in this business talk about.

Lying in the hospital bed, she remembers trying to explain this to her parents. It was in the beginning, her first visit home, and her mother was telling her acting could wait but college couldn't. It was such an innocent, naive argument. Her mother had no idea what was being said, the jobs that were being offered. That Rozzie was like an athlete with a window of opportunity. Three weeks earlier, an agent had taken her out to dinner and told her some major offers were pending and (in the same breath he said it, the same sentence it seemed) would she consider a small amount of plastic surgery.

She nearly laughed and started to explain, *You don't understand, I'm not like that. I don't even wear makeup,* but he spoke before she could. "It's not widely known, but almost everyone's done it. It's the concession you make if you want the good parts." She didn't laugh. He was obviously serious.

"Where?" She'd never thought of it this way. She didn't know her weaknesses until the people who offered her jobs told her.

Afterward, she told no one.

She stayed inside, peeled away her bandages, and studied her scars. It was permanent now, these changes, this distance she was traveling from her own old body. She did as she was told—drank water, didn't exercise, lifted nothing. To fill her empty time, she plucked her eyebrows and watched television. Only later, when her eyes began to really go, did she see the truth: how she'd been misled.

Not everyone does this. There are variations to beauty, permutations possible.

Only later did she see how young she must have been to believe all the things she'd been told.

Jemma, 1988

After her first two movies are released, Rozzie doesn't have to be in a room to alter the chemistry of it—her name alone can. I figure this out my first semester away at college, the loneliest, strangest two months of my life. I arrive and am instantly overwhelmed by logistics, lost in my academic classes, not much better in photography. Participating in dorm life and college activities doesn't come naturally; I don't know how to pump a keg smoothly or get stoned without coughing.

In desperation I start talking about Rozzie any chance I can. I decorate my dorm room with a lobby poster of her first movie and eight-by-ten pictures of her. In truth, she's not that famous, but I act as if she were and I emphasize, anecdotally, the famous people she's met. It becomes an addiction born of the fear that I have nothing else to offer. Eventually it also becomes a series of exaggerated claims and outright lies. "I've met that guy," I'll say, pointing to a movie poster, talking to someone I hardly know, about someone I've never met. "I had lunch with him a couple of times." Even as I say such things, I wonder what I'm implying: that I dated him? My face will go hot with the chance that I am talking to this person's cousin, that I will get caught in this lie, though I never do.

I also never make any friends.

People notice me, perhaps; they go quiet and whisper movie titles behind my back, but in general I am too nervous, too awkward, to be invited to the late-night pizza parties that go on around me. Once I overhear someone say I am really nice, but hard to get to know. I am sure she is right, but I don't know what to do about it. Sometimes, returning from the bathroom, I'll stand outside doors and listen to what other girls talk about, trying to understand what I should be doing.

In November, I go home for Thanksgiving break a day early, and in a gas station just outside of town, I see my old friend Theo working the register. The last time I saw him was maybe six months ago, in an ice cream store. He looks older, more pulled together. He's also pierced one of his ears.

"Theo, my gosh, how are you?"

"Jemma, Jemma, Jemma," he says. Behind him a guy is loading burritos into the freezer. Theo calls over to him, "So, Alan, you want to meet the girl who broke my heart?"

"Oh, please," I say, grinning.

"One of the many," Alan calls.

Theo laughs. "No one but me understands my untapped potential." Alan howls; Theo smirks. "So what's happening with you, lovely Jem? You must be a college girl."

"I go to college. I'm not sure I'd call myself a college girl." I tell him I'm not doing very well so far, but I don't elaborate. I don't tell him there's a danger I might fail a couple of classes. Instead, I ask him what he's doing these days, and he looks around, at the register and the coffeemaker. "Training to be an astronaut." He smiles and I smile back. "No, just kidding. Working here, but hopefully not for long. I have a business idea I'm pursuing. I can't talk about it right now because—" He looks around. "Well, Alan will make fun of it."

"How about later?" I say, surprising myself.

He looks up. "You want to get together?"

"Sure. I'm home for vacation. I don't have any plans."

My mother remembers Theo—the way he used to bag groceries one-handed and talk the whole time. "He was a charmer," she says. "I always liked him."

I blush because it's true and I don't want to make the mistakes I did last time. When he shows up that night at the front door wearing a black turtleneck and jeans, he looks so good it makes me nervous. He may have a bad hand and a limp, but he is beautiful. He really is. "Hello, Mrs. Phillips. Nice to see you again," he says to my mother, kissing her on one cheek. I don't know where he gets this ease with people. It's as if he was born with it along with whatever problems he had. "How's teaching going?"

He hasn't even looked at me yet. I'm wearing my own version of sexy jeans: they've got a hole on one knee and another in back. My mother tells him school is the usual, crazy and good.

"Hi, Theo," I say, standing on the stairs.

He turns and smiles. "Hello, Jem."

Over dinner I try to describe what college has been like. "It's hard. I don't connect to any of the people and I don't know why. It's like they all knew each other for years before they got there, and I came and didn't know any of the inside jokes. So you want to know what I do?"

"What?"

"Talk about Rozzie."

He narrows his eyes. I'm not sure if it's wise to tell him all this, but now that I've started, I don't stop: "All the time. Any chance I can. It's like a sickness. I can feel myself get intimidated by a group of people at lunch, and I'll figure out a way to get the conversation somewhere in the vicinity of Roz so the rest of the meal can be spent talking about what it's like to be her sister."

Theo shakes his head. "That's not good. That's not the most interesting thing about you."

I stare at him. "Sure it is. I mean, theoretically, you're right—I've got, whatever, a good personality—but if you put me in a room filled with nineteen-year-olds, what's interesting about me is that my sister has starred in three movies."

To me this seems so obvious, but he looks surprised. "No, it's not."

Suddenly I'm embarrassed. Why did I start with this? What was I hoping he would say? "Okay, you're right. It's not."

For a long time after that, I can't figure out what to say. We study the menus between us as if they are books we are going to be tested on. I look around for the waiter, the bathroom, someone I might know from high school. Finally I remember I can ask Theo about his business idea. He says he'll only tell me if I promise not to laugh. "I promise," I say.

He holds up his good hand, flat, for me to picture what he's picturing. He takes his time, clears his throat, then says, "Specialty grocery."

I laugh. I can't help it.

He drops his hand. "You said you wouldn't laugh."

"I'm sorry. It's just that word *grocery*. I thought we were trying so hard to leave that behind."

"*You* hated that job, I didn't. I sort of liked it. And this would be different. All gourmet foods—imported cheeses, olives, specialty items, oils, vinegars."

"Where did you get this idea?"

"My mother's Italian and she's always trying to find certain things that she never can. But it wouldn't really be about my mother. It'd be targeted to yuppies."

His saying the word *yuppie* makes me wonder about how different we are. Separate from his limp or his hand, apart from the embarrassing admissions I've just made about my life, he's a guy who works at a gas station and I'm a girl at college, which produces nothing but yuppies.

The rest of the night feels awkward. We keep trying to find our old rhythm and the jokes keep falling flat. After dinner, we go to a movie, crowded with high schoolers out on break, too. It's the night before Thanksgiving and every teenager in town seems to have suddenly taken up smoking. I tell Theo watching them makes me want a cigarette, just as he says he doesn't see why everyone smokes these days. The contradiction is so embarrassing we don't mention it and walk quickly through the parking lot. Walking fast makes his limp worse, more pronounced.

Inside the theater, we wait for the movie without talking. It's hard to tell which one of us is more disappointed.

The next day I tell my parents what's happening at school—all of it: that I'm doing so badly in my classes, there's a chance I may flunk out. I tell them I have no friends, that I'm miserable. So far I have only hinted at this. They listen and nod. "I don't know if I can last," I say a little dramatically.

This has something to do with my night with Theo. I wanted that to be the answer to my problems. I wanted to go back to school with a boyfriend at home so I could leave every weekend, pointing to a picture of a handsome face. And in the end it was a fine evening, but there was no kiss, no declaration of love. If he once had a crush on me, it's waned by now and he's obviously not interested in being a picture I can put on my wall beside my sister's.

My parents tell me to give it time.

"I hated college for the first three years," my mother says.

I stare at her. "That means you only liked it for one year, Mom."

She thinks about it and nods. "That's right."

"That seems kind of sad."

"But I loved it for that year. What made it hard initially made it great later on."

I want to say, *You're not really helping.*

My father tells me to throw myself into my classes, the social life will follow. "Find your passion," he says, then remembers I have one. "Like your pictures. What about your pictures?"

I tell him they're fine, I'm taking photography, but I don't tell him I hate it—that it makes me feel small. By the end of high school, I was head photographer on yearbook and widely regarded as the best photographer in the school. Even our strange, bitter teacher told me he thought I had a future in this, that I should consider art school. Now that I've gotten to college, I've learned only that I'm not as good as I thought. In this class we write critiques of each other's work, which are hard for me to write and even harder for me to get. "I have a problem with some of Jemma's subjects," one boy wrote. "They seem kind of slight to me."

"You're good, but I think you could push yourself harder," another one said.

I assume these people are right about my work. When I got a B+ on my first project, I threw all the prints in a Dumpster behind the art building. One facet to Rozzie's success is that it has made me want to be the best at photography or not do it at all. To be like everyone else—just a student learning—seems sad and ordinary. I've even thought of dropping the class.

Rozzie is in Italy right now, shooting a large-budget Mafia movie that's behind schedule so she isn't allowed to come home for Thanksgiving. On a staticky call from Rome, she says it's okay, the producers are giving them a day off and a turkey dinner. She sounds unfazed about being so far from home. It's not even clear if she'll be home for Christmas. When she asks how I am, I tell her the truth. My life is so sad, I can't seem to pretend otherwise. She listens for a while and then stops me: "You should leave. Drop out."

I assume she's joking. "Yeah, right. I wish I could."

"You can. Come here and I'll get you a job."

She proposes this as if it were a simple matter, a couple of phone calls maybe. My heart starts to race. "Just like that?"

"Sure."

"Really?" This is magic. She has become not only an actress, but a magician. Just as she can enter a room and alter it, so, too, she can change my life.

For an hour I can hardly get my mind around it. Later that afternoon, Rozzie leaves a message on the machine: "Tell Jemma it's fine, they'll send a plane ticket."

I don't even think about what I'm doing, and also don't consider saying no. I stand over the machine, thinking, *This is it.*

My parents aren't happy about the idea, but I'm surprised—they don't forbid me to go, as I might have expected. Recently my mother has begun to concede that, overall, Rozzie's success has been a good thing, an opportunity for her to travel and learn as she works. All the things she worried about early on don't seem to have happened. And maybe this will be better for me, too, my mother says vaguely, making me wonder what she means. After a lifetime of saving for college in large and small increments, of making us contribute in symbolic ways—five-dollar savings bonds, thirty dollars from our grandparents, so that it was always clear, *College matters*—we all seem to be saying, in a single afternoon, *Oh, well, skip it.*

The only person who thinks dropping out of school is a bad idea is Theo, who calls three days after our date to see if I want to go out again. I tell him I can't, that I don't have time, and explain why.

"You're leaving college?"

"I have a chance to work on a movie. I'll go back."

"Like when?"

"When the movie's over," I say, though of course this isn't true. The movie will be over in February after second semester has started.

"I just think you're lucky to be in college. It's a good opportunity."

I've kept expecting someone to say this—to point out that dropping out of college for a two-month job isn't, practically speaking, a strategic move. But no one has until Theo, the only young person I know not in college. "Come on, Theo. It's not the end of the world. You're not in college, right?"

"Exactly."

"Okay, here's the truth." I tell him what I haven't told anyone else: that I'm going to use this chance to become an artist. All the great ones started in Italy, I explain. I'm going to bring my camera and enough film to shoot seven hundred pictures, what Margaret Bourke-White said you need to take to get ten good images. She is famous for running through rolls and rolls of film, for never using a light meter and, instead, shooting every image at five different exposures. I want to go there and seem like one thing—the sister of a star—but be something else: a chronicler, a reporter, the way Bourke-White was. Because Theo doesn't say anything, I tell him about the whole series done on the set of the *Misfits,* Marilyn Monroe's last movie, when she wore that bulky Peruvian sweater and leaned onto Clark Gable's thigh, laughing in a way you never see her do in her movies. I want to capture, in still frames, some truth about moving pictures.

"Huh," he finally says. "Okay."

* * *

When I get off the plane in Rome, Rozzie is there, along with a driver and half a dozen photographers, who snap pictures of us hugging in the lobby just beyond customs.

As we walk through the terminal, they walk backward in front of us and I think of all the pictures I have seen of famous people working their way through airports. We are meant to keep talking, I gather, because Rozzie does—as if they weren't there, as if their walking wall of flashes didn't create a moat of space around us. Everyone else stops and watches; no one comes near.

I wish I could take a picture of how being photographed aggressively by strangers feels. The driver, used to this, keeps the wall moving by eyeing the path the photographers aren't watching themselves. After five hundred feet I want to ask, *Haven't they gotten enough yet?* I want to be friendly—tell them I take pictures, too, and ask about their cameras, how they like the flashes they're using. Instead, I eye Rozzie and say through a smile, "Is it always like this?"

"Oh, no," she says, not looking at the cameras. "They like to get an airport shot. They're worth more than street shots for some reason. Don't worry, it'll be over soon." Indeed she's right. They don't wait around for the car to come or follow us once we are driving on the road. "I'm not quite *Princess Diana*," she says.

Later that night, we go out to dinner with two actors she has met on the set, wonderful, funny men, she tells me. "I feel like I could be friends with these guys for the rest of my life," she says. A bottle of wine appears on the table a minute after we sit down with James, who seems to be about fifty and gay, and Leonard, who seems to be about forty and not. Someone must have ordered this wine when I wasn't looking because Leonard says, *"Grazie,"* and grabs the neck.

They *are* funny. They tell me about what filming this movie has been like, in a flurry of overlapping stories. I pick up the highlights. The Italian crew is crazy, all trying to sleep with each other; the Americans are having affairs right and left, including the director, who everyone says is sleeping with his script supervisor. Progressively the stories seem less funny. Some people are doing heroin. An actor's been fired. They're two weeks behind schedule. I try to imagine how I will photograph these things.

"Heroin?" I say, looking at Rozzie.

"Supposedly." She shakes her head and shrugs.

During dinner, it's obvious Leonard has taken a shine to Rozzie. He stares at her as he tells his stories, his eyes a little watery, the smile on his face unrelated to his words. What I can't figure out is what she's thinking. He is bald and so doughy his fingers on his wineglass look like sausages to me.

"He's very talented," she tells me later, alone in the room I am sharing with her. She tells me the name of his movies, all stories like this one: Mafia, guns, everyone dead in the end. "I think he's just now getting recognized for how good he is."

Are they dating? At the end of the night, she kissed him on the lips, but I have seen her kiss other people on the lips, especially on sets, where people say "I love you" as frequently as they say almost anything else. "I think maybe he likes you," I offer, knowing I sound ridiculous, as if I'm still in high school.

She doesn't snap at me the way I expect her to. Instead she looks out the window, eyes lost in thought. "I guess maybe. Sometimes, I don't know."

I want to bring her back from wherever she's gone—point out that he has very little hair and could really use a gym. I want to say, *Please, Roz. I may be desperate, but you're not.*

But she is, in a different way.

It turns out he's married. He does love her, but he's married. She tells me this the next morning.

"Oh, Jesus," I say.

Rozzie, 1988

She doesn't know what to make of this director who doesn't believe in rehearsal or in actors running lines ahead of time, because all that, he says, is about line readings and he doesn't care about line readings. He cares about the truth, he tells her, pronouncing it *troot*. He never says *troot* without bringing his thumb and middle finger together, stabbing the air.

She is twenty, hardly in a position to argue with a director, but at their first meeting she told him she liked rehearsal, that it helped her feel more confident in a role.

"You don't get the troot by practicing it. It comes from here," he said, using his thumb and finger to stab his chest.

There is nothing she can say to this. She has been in two other movies. What does she know yet, really, about acting this way, producing a performance in one-minute intervals? She often thinks about Daniel, and what he would say of how a scene should be played, of finding emotions behind emotions.

She wants to believe in this director and trust what he's saying, so she sits in these meetings and does as she is told. She closes her eyes, places one hand out in front of her, flat, palm up.

"You've just been raped," he says. "Your mother is dead. How do you feel?"

These things are not in the script as written. She plays a shop girl the two men fight over. There's nothing about a rape or her mother. In the scene they are about to shoot, she has four lines about bread. How is she meant to convey what he is telling her with lines like "Seeded rye or plain?" Instead of speaking, she nods and considers.

Later, the scene gets three takes. She knows she is only good in the last one. For the first two, she is distracted, trying to understand the dead-mother thing, or the idea that she might, out of nowhere, be playing a woman who's been raped. She wants to tell the script supervisor to make a note: *Please use the third take.* She feels desperate about this, almost frantic, but suspects such a plea will make her sound young.

It is a terrifying feeling to learn on the spot the way she is doing— to hit and miss on her takes as much as she has. In twenty-three days of shooting, there is more footage of a bad performance than there is of a good one.

The only person she can talk to about this is Leonard, who says if he had it to do all over again, he would have been a director. He has been a character actor for many years, in countless movies, and in his opinion, actors are props, coat hangers for costumes. "Nothing we do is going to make a difference, really. The director's going to do whatever he wants to do, and after that, the producer's going to screw it up."

It isn't that she likes hearing such cynical assessments, but she feels it's important—that this is the truth she needs to learn. She clamors to be around him, to absorb his knowledge. He steadies her nerves, calms her growing anxiety that this performance will be her last. "Nah," he says, when she confesses her insecurity. "You've got at least five more years, I'd say." He laughs as he says this.

Even though she can see at times he is nobody, really, an aging character actor wrestling with obscurity, at other times an extraordinary feeling will roll through her: *I love him,* she'll think. *I'll do anything to have him.*

Jemma, 1989

The stars of the movie are two men, famous enough that Rozzie and I have seen at least two of their movies together. When we get to the set, though, Rozzie seems unaffected by the fact that we know these faces, have sat in darkened theaters and watched them cry, jump out of airplanes, ride horses. She introduces us casually, as if it's nothing, as if now that she's started making movies, she's pretending to have never watched one before.

After a day or so, I figure out she's right—being around famous people means never alluding to their fame, but talking, for the most part, about them. They speak about their children, about dogs they had growing up, about a time, two years ago, they tried surfing. It is thrilling to pile up these anecdotes and to plan how I will retell them in the future, embellishing the details.

My job as a production assistant is mindless—I stand with a traffic cone and guard parking spots; I fetch coffee and carry a Sweet'n Low pellet dispenser in my pocket. Because I am the star's sister, I am not given the humiliating tasks the other set assistants are saddled with. I am considered different, a bridge between the actors and the crew. The producer puts his arm around me and offers me a stick of gum; the director lights a cigarette for me in his mouth. Though I have only smoked a few times before, I take it, putting my mouth where his has just been.

I quickly strike up unexpected friendships. The fifty-year-old woman playing Rozzie's mother tells me she has never been emotionally intimate with a man; the most handsome actor on the set tells me how much he misses his girlfriend, a model back in New York. It seems that I am more at ease with famous people than I was with the girls on my dorm floor.

Because so little is expected of me in my job, I start taking pictures and no one seems to mind. I shoot all the Tri-X I brought, then find a place where I can buy ten more rolls with the envelope of per diem cash I am given at the end of every week. At first I shoot cautiously, with my camera tucked inside my puffy jacket; then I realize no one cares, and I take whatever I want.

A week after my arrival, it occurs to me that I am more comfortable hanging out on this set than Rozzie is. She watches what Leonard is doing most of the time, waits to see where he sits in the dinner tent, then slides her tray in as close as she can. No one understands this as Leonard seems, to everyone else's eyes, too bald and too old for her. I know only that Rozzie's taste in men has always been unusual, that her heart has been broken by men most women wouldn't consider dating.

This is what seems to be happening here. His wife is expected to arrive in a few days and he's told Rozzie he wants to be her friend, but first he needs to deal with his marriage. She asks me if I think that sounds as if he intends to leave his wife and I tell her I don't know. Neither of us is experienced at this. We look as if we know much more than we do.

One afternoon, I find Rozzie alone in her trailer, sitting in the dark. "I've decided I don't care about him," she says.

"Okay."

"Look at what he's done to his wife. Why would I want someone like that?"

"I don't know."

"I *don't*."

"Good." I wish I could offer her more. She has stepped in and changed my life so dramatically that I want to give her something back. Maybe I can shoot a series of pictures that emphasize his baldness, his doughy white fingers, or point out the crew members who are young and handsome and I know have a crush on her. The next day I realize that none of these things will help, as Leonard's wife arrives on the set and isn't beautiful so much as striking and smart. She is also older, her husband's age, and a professor of comparative lit at Hunter College in New York. She is the sort of woman I suspect Rozzie would someday like to be herself—an hour after arriving, Leonard's wife is talking about politics with the writer of the movie. I watch Rozzie watch every move this woman makes. Maybe she is worried about other things. It's hard for me to tell.

Three days later, Rozzie tells me we're going home two weeks ahead of schedule. It's been decided that the remainder of her scenes can be shot onstage back in Los Angeles. She isn't sure why they're doing this. It may be an attempt to keep the escalating location costs under control, or it may be some people are worried about her emotional state. "We just want you to go home and relax for a few weeks, sugar," one of the producers, a nervous Southern woman, tells her.

Rozzie isn't sure what to think. "Have I seemed weird? Like I'm freaking out?"

"No," I say, though I don't know. Now that others are worried, I worry, too. *Is* she freaking out?

That I will leave with her is assumed without question.

We fly back to New York on the Concorde together, take our first-class seats side by side, accept red roses from the stewardess, who is tall and beautiful and cannot stand up straight in the tiny cabin.

Every hour or so after the flight takes off, we receive another wrapped present. Apparently this is part of the Concorde tradition. We say little as we open them, identical Concorde money clips, identical Concorde writing pads. Have they spotted us for first-timers? Or do regular Concorde riders have boxes of this stuff at home? The surreal speed of the flight doesn't help this feeling that we've done something wrong and are being hustled away, out of sight. These feel like the parting gifts losing game-show contestants take home with them.

Then, as we open the last present, a picture frame containing a photo of this airplane, Rozzie thinks of something. She looks out the window and then at me. "You know what I just realized?" I look at her. "I have no more scenes with Leonard. I'm never going to see him again."

"Oh, you will. You'll see him at some point."

"No. Don't you see? It's great." Her face is lighter; she's smiling for the first time in days. "I never have to see him again."

"Yeah." I laugh. "That's right." Really, I don't understand the hold he has had over her or why she needs to get away to be free of him. Unless it's the way college was for me—and now here we are, breaking the sound barrier to get away from these things that feel like failure.

Jemma, present

A week after the bandages are off, Rozzie starts to see more. I am there, with our parents, when she describes to the doctor what she's seen: "Illuminated figures. Like ghosts."

The doctor coughs and explains to the rest of us that floaters are an ordinary phenomenon, sometimes quite real seeming. Eventually they will go away, he explains.

"No, these *are* ghosts," Rozzie says, smiling. "Attractive men, all lit up." She flashes her fingers open and shut. I smile but don't laugh. I know she's trying to make a joke, and no one is sure if it's safe to laugh or not.

Officially she is legally blind but has enough vision in one eye to see shapes, lights, and some outlines. "It's like looking at the world through a soapy windshield," she describes. "There are these little streaks of clarity. If I move my eyes around, I can get your face in pieces and put it together."

She demonstrates, and her eyes look as if they're rolling around in her head. "I look odd, don't I?"

I hesitate. "No."

Partial vision is tricky, we learn from a woman from the Center for the Visually Impaired, who only speaks candidly when Rozzie is out of the room. "Sometimes people think they see better than they do and take risks they shouldn't," she tells us. Rozzie may think she's ready to do some things independently, but the truth is she shouldn't go out unassisted, we're told. She has to relearn everything, as if she were totally blind, because the sight she has is undependable. At certain times, in certain light, she'll be able to see her money; other times, she won't. She'll need to be ready for the times when she can't. We all nod as if we've thought about this, which we haven't.

"What about reading?" my mother asks.

"No. She won't be able to read. Maybe some very large print stuff. Hard to say." My mother closes her eyes and nods. We're all absorbing this, piece by piece.

"Should she learn braille?"

"Not necessarily. There's so much happening with computers that braille is getting a little outdated. Some people who lose their sight later in life never bother to learn it. There are books on tape, hired readers, computers, lots of other options."

"What about getting around?" my father asks.

"It's conceivable she could manage without a cane, but I wouldn't recommend it. She'll be safer and happier if she learns to use one. Or else gets a guide dog."

I try to picture Rozzie with either of these things and can't. The woman seems to read my thoughts. "A lot of people waste a lot of effort trying to pass as sighted. They'd rather bang into poles and cross streets unsafely than have anyone know they don't see well. Frankly I don't get it."

Later, we tell Rozzie what this woman has said. She listens to it all and nods. Finally she says, "A guide dog? Come on. I don't need a guide dog."

"They're saying that you should learn living skills." We've elected my mother to tell Rozzie this, though we're all here. My mother is trying to sound frank and unemotional, but I can see how hard this is for her. My mother doesn't cry, but her eyes are red.

"Like my plate is a clock, chicken is at two. Stuff like that?"

"That's right."

For a long time, Rozzie says nothing. "Will I be able to live by myself?"

No one says anything.

The answer, at least in the beginning, is no.

One night, when I think she's asleep, I look up and see tears trickling from under her bandages. "Are you crying, Roz?" I whisper.

She says nothing but another tear leaks out.

"What is it?"

She doesn't want to tell me.

"Just say it."

I don't know what's hardest for her about all this: losing her independence or her career or her ability to keep her life private. Because that's what's happening. She has no secrets anymore. At least I don't think so.

"From now on, every man I ever meet will start out feeling sorry for me. That's where it will always begin."

This is as clear and sad a thing as she has said this whole time.

"Not if he's blind, too." I mean it to be a little funny, but I realize, too late, that none of us has said this word so far. Not out loud anyway. We've said "loss of vision" and "sight impairment," but we've never said the word *blind*.

It's decided that when Rozzie is released from the hospital, she'll go home to our parents' house for the summer. The only problem is if they both work, who will drive Rozzie to the classes she needs to get to? Who will make her lunch? We all picture her alone in the kitchen with cans of soup and the stove.

"We could try to hire someone, just for the summer," my mother suggests.

Our town is small; other than a guy who plays professional hockey for the Pittsburgh Penguins, Rozzie is the biggest celebrity it's ever produced, which makes her, to a greater or lesser degree, uncomfortable with almost everyone there. She hates going to the grocery store, hates talking to old friends. "It makes me feel bad," she used to say. "I don't know why."

There is no one we can think of who wouldn't make Rozzie miserable.

Finally, I offer the only choice we have: Why don't I move home for a few months? It won't be so bad, I tell my parents, I still have my darkroom in the basement; I can keep working while I take care of Rozzie.

They hug me tightly. Tears of relief spring to my mother's eyes. This means they can go back to work, return to their old lives. "You are a wonderful person," my mother says, holding my face between her hands. My father thanks me, looking at the floor. He is sad that he hasn't convinced Rozzie to do more medically. Our mother understands Rozzie's impulse to stop fighting for something she may never get and start learning how to live with what she has. Our father doesn't.

Around the hospital I am thought of as a hero. Paula calls me Florence Nightingale sarcastically, then says, "No, really, it's nice. You taking care of her."

The only person who doesn't thank me is Rozzie, which means she must know why I'm doing it. Even the parts she couldn't possibly know—such as what I was thinking.

There *are* ghosts between us—*attractive men, all lit up,* as she says. By not talking about them we are making them bigger, I know. Even though she laughs as she talks about it, I can see she's nervous. We both are.

Jemma, 1989–92

After Italy, I never go back to college.

Instead, I go to New York and, for three years, live in a series of showerless hovels. I bathe in kitchens, above floors warped so badly a marble could roll from one wall to another and, unassisted, back again. I work temp jobs and eat ramen soup to support my photography habit, which has become so expensive I wonder sometimes what I am doing and why I keep at it. I seem unable to give up—I keep thinking if I can get it right, complete what I started, I can put it to rest. But it isn't like that. One good picture keeps me going for weeks in pursuit of another.

I take my pictures to various venues—galleries that run student shows in the summer, magazines with photography internships. I'm good, I'm told, but not good enough yet. "Come back in a few years," one woman says brightly, as if this might sound promising to me.

I turn inward, work harder. Everywhere I go—bars, the subway, the phone boards at temp jobs—I smell like chemicals.

Rozzie also lives in New York, in a two-bedroom apartment on the Upper West Side. Unlike me, she owns a stove with an oven, a mattress and box spring, her own washer/dryer tucked in a closet behind folding doors. As it was in high school, we have separate circles of friends here; we live in different worlds that intersect every other week or so when we have lunch or go to dinner and a movie. She knows my friends, but doesn't like them much; to her, they are an eclectic array of downtown types who go silent in her presence. She doesn't understand why they cut their own hair or dress in all-black outfits and loud, colorful shoes. Sometimes she will even say mean things about them that make me wonder if she is jealous, though this seems far-fetched when they are all so poor.

Her life here mystifies me. It seems at once empty of responsibility and complicated by a countless number of errands to run. When we get together, I watch as she moves down the street with a new imperviousness. She doesn't see pedestrians parting on the sidewalk around her, pointing her out to their friends, mouthing movie titles behind her back. She doesn't seem to notice shopkeepers thanking her emphatically for coming in, or men, midconversation, falling silent at their sidewalk tables when she walks by. I, on the other hand, notice all of this. Everywhere we go, I watch the effect Rozzie has on strangers. Many times, people half wave, thinking perhaps she's a high school friend, someone they once worked with—then they remember and the hand withdraws, the wave withers. Sometimes, there's even a flash of irritation; I can see it in their faces: *Look, look, she's not that pretty.* Or: *She's famous and she's here, shopping for groceries—how can that be?*

Or else the search for the napkin will begin. *One autograph,* the wife will snap to the husband. *It's not so much to ask.* And I'll watch the woman walk across the room, in a hunch around her paper and pen, writing a dialogue in her mind: *It's not for me, it's for my son, who loves you.*

Once, a confused Japanese man asked me for my autograph. Someone at his table pointed to ours and said, "American film star." I saw it happen. I knew why he was mixed up—Rozzie was in the bathroom at the time. And so I signed Rozzie's name; after years of practice, my version was indistinguishable from hers. Even this, unbelievably, Rozzie did not register as odd. She looked around the room, narrowed her eyes at the light fixture, and waited for me to finish. When he left, she smiled. "Where were we?" she said.

I know Rozzie does this because she wants to believe she lives a normal life, that other people share the peculiarities of her existence. In the mail, once a week or so, she receives a free pair of sunglasses that I know to be a hundred dollars or more in stores. She has so many I start asking her for some or else helping myself. She gets other free things: cameras, clothes, videotapes. I'm not sure what they expect to accomplish, sending an already rich person free things. Is she meant to carry them with her on the street? Regularly, she opens boxes from companies she's never heard of and says things like, "Oh, look! A purse!" Invariably she will say, a few minutes later, "Do you want it?"

These companies don't realize they have picked the wrong celebrity, that Rozzie buys almost nothing and hates having things. She regularly gives bags of clothes away—anything she's worn and kept from a movie, she will sooner or later offer to me. Once, I saw one of her movies, accidentally wearing a jacket from it. I was sitting next to a date, and for one long scene he looked from the screen, to the jacket, back to the screen. Finally he said, "That's so bizarre," and dropped it.

She doesn't like buying things because she wants to believe that her life is in transition, that at some point she will travel extensively, through the Orient, to Africa, where she once talked about working with apes. Sometimes she talks about helping poor children or joining the Peace Corps. I don't know if she's serious or not, whether she understands how ludicrous this sounds, coming from her.

"The Peace Corps?" I say. "What would you do?"

"Supposedly they train you."

She doesn't understand. I mean: What would *you* do? You, Rozzie Phillips, in Africa? I don't think she understands that, yes, she is visible now. I have seen her walk by her own face on a newsstand and not look twice, even out of curiosity.

So I look for her. I point it out: "Look, that's you in the *Post.*"

She'll stop walking and look not at the picture but the door of the building we're standing in front of. "What am I doing?"

I squint at the headline. "You're taking off your jacket because the temperature hit eighty-seven degrees yesterday."

She nods. "Okay."

I don't tire of this coverage. Sometimes I pretend people are watching my every move, too. Jemma Phillips buys a bagel. Jemma Phillips rides the subway. I imagine if Rozzie disappears from her own life—to Africa or to Papua New Guinea—I will take over, let my movements be covered, take off my jacket on a hot day in Central Park.

Eventually it's clear to me that I won't get anywhere with photography unless I go to art school. I need to be able to pursue it full-time, not in snatches at night and on the weekend. I need to make connections, meet people who really do this for a living, not ones who talk about it in bars through clouds of cigarette smoke. Three years in New York has left me feeling worn down and unfocused. My friends and I talk a great deal about being artists, and then we spend all day working office jobs wearing clothes we have bought on discount at J. Chuckles. There is nothing artistic about taking lunch orders for ten; nothing creative about typing envelope labels. It's taken three years for me to see this.

My friends understand when I tell them I'm applying only to

schools outside the city. For us, the world is divided into two places: New York and not New York. Though we all came from the latter, we can hardly recall what a grass lawn looks like.

"I need to go somewhere I don't have to work all the time to survive," I explain. Already, I am picturing a shower, a real bed, time.

"Sure," they say, seeing for a second the freedom I am talking about.

To my surprise, the person who doesn't understand my leaving is Rozzie. When I tell her, she starts to cry, which takes me almost completely by surprise. "I don't know what I'll do without you," she says.

I want to say, *You don't?*

I see her maybe once a week, sometimes less than that. In the past, she has been gone a great deal, though for the last six months this hasn't been true. Miriam, her manager, calls this a temporary work dry spell. Surely this is why she's crying, I tell myself. She's anxious about work, restless.

I look around the restaurant we're sitting in, then lean across the table. "It's okay, Roz. You have a life and money. You can buy furniture if you need it. I can't."

"I'll buy you furniture if that's the issue."

"It's *not*," I say so emphatically we are both surprised.

She looks up at me, eyes rimmed red. What is the issue, then?

Rozzie, 1992

In her worst moments—there have been three to date—the physical world dissolves. Colors take flight as if the street she stands on has been, the whole time, a painted muslin backdrop loosed by the wind. Everything flaps. Sounds intensify. A single car horn becomes a shadow bearing down on her.

This is different from her high school episodes.

These are terrifying. They always happen outside, in the sunlight, and she is obliged, most times, to move on, forward through a fog threaded with broken shards of color. She must read shadows, feel for sunshine, determine when buildings begin and end. Sometimes she will move ten feet in twenty minutes. She loses all track of time. She forgets where she is going. By the time her eyes clear, she is so exhausted she wants only to find her way home and fall asleep.

A week after Jemma leaves for art school, it happens again, this time for an hour, and is followed by a headache so severe she must beat her way into a drugstore and buy some Advil. She takes four on the spot, two more at home. She has never before experienced pain like this.

Afterward, even more troubling, there is a permanent clouding on the periphery of her vision. The cloud moves with her, to the store, to auditions. Sometimes she will forget and then look and see, yes, there it is. Without mentioning it to anyone, she makes an appointment to see her first specialist.

To her surprise, she finds it's a relief to finally speak about this. Such a relief that in the doctor's office, she starts to go on a bit, describing her sight in the language of poetry—shattered images, veils pulled and loosened across her eyes. It's a new kind of challenge—not disguising this problem but describing it precisely, finding the words for what has been, so far, only vague and menacing. She almost feels like laughing, until the doctor who has been staring into her eyes for nearly an hour with various machines stationed between them responds with the name of a disease, a dead word that flattens everything she has said.

Jemma, 1992

The great joy of art school, I discover after a month, is that no one cares if I spend fourteen hours a day in the darkroom. My impulse to do little besides work is celebrated here, as is my inclination to talk only about photography. Sometimes over a beer, or sandwiches in the deli, someone will say, "No shop talk," meaning no one is supposed to say *Mapplethorpe* or *grain* or mention the store selling paper, cheap, one town away. These are the only times I feel awkward, when I worry that in desperation someone will ask me a question about Rozzie.

Mostly they don't and mostly I'm alone, working.

My favorite place is the darkroom. In the fuzzy amber glow, every print is flawless and ethereal, a joy to look at. I could stand in this nonlight and study the beauty of my own work forever, an embarrassing private thrill that comes just before stepping into fluorescence and seeing, all too well, the hair on the negative, the shadow of the bystander, the shot-spoiling spray of light. This is the room where I first meet Matthew, doing the same thing I am: studying prints. I can't help noticing he is two inches from the door and he has finished printing but he still doesn't step outside. He has a smile on his face as he peels one picture off another. At one point, he laughs out loud, almost a bark of joy. I can't help it: I laugh, too. "What'd you get?" I say.

He looks up, surprised. He knew I was here but must have forgotten.

"Sorry." He looks down sheepishly.

"It's okay. Can I see?" I hold my hand out. He looks at me, and back at his picture. I know I would do the same thing. Hesitate forever. "Come on. I'm sick of staring at my own stuff. Nothing's coming out."

He unpeels the picture and hands it, bent under its own wetness, across the tray of chemicals between us.

I laugh. It's a human moment between animals: a dog squaring off with a flock of ducks; they're all scared—the ducks, the dog—but the best part is in the background, the impervious human bystanders who turn away from the drama. I have tried to go for humor in my own pictures and it's hard. It so quickly turns mean, into something that makes fun of the subject.

"Can I see more?" I'm not usually this forward with other people in the darkroom. There's no privacy as it is, so there seems to be a tacit agreement not to speak. I can spend hours sharing tongs with a person I haven't looked at once. But this time, it's late and it's Friday night. That we are both here means we've got something in common.

He hands me the others, all shot in the same park, which looks like some place in London, maybe. The people have a European air of nonchalance, and the animals all seem vaguely exotic, even the ones wearing leashes. He shoots the way I do—unplanned, chaotic. All of these have animals and humans, but he couldn't have planned it; impromptu shots like this can never be planned. They are terrific, one story after another. A roll like this is one in a hundred, I know that well enough. "You should look at these outside," I say. "They're really good."

He laughs and I do, too. "They're always better in here, aren't they?"

"Yes," I say, looking up long enough to catch his eyes.

*   *   *

That night, Rozzie calls me in my dorm room and tells me she hasn't left her apartment for three days.

"Why not?" I say. This seems like a long time, a little scary.

"I don't like my friends here. I don't want to see them."

I don't like her friends either, but usually she never says things like this.

"I'm sick of the pretension."

What pretension? I wonder. Most of them are crew types, makeup artists or wardrobe fitters, people she talks to while making eye contact in mirrors. She doesn't have other actress friends, so when she and her friends are together the only one in danger of being pretentious (I would never say this, of course) is Rozzie. Recently, she has been training herself in accents. Sometimes, for practice, she will spend a whole lunch speaking with a thick Dutch accent. She doesn't mean to sound affected, she means to be serious about her *r*'s and *l*'s, but the end result is the same.

"You can go out by yourself," I remind her. This is one of her great strengths and one of the things I've admired most about her in the last three years. She eats alone in restaurants, goes to movies by herself. In times when she doesn't have a boyfriend, she can be admirably self-amusing.

"See, that's just it," she says now. "I *can't*."

Her voice has a worrying edge to it.

The first time Matthew and I go out it's four in the afternoon and neither of us is sure what to order. "Gosh," I say. "It's too early for a beer and too late for coffee."

He smiles. "How about a milk shake?"

He seems so sweet—so childlike—saying this that right away it's what I want. We are sitting in a restaurant bar that has shakes on the menu. No doubt they won't taste good, but what difference does that make? I'm thrilled to be here, in this new life, with this new person who seems so promising. He looks happy, too, as if he has dressed up for this date. He wears a button-down shirt; his brown, curly hair is still wet from a shower; his hazel eyes are bright.

"So I've been hearing about you," he says after we place our order.

This surprises me. "Hearing what?"

"That you're good. The award. All that stuff that's not supposed to matter. It made me feel bad because I hadn't asked to see your prints the other night in the darkroom."

The great turning point of my life—or at long last the acknowledgment I'd been waiting for since high school—came two months after I got here, when I won an award usually reserved for a junior or senior. I was thrilled and also self-conscious because it was for my series of movie-set shots. Though I'm careful not to emphasize the stars, you see them when you look closely—Alan Harmon drinking coffee, Leena Westover blowing on her hands to keep them warm—surrounded by crew people wearing tool belts and bracelets of duct tape. Usually the celebrity is set off just a little, the only one in a costume, the only one not talking. There's an indefinable tension, almost an electricity. Initially, winning the award made me feel like a celebrity. Now it has had a strange effect. I'm working harder and producing less that's any good. I'm self-conscious because I don't want to be thought of as someone who may have talent or may simply have access to a world most people don't have.

I don't talk about this with anyone here because it scares me too much. "That's okay," I say to Matthew. "I wasn't getting anything terrific. Trust me."

I tell him I'm trying to expand my subject matter, that I've always taken portraits of people at work and I'm trying to go for something different.

He narrows his eyes and thinks for a minute. "Are you the one who does stars?"

I nod.

"Huh. I didn't realize that. So what? You know someone?"

I nod again, surprised. Even though I don't talk about it anymore, most people know who my sister is. I tell him and he thinks for a while. "Was she in *Seven Serpents*?"

"No."

"I don't know her, I guess. I'm terrible about seeing movies."

Of course I love him for this. Then he surprises me again. "My father is famous. Or sort of. He's a writer. So I guess I know what it's like . . ." He turns to the window, as if he's looking for a thought. "Watching all that. Standing outside it. You hold your breath, like any minute it could turn on you. It could all be about *you* and then— my God—it's not even about *them*. It was never about my dad."

I have never met anyone who might understand what it's like to be me, that I have taken pictures of celebrities not because I love them but because it's what I know now, where the light shines brightest and my vision is the clearest.

Afterward, we walk slowly back to school and talk about what brought us to photography. I tell him that for me it's been a way of participating in a world I am sometimes shy of. Behind a camera I feel shielded, less watched, less self-conscious. He nods as if it's the same for him. "That's right," he says. "Exactly."

And even though it feels as if something has passed between us— a current, an understanding—when we get to the path for my dorm, I don't ask him up. Suddenly I am what I've just talked about being: shy, at a loss for words.

We start meeting in the darkroom, keeping the same hours, Friday night, Saturday night, alone long enough to tell our life stories. "I'm so tentative about everything I do," he tells me. "I don't know if being a sibling is different, but if you're the kid of someone famous, you're usually either incredibly reticent or a completely screwed-up drug addict. It's almost a rule." He looks up and smiles. "I'm the former."

"Why do you think it's your father that made you reticent?"

He hands me the tongs. "Everyone's expectations. Even when I was a kid, everyone used to say, 'Oh, you must write, too. Can I read your story?' In elementary school, I had this thing where I couldn't speak in front of the class. I'd open my mouth and nothing would come out."

"You want to know what people expect of sisters? Nothing. I would go to her sets, do nothing but make chitchat, and everyone would tell me how amazing I was. And so together."

"You are together," he says. I look up. He's looking at me in the red glow. "You *are*."

In a bookstore, I find his father's books, all about Waspy New England families falling apart over secrets and alcohol. One is dedicated to Matthew with a Latin phrase translated to read: *My boy, my heart.* Even though I know better—that when my sister talks about me in magazines, it has nothing to do with me—I can't help it, I'm still impressed. Our next night in the darkroom, I mention the dedication.

"Yeah. I was terrible about that. I was a teenager. I thought he was trying to take over my life and I told him I didn't want any of his fucking books. Nice, huh?"

"What did he say?"

Matthew thinks about this for a minute. "I don't remember. That it was too late, the book was already at the publisher."

I want to kiss him. I even plot strategies: hold on to the tongs and pull him closer, reach across chemicals in the red darkness, touch his hair, his face, tell him not to be so shy. I want to point out we have everything in common—that our souls are twinned: this passion for work, this shadow we've both spent our lives standing in. This feeling is so strong, I believe if he resists, I can talk him into it. Unlike Rozzie, who falls in and out of love with every set she works on, I have only dated a handful of men and have never felt anything like this before. My armpits tingle at the thought of him, and the fantasies I construct of us being together.

Once, walking home, late at night, I ask him if he wants to come up to my room. "I have some beer," I say, which I do, bought with this proposition in mind.

"I probably shouldn't," he says. "I'm sort of in the middle of a lot of stuff. But next week. How about that?"

Days go by. We spend more and more time together. One night, he kisses me under the eaves of my dorm—a fast kiss, as if it hasn't happened at all, as if he were going for my cheek and instead hit my lips. I keep thinking this is it, and then it isn't.

I half wonder if his hesitance in getting involved with me has something to do with my work, which is going badly. The problem, now that I am in school, away from sets, is finding something else to photograph. In pursuit of the artistic vision everyone talks about in class, I have tried no less than seven concepts out on my teacher, who is a lover of the concept. "Anyone can take an image and print it," she tells us. "Fotomat can do that." She shows us slides of work that is exciting to her, cutting edge. She doesn't name the photographers, which makes us all a little nervous, as if maybe they are other students in the class. One frames her pictures in Emily Dickinson poems written in tightly printed rectangles of words, dashes, and slashes; another makes a collage with visible Scotch tape. "We're seeing the process, not the product," she tells us, pointing to the tape. "I think that's very exciting."

I get the drift. Photography needs an idea driving it, and it needs to do what hasn't been done. My problem is this passion I have for the old-timers: Cartier-Bresson, Brassai, the ones who talk about composing a moment, freezing time. The ones who worked with amazing images of people you can never forget and never considered gluing pieces of pinecone to photographic paper.

I'm trying my best, though. I get different ideas—for a while I shoot images in my rearview mirror: women's faces, church steeples, all cropped haphazardly by the narrow rectangle of the mirror. I even speed to get a picture of a police car, which sadly doesn't come out very well. All I have is the ticket to show for that one. Laid side by side, they make no point except that I do an awful lot of driving. I try still lifes—compositions of disparate objects neutrally arranged: a doll's dress, a tape measure, a golf ball, two clothespins. It's an interesting idea, everyone says, but the pictures don't move anyone, and why should they? one person points out. That's not the intention. I try to be stronger-willed than I was back in college. I explain my intention—to see if a narrative will emerge from six randomly selected objects. I've stolen this idea as I've stolen all my ideas. I'm hoping to give objects weight and resonance by juxtaposition—that seeing child's pajamas next to a rolling pin will be unsettling without being overtly violent. "A rolling pin could also suggest homemade pies," I explain before the class, which blinks back at me blankly. They nod. They get it, but their expressions beg for celebrities, for my old stuff.

After the still lifes, I begin a series of arranged landscapes, with objects to suggest recent human habitation: a picnic basket, a broken wineglass. I mean these to be more narrative than the still lifes, to tell a story. There's supposed to be a set of subtle clues in each. I imagine people gathered in little horseshoe clusters at every showing, spending twenty minutes on each one, trying to figure out what has happened, why there's a running shoe, a calendar, and a corsage. But they've all come out wrong; mostly they look like litter strewn on grass.

Matthew tries to be supportive. He studies them in the yellow light and then steps outside as if, God help me, that will be better. He suggests reshooting with different placement. He points to one and says enthusiastically, "This almost works."

The blander the reception I get, the harder I try, the more hours I log at the darkroom, hunching into the enlarger, burning and dodging, double- and triple-exposing, piling trick upon trick until my prints bear almost no resemblance to the negative they came from. "These are questioning the accuracy of our visual perception," I explain to the class, holding up a silhouette of a building printed to look like a person's profile, with the vaguest suggestion of brick and window. Too late (when I'd arrived at class in the morning) I'd realized it also looks like a Thanksgiving turkey. This is the problem: my tricks play tricks on me.

One night Rozzie calls and, out of the blue, says she is thinking about coming to visit.

"You are?" I've never invited her.

"I need to get away." She adds, again mysteriously, "Bad things are happening here."

"Like what?"

"Never mind. I'll tell you when I get there." Her voice sounds edgy and desperate.

I tell her to come, hesitantly, scared of what this will mean. As it is, my work has so little foundation apart from her. I'm afraid if she comes, I will never get good at anything else.

Two days later, I pick her up at the airport and see that she has brought three enormous suitcases. How long is she planning to stay? I don't ask. She is obviously in a state of mind where the wrong question might set off an unpredictable reaction. Better to wait—to wrestle these suitcases out to my car and say nothing at all.

In my dorm room, when she takes her coat off for the first time, I can see by her arms how thin she is. Her collarbones stick out, her shirt looks empty. I know enough about such thinness to be afraid of it. She's never been like this before. As if this will help, I open a box of crackers and start to eat.

She looks around the room. "So this is a dorm room. I've never been in one before."

"They're not that great."

"No, this seems neat. With all these other people right next door." She taps the wall behind my bed, which is buzzing with the base line of a neighbor's stereo.

"I'm going to get an apartment next year."

"Oh." Obviously she is expecting me to say something more. For a while we don't speak.

She sits down on the bed and stares out the window.

"Is something wrong, Roz?"

"Last week I went to an audition and the director said he wanted to hire me but his producers wouldn't let him because of my last two movies. He said they needed a box-office female." Her voice is as thin as she is, like a thread fluttering in the breeze. "I've been on seven auditions in the last month." I know that for a long time she didn't go on auditions. She got offers or had meetings. Now she is in the trenches, I guess, struggling to get work like everyone else. "I got two offers for cable movies, but my manager says accepting them would be admitting I've fallen off the A-list."

I don't know what to say other than to hold out the box of

crackers I've got on my desk and offer her one. She shakes her head. I should know the food that is a comfort to me is part of this battle she's fighting right now. It's her enemy, and this thinness is her only weapon. "My manager thinks the problem is that I'm too tall."

"Why?"

"A lot of actors are short. Shorter than you'd think. Did you know Ron Parkman is five feet four inches?"

"Aren't you a little young for Ron Parkman?"

"No. Just too tall."

She stops talking and stares into the sun setting over the top of the building across the quad. "Pretty sad," she finally says. She seems to mean the way the building blocks the view, but really, there's no telling.

For the next three days, I try to think of solutions: Write your own script! Be a director! Start a theater company! She listens, thinks for a minute, then shakes her head.

I go about my day, go to classes and, some afternoons, come back to my room to find her sitting on the bed with the lights off, still wearing her pajamas. She will blink at me, confused. "What time is it?" she'll say.

She eats little, rarely leaves my hall, spends her time on my bed opening and closing books. Once, when I ask her if anything is wrong, she says, staring at the carpet, "Sometimes I think I should have gone to college."

After three days, I can take it no more. I make a date for us to meet Matthew for dinner. "We'll just get out for a little while," I say. "Try to have a good time."

I want to get us away from my dorm room, where she seems to do nothing but stare out the window, one hand resting on the pillow on my bed. Once we get to the restaurant, though, I'm not sure this was such a good idea. A few minutes after we sit down, she starts to cry. "I'm sorry I've been acting so strange." She shakes her head and blows her nose. "I don't know what's wrong with me."

I can see over her shoulder, people are staring at her. "Do you want to go back to my room?"

She keeps crying.

"Let's go back to my room, Roz."

"No. I want to be out. It's good for me." She uses her own napkin, then mine, then one from the table beside us. "For some reason, I keep thinking about Grandma Ann. Do you ever think about her?"

I shake my head. Grandma Ann died about ten years ago.

"I found these pictures of her when she was our age, in the newspaper modeling old-fashioned bathing suits. She looks so vulnerable, wearing little high-heeled shoes, with her hands spread on her legs like she's trying to cover them. It makes me sad."

"I don't think she was sad," I say.

She's not listening; she's lost in her own thoughts, face blotchy, cheeks wet. "When I started acting, I thought it would be about getting into other people's skins. I thought I'd be crawling into voices and wigs and disappearing the way Meryl Streep always did. And what it feels more like is standing in front of a camera with no clothes, trying to cover yourself up and all you've got are your hands." She blows her nose. "It has nothing to do with Meryl Streep. Everyone started out wanting to be like her, and instead all we're doing is being told our face photographs too large. I don't think Meryl Streep feels like Meryl Streep anymore."

I understand what she's getting at, but I wonder why she has waited until now to say it. Just then, Matthew walks up. "Hi," he whispers, touching my shoulder. He obviously doesn't want to interrupt.

"Hi," I say, sliding over in the booth so he can sit down next to me.

Rozzie looks up, startled. She's obviously forgotten we were meeting anyone.

"This is Matthew," I have to explain. "Remember? My friend."

She nods and tries for something that resembles a smile. "Oh, yeah," she says. In the silence that follows, when no one knows what to say, I think about suggesting we do this another time. Then Rozzie says, "I don't *always* cry."

Matthew laughs. "I do," he says, smiling. "Or a lot of the time anyway."

Maybe because of this joke or because she senses Matthew's innate goodness, Rozzie loosens up quickly. She orders dinner: a large salad, no dressing, extra rolls, and asks Matthew about his work. On this topic, Matthew isn't shy. He describes what he does, which is to shoot street musicians. The title of his portfolio is "For Free." He talks intelligently about these pieces, can describe his vision with a clarity that I envy. Rozzie gets the reference at once: "Like the old Joni Mitchell song," she says. Though she can't sing, she does, the entire song, loud enough that the people sitting at the table next to us stop talking and listen. Aware she has an audience, she closes her eyes and puts one finger to her ear as if she were in a recording studio, laying tracks. She is not on tune, but regardless, everyone applauds when she finishes. She beams and nods to the clapping audience.

The food arrives and we start talking about my work. "Jemma's very talented," Matthew says, even though the only work he's seen is my last three months of failed efforts.

"I *know*," Rozzie says emphatically. "Believe me, I know. I'm the one who always thought she should do this professionally."

It's true, she is, but suddenly I don't seem to have a place in this conversation. My recent work failures have made me feel a conversation like this is going to jinx me. I get up and tell them I have to go to the bathroom, where I stand in front of the sink and stare into the mirror.

When I walk back out, Rozzie is telling an animated story with big gestures, her arms raised out like branches. I wonder if she is telling the tree story. Or the one about our father holding up the ceiling of our house for two hours until the plasterer could come. When I get to the table, she looks surprised and lowers her arms. "We were just talking about you," she says. I sit down again. I can't imagine what they were saying.

"He's nice," Rozzie says on the walk home, stopping to look up at the stars. "I approve of your liking him."

I haven't told her too much about it, but even in her current state, she can see how I feel. I tell her who his father is. "You're kidding," she says. "That must be so weird. The families in his books are always so screwed up."

"It seems like it's hard for him."

After this one dinner, Rozzie seems better. She takes showers, gets dressed in the morning, leaves my room. After she's been here for a week, I run into her in town, taking walks, going to the bookstore, drinking coffee. She even makes a few friends and talks about getting together with people I have never met. "There's a book group I might join," she says, which makes me nervous, as if she is planning to stay indefinitely, or long enough to read a novel, anyway.

One day, coming out of the post office, I see her eating a sandwich in the deli with Matthew. She looks up, smiles, and waves me over to join them. "Look who I ran into! Come join us." Her voice is so hearty I have to wonder: Had they made a date?

I order a seltzer, sit down, and within thirty seconds, conversation feels oddly strained. "I was telling Rozzie here how we met," Matthew says, and laughs though no joke has been made.

"In the darkroom?" I offer, looking at her and back at him. Is that what he means?

"Right," he says.

"Matthew has a theory," Rozzie offers. "Go ahead. Tell her. It's about people who work all night in darkrooms."

Just the night before I had stayed in the darkroom until two, trying to rescue another doomed project, this one a series of embarrassing nudes.

He smiles shyly at Rozzie. "No."

My stomach contracts. "What about people who stay in the darkroom all night?" I stare at Matthew—this is how we met, what we both have in common. Whatever he's said applies to him, too.

"Pent-up sexual energy." Rozzie doesn't mean to be cruel. I see her eyes fly up to mine, worried that she's made a terrible mistake.

"Oh. Nice." I stare at Matthew, who won't look at me. All the intimacy at the table is between them. I am the outsider. "I should go. I have work to do."

"No." Rozzie grabs my sleeve. "Please don't. I'll go." She picks up her bag and stands.

Suddenly this is unbearably awkward. As if it has been planned. My sister disappears and I'm left alone with Matthew.

"So, Jemma, there was something I wanted to talk to you about."

Whatever it is, I don't want to hear it. "You don't have to say anything, Matthew."

"No, I do. I like you so much. You've been such a good, important friend to me, and I was never sure how I felt, if there was more there or not—"

I picture our kiss and suddenly this is too awful. "It doesn't matter."

"The truth is, I'm scared to be with another photographer."

I look up, surprised.

"You're good, Jemma. I've seen your portfolio, which is so good I couldn't even say anything. I feel terrible about that. It stunned me, though."

"Everything I've done in the last three months is terrible."

He smiles and doesn't deny it. "So? You're experimenting. You're not afraid to test yourself. It's going to make you even better. The truth is, I'm insecure. And the idea of being involved with you makes me more insecure."

Instead of answering, my hands fly around the table, cleaning up straw wrappers and used napkins. I want only to leave, but feel compelled, for some reason, to tidy up before I do. To my surprise, Matthew grabs my hand. "I like Rozzie," he says, and for a split second I look up into his eyes, which are dancing with a different fear from what he's describing, something I haven't seen in his face before.

Back in my room, Rozzie is waiting. "I'm sorry," she says the moment I walk in. "I'm so *sorry*. I didn't mean for it to happen. I didn't want it to happen, I swear to God. I kept thinking, 'No, Rozzie, leave this man alone. He's Jemma's friend.' And then, I kept seeing him and we kept having these great conversations."

I hold up my hand. I don't know what to say or do. Nothing like this has ever happened before. "I don't really want to hear about it," I say.

Without planning anything, I pull out a duffel bag and start packing clothes. Rozzie watches. "What are you doing?"

"Packing."

"To go where?"

"Home. To Mom and Dad's. I need to do an assignment back there."

"What assignment?"

I think fast. "I'm shooting a series on Mom and her students." It's the first thing that comes to me. Recently our mother has won another award and was in the newspaper again. It's not a terrible idea.

"Wow. I didn't know that." She watches me move around the room as I find underwear, shirts, all my equipment. "So what should I do?"

"Stay here. I don't care. It doesn't matter."

She thinks about this for a long time. "Really?"

Jemma, present

I still can't get over how I went so long without noticing that Rozzie couldn't see. When I ask her about this, she leans back in bed and tries to explain what it was like: "I could tell if someone was standing right here," she says, holding her hand in front of her face. "Usually I could tell if it was a man or a woman." To me the implication is shocking: she couldn't tell who it was, didn't see eyes, couldn't read expressions. How could she act without being able to see the other person's face?

I think about those years in high school, when she spent so much time studying her reflection in the mirror. Was she memorizing the face she would later lose sight of? Expressions she would need for acting later on? But how did she continue, all of these years, to seem fine?

"It wasn't easy," she admits. "There was a trick to it. That's why it was nice to have you around. It didn't seem odd if I stood close to you or put my hand on your arm to go to dinner. And some days it wasn't bad. Those were the days I'd memorize my lines, and people's voices. I'd get out as much as I could, try to look as normal as possible."

I'm stunned by the energy this must have required—years spent in the practiced art of seeming fine. Then to take on roles on top of this role. I think of one movie where she is supposed to be so nearsighted she can't find her glasses on the bathroom counter. The scene always makes me laugh, the way she gets down on the floor and gropes, eyes pinched into Mr. Magoo slits. I've always thought it was her funniest scene on film. Now of course it seems sad.

In the end, I keep coming back to one question: Why didn't she tell us?

One time she says: "Telling you would have made it true. Not telling meant maybe it wasn't."

Another time she says, "I thought I was going to be all right. Sometimes I was."

I can guess at another reason she doesn't say: I haven't let her. I have never let her be anything less than what I want her to be. She is my horizon, the line I've been moving toward even while I sit, motionless in the shadows. How could I reconcile my impulse to follow her with the fact that she might not know where she was going? Now when I look at her future, I see my own life narrow and darken.

In the three weeks Rozzie has been in the hospital, I eat more meals and spend more time with my parents than I have since high school. We have adjoining hotel rooms and eat dinner together every night, more often than not at a pancake house next door to the hotel. Because there is so much time and so little to say about Rozzie's progress, by necessity we must come up with other topics of conversation. I ask my parents about their lives, details about work, about memories from their childhood. Eventually, we start asking straight, open-ended questions. "What was the most scared you ever remember being?" I ask my mother. Without saying it, it's clear I mean *before this*.

She doesn't need to think long. "Oh, God, when I got that terrible biopsy done."

I look at her. "What terrible biopsy?"

She seems surprised. "I told you, didn't I?" I shake my head.

"When you were—what would it have been?—ten maybe, I had a lump in my armpit removed, which they told me was cancer. They said it was a fairly aggressive form and that I'd have a long, hard fight ahead of me. Then, three days later, they apologized and said they'd gotten my file mixed up with someone else's—that my lump was benign and I was okay."

"My God, Mom. Why didn't you tell us this?"

"I thought I *had* told you afterward. Isn't this funny? I've always known I handled it badly." She shakes her head. "When you're really scared, the thing you're most afraid of is not being able to protect your children." She looks out the window, away from me. "It's a terrible feeling, not being able to protect you all."

This isn't typical of my mother at all. Usually if she says *my children,* she's talking about her students. I've never thought of us being so large a part of her inner life that she'd have to hide the darkest part from us. It's interesting, I realize, how secrets can be a measure of how much you care. And how telling them is the beginning of caring less.

Another thing I learn about my parents: once, they almost separated. My father tells me this. *"You're kidding,"* I say.

"It was right around your junior year in high school. You were home, but Rozzie wasn't." He stops talking.

"Yeah," I prod him, "what happened?"

He shakes his head. "Your mother fell in love with somebody else."

"No way."

He nods.

"With who?"

"It was someone she worked with. Nobody we knew."

"Did she have an affair?"

"No, no. They were friends. She felt a companionship with this person that she and I had lost."

"So what happened?"

"It was horrible for a long time. Very painful. We hardly spoke for a week once."

What I can't believe is that I was there and didn't notice.

"Finally I told her to go ahead, it was fine, be with this person, and miraculously, he vanished. Got a job in Connecticut and left."

This must have been around the time my father started the play-reading group, when he transformed himself into King Lear for a night and stormed around our living room with a bath-towel cape. At the time, I had thought he was doing it for Rozzie, his absent audience, his star daughter. Now I understand he was doing it for his wife.

At night, when she is almost asleep, but not quite, Rozzie describes what she sees: sometimes it's like a soapy window, sometimes it's beautiful. Once, when she is almost asleep, she whispers, "Sometimes I see things that aren't there."

"Like what?" I whisper.

"Flowers. Birds. Certain people."

"Who?"

"One time I thought I saw Grandmother Ann. She was smiling and waving hi. Once I saw you. As a little girl."

"Doing what?"

"Playing jacks."

My heart freezes. Is this a memory for her, too? I remember the rings, the way she used to fly around them. "Are you moving?"

"Sort of," she says, squinting, as if to see her thoughts more clearly. "It's blurry."

I remember once believing a line connected us. Now, it's as if we're at two ends of it, holding on.

Jemma, 1992

I drive straight home, three hours, where my mother runs a bath for me, tells me I need to be alone, and then sits the whole time on the toilet lid and points out a few things: This isn't typical of Rozzie (which is true). Rozzie hasn't worked in a long time (also true). She thinks Rozzie may be depressed or that something else is going on we don't know about, something with her work. Their conversations have been strained, my mother says. "Everything I say seems to irritate her. Was she like that with you?"

"No. She just seemed sad until she met Matthew, and then she seemed charming. I hate her, Mom. I swear to God, I hate her."

My mother shakes her head. "There's more to this. Has she been making cryptic comments to you?"

I think about her phone calls, talking about pretentiousness and bad things happening. "A little. I don't know." I think about her sitting for three days in my dorm room, becoming, as an adult, the child I once was: so scared and overly cautious. I picture her watching me from the window the way I once watched her from the porch.

"I'm worried. I think she's very alone right now and very angry."

"What does she have to be angry about?"

"Well. A lot. She doesn't have a very easy life. Except for you, she doesn't have very many friends."

I put a washcloth over my face. "Now she has one less."

"That's exactly why I don't understand this."

Later I lie in bed and listen to her tell my father the story. I don't hear the whole version. I hear her say, "This worries me, frankly. . . . I've never seen her like this before." I don't know if she means Rozzie or me. Tears fall so steadily from my eyes that my ears get wet.

My mother has spent her whole life directing children to look at her, to find her eyes with their eyes. Sometimes she will count: one second, two seconds. If they make it to three, looking right at her, they get a pretzel. When I tell my mother I want to do a series on her students, I know she won't love the idea. She'll think about the kids and worry about its interfering with her work, the way that television special did so many years ago. So I argue that it could be a good experience for them, relating to someone other than a teacher, learning about a camera, following instructions. Because I badger her about it and am otherwise so morose, she finally relents: "Just come and bring your camera. We'll see how it goes."

I want this to be the opposite of shooting celebrities, who know exactly how to flirt with their eyes and what to do for a picture. I want this to be about kids who don't know enough to look at a camera, who believe eye contact is something to be scared of, maybe because I understand now that it *is*.

I haven't been to my mother's classroom in a long time. The last time I visited, there were no computers, just tables and chairs and Naugahyde napping mats. Now there's a whole battery of equipment, even clothing to help these children focus: weighted vests, prism glasses. Regina walks in, bouncing on her toes, hands fluttering around her face. I vaguely remember her as a kindergartner. Now she is fifteen, beautiful and tall. "Good morning," she says to the air. "I'm walking on my heels. I'm at school now, I'm wearing my vest. Hi, Jemma, you changed your pants."

My mother smiles and shakes her head. Regina must remember me from almost six years ago. "Hi, Regina," I say.

"You had on a green shirt, brown pants. Now it's different. I have a dog. That's different. I've also had seven fish die. Do you want to see my pictures?"

Over the course of the day, I meet them all, one by one, and talk to each of them as best I can. One boy tells me he loves Ginny. When I ask him, "Who?" he says never mind, to forget he said anything, he doesn't want it to get out. "That's what happens. It gets around and then everyone *knows*."

Another girl tells me she wants to be a drawer when she grows up. "A drawer?" I say, ready to go along with it, ask if she'll hold socks or shirts. "I want to draw," she says, rocking slightly, rolling her eyes.

Another boy asks if I'll take pictures of his watch, rather than of him. Only one of my subjects wants to have her picture taken or understands the usual procedure. She studies the chair I've set up, settles into it, hands on knees, and smiles broadly before I've even gotten my camera out of the case. Her eyes are two slits; she looks as if she is hang gliding or leaning into a strong wind. "I need just a minute, Ann. I'm not quite ready yet."

Her smile doesn't fade. Finally she says, "One minute," stands up, and walks away.

The rest understand what I'm doing enough not to like it. "No picture, please," one boy says, his face to the wall.

"Okay," I say. "Do you want to take a picture?"

His shoulders turn a fraction of an inch. "I'm not allowed to touch Dad's camera."

"This isn't Dad's camera. It's mine. You can touch my camera."

He turns around but doesn't face me. "All right. I'll take one pic-ture." I hand him the camera, and even though he's not looking at it, I point to the different parts. When I give it to him, the weight seems to surprise his hands. He watches the clock while his hands explore what he has not been allowed to touch until now. Finally, he takes a picture of the floor.

After that, they all want to try. One boy asks if he can take a pic-ture of the toilet flushing. "I don't know about that," I say.

He looks confused. "Does that mean no?"

I tell them to shoot whatever they want. Lack of eye contact is such a defining facet of autism that trying to capture what they're looking at, instead of eyes and faces, could be an interesting idea. It's a long shot, I know. In all likelihood I'll have wasted a lot of film on underexposed pictures of dust motes and linoleum. But on the chance that it works—that I can pair a portrait with a photo taken by the child—it's worth a try.

Though I have spent most of the morning focused on my own work, by the end of the day it occurs to me that what I have always heard about my mother is true: she is remarkable with these children. And it's not easy. During the day, three children have broken down. One because his aide will be leaving in a week, one because his jacket won't zip, one for reasons no one can discern. My mother sits behind this last one, a six-year-old boy, holding him to her, rocking him with her eyes shut. Into his ear, she softly sings "Itsy Bitsy Spi-der." It takes a long time and many choruses to calm him down. I lose count on the tenth, just as it occurs to me what this song is about: regrouping, drying off, starting over.

That night, I get an idea. What would happen if I took the chil-dren's picture and then had them take a picture of me? I wouldn't give them too many instructions; if they shot the chair before I got there, so be it; if they shot my foot, fine. When I ask my mother what she thinks, she says, "It's not bad, but I'd say only about four of them could really do it."

I'm taking ten in all. "What about the others?"

"They'll still take the toilet flushing or not take anything." She thinks about it for a while. "Actually, I don't know what they'll do." She laughs. "That's the truth."

This makes me think it's a good idea. There's an unknown element, even a scary one. This equipment is expensive and it's my livelihood right now. I'm placing it in the hands of kids who are not known for their ability to regulate their impulses.

The next morning, I start with Steven, who is twelve, and one of the most advanced in the group. He spends three hours a day here and three hours a day in a regular fifth-grade classroom. He straddles two worlds; in the other, he controls his impulse to rock and flap his hands; here he relaxes. He rocks and flaps and smiles at the floor when my mother comes over. "Hi, Maureen. Karen said you had a good day."

My mother runs her fingers through his hair. "Karen *did* say you had a good day."

He grins and for a fleeting instant lets his eyes meet hers.

Steven has been told to keep his hands from flapping by putting them in his pockets. I take two exposures of him, smiling into the air, his arms straight as canes at his sides, his hands dug into the bottoms of his pockets. He looks pained, as if he's wearing an invisible straitjacket. Then I tell him to take them out. I have a long exposure on the camera and I know what will happen: his hands will disappear into a white blur and his smile will be a true one.

That night, when I print a test strip in the old basement darkroom in my parents' house, I know before it even comes up it's good. His eyes are up at the light, shining merrily, his hands invisible, his expression a simple reflection of joy in the moment. It's not a child staring hard, deadpan into a camera, giving back what the adult behind the camera is giving him. It's entirely his own expression, including the hands, which are unsettling, but his. By the time I get it into the fixer, I know it's the first thing I've done in months that's not imitative or the result of a desperate grab at a concept. It is different and good—an image of a child we haven't seen before.

I get so excited I stay up late printing more. The ones of me are an interesting mix. Vanity compelled me to dress nicely and wear makeup, and the joke is that my face never makes it onto a negative. In one you can see my hair; in another, my mother. Mostly I am flying from the camera to the chair—a blur of shirt. The more I look at them, the more I think there's something interesting about this. A conventional portrait of an unusual child is juxtaposed against a chair someone keeps trying to get to. The chair looks fine, the person looks ridiculous. Or as if she is trying to fit into a universe that isn't accommodating her need to walk between the camera and the chair.

I work at the pictures, dodging and burning, to make my blurred figure more mysterious and more frantic. I love the effect: the universe is skewed; I am forever in motion, a chair eternally out of my reach.

For the next three days I do nothing but shoot and print pictures. When my mother finally asks if I've talked to Rozzie, I snap no, I don't want to, so tersely it's clear: I don't want to think about it either. I want to put it out of my mind entirely.

But I can't.

My fourth night home, I leave my prints drying downstairs and go into Rozzie's room, which looks exactly as it did when she was seventeen, the summer she left for L.A. and ever afterward, returning only for visits. The closets are filled with her high school leotards and tapestry skirts. Over her desk is a bulletin board with all the buttons she used to pin on her backpack: ERA Now; Keep Abortion Safe and

Legal. Now that she no longer does anything political, all this seems especially irritating to me, a contrivance. I sift through her desk to find more evidence of her phoniness. I want to pile up reasons for my anger, proof that she doesn't mean what she says, that over and over she talks about how important I am, but when a man enters the picture, she forgets all that. In a drawer, I find a high school history paper, a syllabus for Spanish Two, and then a letter, undated, written on pale blue stationery:

Dear Daniel:

I'm sorry for taking you by surprise yesterday. I know I shouldn't do that, but I can't help myself. I am drawn like a magnet to your house. I vow not to stop by and suddenly, there I am, on your grassy walk, approaching your front door. It is always so good to see you and talk to you, even if we can only drink iced tea and sit across the room from each other. I love telling you my stories. I practice them so my timing will be right, so I know you'll laugh. You were always right about timing. I've learned that over the years.

Even when our times together seem as stiff and as formal as that glass of iced tea was, I still love seeing you. You are the voice in my head that I always

I turn it over, look for the next page, which I can't find. This must be to Daniel Wilkenson, her old drama teacher, but I reread it to see if I am right. I can't get over it: *I am drawn like a magnet . . . ? You are the voice in my head . . . ?* My heart does a little dance in my chest. I feel as if I have stumbled onto a gold mine.

I know Rozzie visits him when she's home, though she always makes it sound like a duty, always says, "I should go see Mr. Wilkenson," with a sigh as if she means *poor Daniel.* Once I went with her, not by choice—she was giving me a ride to the pool that turned out to be closed—and we found him mowing his lawn without a shirt. I remember being embarrassed by his pale white arms and brown chest hair, a body not meant to be seen. He quickly found his shirt and covered it up. We sat and drank water that his wife brought to us without speaking once. She was tiny, like a bird, with short brown hair and no makeup.

Now it means I know where he lives.

In the wake of Rozzie's waltzing out to my school and ruining my life, I have had no recourse and no place to put my anger. Calling her at school would do no good. It would just be a conversation she could have with Matthew. Now I know her vulnerability; now there's something I can do.

Because I have brought so few clothes down, I wear an old shirt and pants of Rozzie's. Maybe he will recognize them—I certainly would; to me they even smell like her—but I don't care. It feels like a costume and gives me the power of disguise. This isn't me, ringing his bell with the letter in my pocket. This is someone else.

The porch light comes on. I don't know if he'll remember my name, so when I hear him call, "Just a minute!" I say, "It's Jemma, Rozzie's sister."

He opens the door wearing shorts and a T-shirt and no shoes. "Jemma, how nice to see you. Come in, come in."

I follow him inside. The house looks different from what I remember. There seems to be less furniture around the room and more plates on the floor.

"Sit down. What would you like? I think I might have some iced tea. Would you like iced tea?" I think about the letter and wonder if there is a perpetual pitcher sitting in the refrigerator awaiting visits from younger women. A moment later, he returns with the sweetest iced tea I've ever tasted.

"So you're doing photography, I hear."

"That's right."

He sits down across from me in a folding chair with his iced tea resting on one of his pale knees. "Wonderful." He looks sideways at the door and pauses as if he's listening for a particular sound.

I can't waste time, I realize, his wife might walk in at any moment. "So, Mr. Wilkenson—"

"Daniel, please."

"Daniel. I stopped by to talk to you about Rozzie."

He nods and closes his eyes in a gesture that's hard to read but I hope means, yes, go on.

"I'm not sure if anyone has told you this or not, but she's having a sort of hard time right now."

"With work?"

"It's more than that. She's very . . ." I hesitate. I need to do this right. "Alone. She has a hard time reaching out to people. Believe me, I wouldn't be here if my parents and I weren't very worried about her."

His forehead corrugates; his hands move together. "Tell me more."

"We think she's having kind of a nervous breakdown. I'm not sure what else to call it. She came out to visit me at school and now she won't leave. She says she's scared of going back to New York. I came home to discuss it with my parents, and then we found this letter on her desk."

I hold it out to him. Because I know her handwriting so well, I have given it an ending: *You are the voice in my head that I always hear, you are the love of my life, the man I am waiting for.*

I know this is bad, but I keep going.

He reads the whole thing and looks up at me. "When did she write this?"

"I don't know exactly. Recently, I'm pretty sure."

He stares down at the letter in his lap.

"We were wondering if you would mind going to see her," I say softly. "I know it's a lot to ask." I say this fairly certain he won't do it. He's a married man, after all, and a teacher. Even being a celebrity can't change some facts. I don't really want him to do anything; I just want to humiliate Rozzie as much as she has humiliated me.

"You want me to drive up to your school?"

"We don't know what will help. I know she's always cared for you a great deal, and then I found this letter. And it occurred to me, maybe this is what's confusing her right now. Maybe she needs to see you and sort out her *feelings*." I put a soft emphasis on the word *feelings*. "She has always liked you. You may not realize how much." I lower my voice to a whisper in case his wife is standing outside the door, listening. "I know she seems to lead this glamorous life now, filled with celebrities, but the person she's always really loved is you."

I stop speaking and sit back. My face is hot and my heart feels as if it is about to beat its way out of my body.

For a long time he doesn't speak. Then he takes a sip from his glass, looks up, and says, "You may not know this, but my wife left me about seven months ago."

I stare at him. "No. I didn't know that."

"She was never happy living here for a variety of reasons. I tried to make her happy, but there's just so much one person can do."

I don't say anything.

"After it happened, I went to see your sister. I told her I was free now and she told me, in no uncertain terms, to leave. That she didn't want me to visit her ever again."

What? My knapsack slips off my knees. "When was this?"

"About four months ago. I haven't heard from her since."

"Oh, my God." My mouth goes dry.

*　　*　　*

That night at dinner, I am so quiet my parents say they're worried about me. My mother thinks I've been working too much, that I need to take a break. "Let's rent a movie," she says brightly. "Your choice."

In the car ride to the store I try not to think about sitting across from Daniel Wilkenson, watching his face spasm as he told me about Rozzie's rejection. I honestly thought the letter would come as a surprise to him, be as simple as news of an old student's infatuation. I thought he would laugh, hopefully at Rozzie. That they have discussed their feelings, and his marriage, comes as a hideous shock to me. I went there intending to hurt Rozzie and fear now I've only opened an old wound for him.

At the video store, I wander around distracted and disinterested. When I hear a voice behind me call, "Jemma?" I pretend, for a second, not to hear. Then I turn around and it's Theo, whom I haven't seen in years, with his hair cut short and surprisingly stylish. At first, I can't think of anything to say, and then I point to the movie he's holding, *Children of a Lesser God*. "That's the one where William Hurt teaches a singing class for deaf kids."

Theo smiles and touches the box. "Please, Jemma. My favorite movie."

I laugh and he does, too. "I can't believe it's you," he says. "You look so different."

"I do?" I look down at myself, surprised.

"So big-city, I guess."

I am wearing what I always wear these days: black jeans, black turtleneck, red shoes.

"Really?"

"You look like one of those very cool people in a Gap ad."

I grin. When he asks what I'm doing now, I tell him I'm in art school and he looks impressed enough that I keep going and tell him about the award.

He raises his eyebrows. "Two months there and you're winning awards?"

"Well, small ones."

"What do you take pictures of?"

I start to tell him and then I realize I already have. The last time I talked to him I described the pictures I've spent the last four years taking. "Movie sets, so far. Do you remember, I told you?"

He nods. He remembers. "Sure."

"I've been doing that for a while. I want to move on to something new now."

"Like what?"

"Well, I'm home now shooting my mother's students."

He looks interested. I want to keep going, tell him all about what I've been getting, except that a woman walks up, blond, a little plump, holding a box. Theo slips his hand into hers. "Hey, Stace, this is Jemma. Jemma, this is my girlfriend, Stacey."

"Hi," I say, holding a smile for so long, my lips stick to my teeth.

I spend the rest of the night watching a movie with my parents and thinking about Theo. Did I not date him years ago because he had a limp or because maybe, I knew, I might really have liked him? I don't know. Eventually I look up his telephone number in the phone book and call just to get a machine and see if he is living with this Stacey person. I tell myself I'm curious, in a sociological way, how many people my age are living together. Then he answers and without even thinking I say, "Theo, it's me."

He knows. "Hi. I was thinking about calling you, too."

We get together for lunch at a restaurant down the highway that he claims has great pasta, but he must have chosen it because it is almost ten miles outside town and the likelihood that he will see anyone he knows is slim. When we walk in, the place is filled with old people. After we order, Theo doesn't beat around the bush. "So, I've got to say, it threw me off a little bit running into you like that."

I had planned to be casual, keep the conversation light and friendly. I was even going to be generous and ask him about Stacey, what she did for a living. "What do you mean?"

"The strange part was, I'd been thinking about you earlier that day. And then all of a sudden, there you were. It was weird."

"What were you thinking?"

"I don't know. Sometimes I just think about you. And I do stuff, like once I rented *Green Card* because Andie MacDowell's hair looks like yours. Or I'll rent a movie because the woman's a photographer. I've done that, too. I probably shouldn't tell you this."

What I can't get over is that he's talking about movies, but he doesn't mention Rozzie's. "Do you ever watch my sister's movies?"

"I've seen them. Or some. I don't know. I like them. She just doesn't really remind me of you. Other things do."

I feel my heart crack; I have one chance to do this right, I think. I ask him if he's serious with Stacey, and he says, sort of, yeah, that's what makes seeing me again hard: "We're talking about moving in together." I want him to keep going. He has admitted so much, I want him to add, "We won't now, of course."

But he doesn't.

Instead he says, "We're good together."

What he's said earlier makes saying this worse. Seeing that he can speak his heart so much better than I can speak mine makes it all the sadder to be told I won't have it. But in my own way, I am an actress, too. I know how to slide through these moments, to not look as if I'm dying, even if I am. I tell him I'm happy for him, that it's a great thing to find someone you like that much. I don't say *love*. I haven't given up all hope yet.

Two days later, I call again. My parents have extra tickets to see a play at the college, I tell him. I know it's last-minute, but would he like to go?

"Umm . . ." He waits forever.

"I'm not trying to screw up your relationship. I just want to be friends. I swear."

"Okay. Sure."

The play is called *Burn This* by Lanford Wilson and is so good I almost forget Theo is beside me, that the play is just an excuse to go out with him. At the center is a dancer named Anna who has lived for years in New York with her best friend, a gay man. The play starts after he has died in a boating accident, and his brother, a crazy, charismatic restaurant chef, blows into town. He is loud, coarse, and incredibly compelling. The actor who plays him is short and dark—though his character's name, ironically, is Pale. He circles the edges of the set like a caged animal, banging on the walls, drinking, popping pills, swearing at everyone. Her character, however, is the one I recognize; I feel as if I'm watching some parallel version of myself—a woman who has chosen an impractical career and then made all her other choices safe and cautious. When she admits she hasn't had sex in years, she tries to explain how dancing for her is like sex, and the love she feels for friends is as valid and sustaining as any sexual love. Pale touches her for the first time and says, "Bullshit."

I have been telling myself some version of this for years: that I am happy with my life as it is, even when I know it isn't true. Part of being mad at Rozzie right now is really about closing one door to open another, about cutting away safety nets to really, finally fall. I don't say anything for a long time after the play is over. Finally, outside the theater, Theo says, "Boy, there was a lot of swearing."

I shoot him a look. In the past, I've been grateful when a man says something like this because it means I am safe, I don't need to like him anymore—I can go back to my lonely life without the mind-occupying crush because clearly he isn't very smart. But this time feels different. I want Theo to understand why I liked it. "I think there had to be. He was trying to shake up her world. She had this life that was ostensibly successful, but was really carefully constructed and very limited." I hesitate and keep going. "I've felt like that sometimes. Like I've been afraid to take certain risks and I'm not even sure why. It's been so long I'm not even sure what I was so afraid of anymore."

Theo doesn't say anything, and I wonder if I should feel stupid if he realizes I'm admitting I haven't had sex in a long time. Finally he says, "You're afraid of getting hurt, I'd imagine."

"Yeah. I guess so."

"I don't understand why, to be really sexy, a guy has to rage around and take cocaine and be like that."

I can tell it bothers him. Or he's worried. I've liked the play for my own reasons and he hasn't for his. "You don't," I say simply.

Though I paid for the tickets and dinner, he has driven, so it's his car we're sitting in at the end of the night. I tell him I'm going back to school on Monday so I might not see him again for a while, but it was great to get together, to have him as a friend again. After I say all this, I lean over and kiss him. I know I seem ridiculous, my mouth saying one thing, my body doing another, but I also know how it feels to regret not trying. Right away he kisses me back, pulls me closer so our hips are touching. It feels better than I even imagined, as if he is reaching into every lonely part of me and erasing the pain. I can feel his erection, but I have it, too, whatever the equivalent is. I want to keep going, lie my seat down and pull him on top of me. "It's not like this with Stacey," he says.

"Like what?"

"Like my heart is coming." After he says this, I feel his body shift, as if he's changing his mind. "But I don't want to do this if you're just leaving."

I don't know what to say. What I hear is *I don't want to do this.* "I guess we should stop, then," I say. "I mean, right?"

"Right."

Rozzie, present

She admits to seeing some things, but she doesn't tell anyone this startling development: that on the fourth day after the bandages are off, she opens her eyes and sees a man standing beside her bed—short, wearing white, with dark, curly hair.

At first, she assumes it is her imagination. Jemma has described her doctor, and this is her mind's picture come to life—talking, reading, pushing up his glasses. Then she reaches out and touches where she believes he is standing. And he *is*. She can *see* her finger and the cotton of his coat—can feel it at the same time. Her heart begins to race.

This has happened once before—this gift of clarity—and she knows enough not to say anything. She knows that it will come and go, which it does. Sometimes, she will see flowers on the windowsill—smell them even, she is *sure*—but when she gets across the room, she finds nothing, warm air, a patch of sun.

The mind and memory are powerful tricksters.

If she tells the doctors, she will fail their tests. She will see a blue jacket on a doctor who will tell her he is wearing only a yellow shirt. And even after he's told her, after she *knows* the truth, the jacket won't change. It will be there with details: buttons, stitching. She will see what she sees, as she always has.

She has learned, over time, not to trust male authority figures. Or at least not to trust herself with them. She has believed too much of what she's been told. If she lays herself open, tells them everything she believes she can do, the power will diminish. She'll be told she's not really seeing; she'll be tested with their machines and will score poorly. What she sees will become their explanation of what she is seeing. Far better, for now, to keep it to herself—to fail no tests and instead take pleasure in what she is given: a Docksides shoe, a mug, the cord of the telephone that sits by her bed.

She doesn't think about death anymore, or moving quietly into a darkness like death. This trick is far too titillating; it's like acting again, pretending not to see what she does see, or might.

One afternoon, Jemma comes in wearing what looks like a green-and-white checked shirt. She hasn't seen green in ages, since New York, where you could only find it on clothes or in Central Park. Now here it is again, on a shirt, she's almost sure.

She doesn't know how to ask without raising suspicions. She tries another approach: "What are you doing for clothes? You only packed for a couple weeks, right?"

"I'm rotating three shirts and some pants I bought last week at Kmart."

"Lovely. Which three shirts?"

She waits to hear green-and-white, but none of them are. Instead, Jemma describes three different shirts and Rozzie holds her breath. This must be her imagination, she thinks—tricks one side of her brain is playing on the other. She feels like weeping for how little she understands herself now.

Then Jemma moves. She must be looking down. "Oh, and this hideous plaid. My kelly-green-and-white beauty."

Rozzie exhales.

Jemma, present

In the last few days, a new issue has emerged. Suddenly there is a question about Rozzie's finances. It is odd to hear this—for years, she has been the richest person anyone in our family knows. Now Miriam, her manager, tells us that in six months Rozzie's money will be gone.

When I first hear this, I feel a flutter of satisfaction. I think, at last Rozzie, who claims not to care about money, will see what it's really like to have none. I picture her living in the apartments I used to, with silverfish and cockroaches, bathtubs decorated in cosmic rust stains. Then it's quickly clear the issue isn't living in the luxury that she once did, but surviving at all with the expenses her new condition will incur. She will need equipment, expensive and electronic, and she will also need regular hired help. There will be a steady drain on her finances and, as Miriam has gently pointed out, fewer job offers.

I start to worry. I overhear my father talk to an investment counselor. On another call, I hear him nervously ask how residuals work. He nods, runs his fingers through his graying hair. "We were hoping for more, of course," he says with a cough. Then a strained laugh.

Our parents have never been wizards with finance. We grew up with some money, but not much, nothing like what Rozzie is accustomed to living on. Presumably our parents still have the money that was meant to go toward our college, but my father seems so nervous,

I wonder. Maybe in the flush of Rozzie's success, they, too, over-spent. We talk about it cautiously, in experimental probes. "How much are these things?" my mother asks Carol, a counselor from the Center for Visually Impaired who has been describing computer equipment to us.

"They range. Eight to ten thousand," Carol says blithely.

Dear God, we all think. For one piece of equipment? I look over at my father, who stares into his lap, his expression unreadable.

Miriam makes one suggestion, half joking. "I'm not getting any job offers, but I *am* getting calls from magazines who want her story." Even as she laughs, she says this with a question mark that only I hear. As if she's feeling us out. My parents miss the implication or else ignore it. When I'm alone with Miriam, I ask if the magazines will pay for the story. I'm not asking anything she hasn't thought of. "Occasionally they do. But it has to be exclusive, and really it's only the tabloids who pay. I can't see Rozzie agreeing to that."

No, of course not. Rozzie has spent the last three years ducking away from photographers and avoiding publicity, so why would she start seeking it now that she's so fragile? My parents would instantly dismiss this idea, but I see another side to it: her story is worth some-thing now and it won't be forever. A year from now or even six months, when she really needs the money, it will be old news. She may be looking for *any* way to make money and have none.

In the afternoon, while Rozzie sleeps, I sit in the smoking room of the hospital and flip through back issues of the *Star* to find hospi-tal shots of other celebrities. I find a few. For the most part, they all have the blurry, poor quality of paparazzi photos snapped on the sly, a bent brunette head said to be that of Elizabeth Taylor sitting in a wheelchair, but really, it could be anyone at all.

To me, it seems that the poor quality of the photos has become part of the story, the expectation for a celebrity felled by disease. Illness is the great leveler of society, all glamour erased in its wake. Mary Tyler Moore gets diagnosed with diabetes and every paper runs a blurry picture of her with bad hair, as if getting diabetes means forfeiting your combs.

The more I look, the more I think: Maybe the pictures don't have to be so bad. Maybe there can be a different version to this story— one that chronicles, in focus, the path of disease, how a body accommodates it, and how a person, given strength and conviction, can accept it.

I imagine the shots I would take. For the first time in months, I think about finding my camera and using it.

I want to say I have forgiven Rozzie for what happened with Matthew, but the truth is I haven't. We never mention it, and have never talked about what happened later, how on his third visit to New York, she broke up with him suddenly and he returned to school a shadow of himself, desolate and unshaven. For a while, from a distance, I watched him slump around campus in disheveled clothes and then I sought him out, told him she did this all the time, to many men. I told him other stories of the people she'd flattened with her disregard. "She doesn't think she's being cruel. It's just the way she is," I said, going on and on, losing track of what I'd meant to say.

Theoretically, this was an offering, a solace, an act of friendship, but anyone listening might have said otherwise. Even Matthew must have sensed this. A few weeks later, we stopped talking altogether.

Alone in the hospital, it sits between us. I wait for her to bring it up, to offer an apology or an explanation. Sometimes I wonder, if she does apologize, what will I say? This anger protects me, keeps me the same distance from her that she's always been from me. Would I give it up just like that, with a simple *I'm sorry*?

* * *

That night, I'm killing time in the gift store and it occurs to me: maybe Rozzie would never have to know. The shelf life for these papers is a week, at best; nothing, really. What are the odds she'll recover enough sight to go to the grocery store in the next month or so? I also tell myself that in all likelihood these papers are going to run this story anyway. Better to have some input beforehand. Better to negotiate some control up front.

I get the phone numbers and leave messages. I don't tell anyone what I am doing. This is just an experiment, I tell myself; I'm calling to see how much money they're talking about. It takes several tries, but finally I get an articles editor from the *Star* on the phone. I tell him I am following up on a call his newspaper made to Rozzie's manager.

He sounds confused. "Wait, what's your name?"

"Jemma Phillips?" I say with a question mark, my old, horrible habit.

He puts me on hold and returns a minute later. "Hello, Jemma," he says, his voice altered, as if he's checked some file and found my name. "So you're her sister, huh?"

I can hear in his voice, he's *very* interested. Suddenly I get nervous. I need to play my cards right. "Yes," I say. "The thing is, I'm not sure if she's interested. We'd need to know how much money it would mean and she'd want to make a few stipulations."

"Such as?"

I have him. I know I do. "Such as she'd want me to take the pictures."

"*You?*"

"I'm a professional photographer," I say with no question marks anywhere.

Another pause. "Okay."

After I hang up, I try to decide if this idea has come out of my anger or from my other, better side that genuinely wants to help. It *could* help, I think—by putting Rozzie back in the spotlight, letting people see she is still beautiful, still herself. Maybe it will even be a way back into movies, which she talks about now as if they were a distant part of her past. Maybe my pictures can now do what I wanted them to do so long ago: show Rozzie who she is. Show the world, too.

Then again, I don't know. I've been angry for so long, I've lost track of it now. It's like a distant memory, or something I can't see very well, but I know it's there. It comes out in dreams, where I yell so loud, for so long, I collapse into chairs, hardly able to catch my breath. Chest heaving, I grope for the words that slide in and out of my dream mouth. *"You!"* I scream. "Don't understand," I say softer. Nothing is a sentence. Nothing makes sense.

Jemma, 1992–93

After I finish with my mother's students, I go back to school. I find a dozen roses Rozzie has left in my room with a long letter, talking about how I matter more to her than anyone else on earth. Halfway through, I stop reading and throw all of it—flowers and letter—into the trash.

I don't want her apologies or her empty declarations of how important I am to her. I love the novelty of being angry, and I know to hold on to this anger, I must pretend to let go of it. I must speak to her occasionally, superficially, about nonevents in our lives: meals we've eaten, movies we've seen, which I do. We talk every week or every other week. I know she feels the distance and tries to bridge it with platitudes. "It's good to hear your voice," she'll say, segueing from nothing but my own reticence.

"Yeah," I'll say.

In distance there is power, I learn. Every time I tell her I have to get off the phone, she works to keep me on, which has always been my role: getting less, wanting more. Apathy gives me an edge. I love every yawn I produce, love saying twelve minutes into a conversation, "I should probably go." I know this works and I know why it matters: she's had men off and on all her life, but she's never not had me.

"Go? Already?" she'll say in a panic.

"I'm really busy right now."

In between these conversations, I throw myself so completely into work, my fingernails go soft and turn a shade of yellow I have never seen before. I don't want to do or think about anything else. I need all of this to pay off in a phenomenal work triumph, to make the end of a sordid story be a portfolio I can finally show with some pride. My last two days at home, I brought in a four-by-five portrait camera I had borrowed from school and only used experimentally before. It is cumbersome and hard to work with, but the negatives have turned out well. Fine-grain, unbelievable detail, they beg to be blown up larger than life, and so I experiment making bigger prints. In the past, I've always shied away from the large prints. Now I stand in front of the light image projected against the wall, so my picture falls on my own face, flush with the excitement of taking risks like this. Burning through paper that costs five dollars a sheet, saying, yes, this is worth it, all my time, all my money.

I love what I get.

My teacher isn't a fan of big prints so I'm running the danger that she'll do her usual critique on gallery-style printing before any of us are ready to be in galleries. It is an act of confidence to print up faces twice the size of my own. Still I keep going. I do all my portraits big as sofas, and then I do the pictures of me almost the same size. I stretch the rules of my premise—one of the best "kid" pictures, as it turns out, is the toilet flushing, mostly because it's a toilet and a tiny face in the corner, another child, peering in, as enraptured as the photographer obviously is. It's the closest the images come to showing what an autistic child might be thinking. Though it wasn't shot with the instruction to take a portrait of me, I print and include it as if it were. Admittedly this is unfair to the child, makes him look more confused than he is, but for now, so be it, I decide. Professionals and artists have been making choices like this for years. It's how you get good.

Finally, I am excited enough to show my friend Maya.

"I don't know," she says, staring at two, side by side. "Freaky kids is tough. It's kind of been done."

My stomach does a somersault.

"I mean these are really good, don't get me wrong. Really good. Seriously. They're fantastic. I don't know why I said that first thing. They're great."

My anxiety catapults. I don't know what to make of this. Maya is a complicated friend. She's ambitious and self-critical at the same time. She is capable of crying in public in a way that I never would. She can stand in a darkroom and talk to no one about problems with her prints. I wonder if maybe she is applying that same worried hypercriticism to me. The next day I decide to take the prints to show my teacher, even though I know this is a risk, that I have too much riding on this work.

"Okay. Not bad." She hands them back. "But I think you could go further with this."

"Further how?" I ask, my voice tiny.

"What you are doing right now is too limited to these particular kids. Right, they're unconnected, they see the world funny, but what does that have to do with me? There's got to be a connection to a universal truth outside the particulars of your subject matter. Otherwise we're just being voyeurs; we're gawking at the autistic kids, we're not participating in the picture at all."

"What should I do about that?"

"Think about what this has to do with people who aren't autistic. What do these kids have to do with me, for instance?"

Nothing, I want to say. You don't need to be a stripper to be moved by Brassai. You don't need to be a freak to be touched by Diane Arbus. I want this woman to think about what she's saying and take it back. Or else I want her to drop dead. She is cutting out my heart. Taking the only happiness I've felt in months. I walk outside and think: I can't stand being here. I'm going to leave. Take my award and immolate myself on the central quad. I'm going to leave a note saying I killed myself because no one liked my work enough.

Instead, I decide I will prove this woman wrong. I take slides of these prints and start the arduous, unimaginably expensive process of submitting to galleries. I walk between my house and the post office clutching a fan of padded brown mailers every other week or so.

Though I have made a few friends here, I begin to distance myself from them. Being angry at Rozzie means being angry, in general, most of the time. After a brief rapprochement with Matthew, he and I drift apart. He clearly wants to move on from his pain, and seeing me obliges him to think about it again. If, for a brief instant, I imagined their breakup would open the door for me again, I can quickly see all doors are closed, even our old, lovely friendship. He works in a different darkroom now, across campus, a mile-and-a-half bike ride away.

I grow so isolated I begin to wonder if people are talking about me. I stand outside of doors, as I did in college, holding my breath, trying to hear what's being said. When people see me, they startle, as if I look different or they thought I wasn't here anymore.

One night I leave the darkroom, and walking home late, I see Maya, Matthew, and another woman walking up the street. My heart stops. They are laughing about something, illumined in the warm glow of a storefront. Maybe this is just a coincidence, maybe they haven't gone out to dinner or drinks together, but all the same, I feel closed out of every circle I've ever been a part of.

All winter, rejection letters dribble in. My slides follow in self-addressed, self-stamped body bags. Other people hear good news: Maya gets an internship on a magazine in New York, Matthew gets an honest-to-God job offer from a small college in Ohio. People tell me their plans with affected shrugs and throwaway disclaimers. ("The school is actually in a cornfield," Matthew says. "Not just near one.") I can see them tempering their enthusiasm, editing their news because my own is nonexistent.

In March comes the crowning blow in the form of a letter from my adviser. My work will not be shown in the spring show put on by the Art Department. I have gone, in the same year, from being a first-year student singled out for an award, to one of two or three in the department who will not be represented in the final show. I go to my adviser's office early in the morning when I am certain no one else will be around. "What is this?" I say, holding the crumpled letter.

"We just didn't think your work this semester was strong enough."

I stare at her and she returns my gaze, unflinching.

She must be right—I am getting only rejections—so why did I think these pictures were so good? When did I lose sight of my own work?

I know my adviser doesn't mean to be cruel. This is meant to be a challenge to me. All artists suffer rejections; the ones who succeed are the ones who get past it. I tell myself this, even though Rozzie, the one success I know, the yardstick by which I measure my own life, has never suffered as I suffer now. Then I remember the first few days of her visit, when she seemed so disoriented and removed from herself, just as I have felt these past few months. She has gone almost a year without work, more idle time than I have ever had to face. I have kept our conversations so minimal and distant that I have no real idea what she's doing to fill her days.

For the first time in months, I feel bad about this. I wonder if it's possible for us to commiserate. I call her up, prepared, for the first time in six months, to have an honest conversation, and her voice is different, lighter than it's been in a long time. She was just about to call me, she says, a little out of breath.

"Oh? Why?"

"I got a job. A good one, a good part." She tells me the story of the movie, the name of the director. Listening to her, I feel the way I have all winter long: shut down, shut out. I want to slip the phone back onto the cradle; hang up without making a sound.

Then she says, "Here's the funny part. There's a role for someone to play my sister. I was thinking about asking them to hire you."

Come on, I think. Not again. After all this time, is Rozzie still capable of getting me jobs I don't need to interview or be qualified for? Does she still wield that kind of power?

Apparently.

I don't even say yes. I say maybe, which everyone must assume means yes.

A day later, my phone rings all morning with producers and costume people, scheduling fittings and airplane tickets. My anger has mutated; turned inward and then back out again. This is my revenge against my teacher, against Matthew, even against Maya. They have their opinions, their criticism, their job offers and internships, but none of them has a movie set they can be on four days later.

None of them can leave, just like that, without saying good-bye.

But I can and I do. Just like that.

Two weeks later, I am standing in an unflattering, floor-length pink dress, playing a bridesmaid. Rozzie is the bride, stunning in an antique lace dress, rumored to have cost ten thousand dollars and to be one of a kind, though I've seen two of them in the costume trailer. The dress takes forty-five minutes to put on or take off, so to save time and her dress, she eats with a tablecloth spread over her shoulders.

The spirit on this set is jolly; everyone thinks this movie will be good, and some are saying it will establish Rozzie's career as a serious actress, not just a pretty face. "Finally she'll get a chance to sink her teeth into something and *act*," says Miriam, visiting the set.

The only person not caught up in the enthusiasm is Rozzie, who floats through the day, from scene to scene, meal to meal, with an empty expression on her face. She talks to people, listens to their stories, and when they walk away, her eyes don't move. Even crew people notice this new, inexplicable seriousness in her mood. I overhear the wardrobe girls say Rozzie seems a little withdrawn. "It's a hard part," one says. "She's got to stay focused on that."

It's not the part, I suspect, but I don't know what else it could be. We have slid into a rhythm, careful and polite with each other. We find our old quiet ground and occupy it side by side, books in our hands, ice melting in our drinks. This goes on for days. In this time, the only thing I learn is that acting is much harder than it looks. My makeup is so thick I can feel my cheeks fold when I smile. My hairstyle makes me appear, in shadow, to be wearing a helmet. I am so conscious of these physical alterations, I'm unable to deliver a line without looking at my reflection in the lens of the camera. Many takes are wasted by this amateur tic, and I realize, all this time, I have thought what Rozzie does is easy. Now I see it's not.

Once I try to tell her this, but it comes out wrong. "Good at what?" she asks, staring down at her plate of food.

"This acting stuff. It's hard."

"Oh. Right."

I don't know what she is thinking about, or what her mind is on, if not this job. Once I overhear her tell someone she has gotten into meditation recently. Later, I notice in the back part of her trailer, above her sofa bed, she has taped a picture that looks like an elaborate black-and-white snowflake. Underneath is written: *Tibetan Prayer Wheel.* Good God, I think, nervous suddenly, remembering my mother's old fears about Scientology. Maybe this work has taken her so far away from where she began that a religion might feel like a new, better family.

I want to not care; to be able to say this is *her* life to live and throw away as she chooses. Then I overhear her tell a makeup girl that she's been having a hard time lately, problems with her health. I am sitting two chairs away, getting my own makeup applied, but she speaks as if I'm not in the same trailer, or she doesn't know I'm here. "My sister's been a big help," she says. "She's really gotten me through it."

My heart speeds up. Gotten her through *what?*

I want to ask someone if they know what's going on with Rozzie, but theoretically, I'm the one who knows her best.

My first real scene is with an actor named Adam Baker, who's been in three movies and is the best-looking man I've ever stood beside. He plays the groom's brother and we're supposed to be fighting in the middle of a cocktail party.

His line: "I give it six months."

My line: "Shh. It's their *wedding*."

His line: "You really think it's going to last?"

Mine: "Of course I do. They love each other."

In the movie, the newlyweds will get in a car accident, driving away from the wedding, in which the groom will die and the bride will be forced to take over his business with this brother she loathes. By the end, Rozzie's character emerges as strong, opinionated, and unafraid of disapproval. My character represents where she comes from. I'm meant to be conventional and humorless, which is fine because speaking lines makes me so nervous, I can't imagine trying for a joke.

On the first take, the camera dollies up the aisle ahead of us. I make my old mistake and look in the camera. Before I get to my first line, the director yells, "Cut!"

I blush. *I'm new at this,* I mouth to the guy sitting behind the camera. He has headphones on and doesn't seem to care.

We set up again—the makeup girls touch our noses with sponges, our hair with combs. Two lines into it, I look into the camera again. *"Cut!"* the director yells. I try laughing, but the schedule is too tight, the pressure too high. No one smiles back.

"I've got an idea," Adam says. "I'll keep looking at you, and you look right at me, into my eyes, both lines." He holds up two fingers to indicate where his eyes are.

I feel like an idiot, of course.

We set up again and this time I do fine, until we get all the way up the aisle and I turn and see a familiar face in the crowd of onlookers watching us shoot.

I don't look at the camera, but I look at the face: it's Daniel Wilkenson.

Over dinner break, Rozzie tries to tell me it's not that big a deal. "So you're never going to be an actress. Do you care? Did you want to be?" She narrows her eyes at me. "I mean, did you?"

I don't answer for a minute, because I am too busy scanning for Daniel in the crowd that lurks beyond the food-catering tent. It's not a big crowd—curious neighbors, mostly, and a dozen or so girls trying to see Adam. I'm sure Daniel was there twenty minutes ago, so where is he now? We are in the middle of nowhere and he has found us, and I know already something awful is going to happen. The truth will come out, the letter will appear, Rozzie will kill me.

"There's something I need to tell you," I whisper to Rozzie. I can't put it off. He's going to walk in here any minute.

"What?"

I look up and realize it's too late. He's here, inside the tent, headed toward us trailed by an anxious-looking PA who holds one hand on his walkie-talkie.

"Rozzie!" Daniel shouts, grinning crazily.

She looks up and sets down her fork. I can't read her expression. "Daniel," she says.

He arrives at our table, looks at her, then at me, then back at her. "Rozzie, this man claims he knows you," the production assistant says anxiously.

"It's fine." She nods. "He does."

For a long time, she and Daniel stare at each other, and then, as if something has been said—which it hasn't—she slides over on the bench to give him room to sit beside her. When he does, she leans over his shoulder. "I'm glad you came," she whispers. He grabs one of her hands and kisses the back of it.

"My dear," he says. "Of course."

What is this? What's happening? Suddenly nothing makes any sense. I watch as she buries her face into his turtleneck, forgetting her makeup so it leaves a smudge the color of flesh.

For the rest of the night, I don't see them. We are trying to finish my scene and Rozzie isn't in it, so she's free to go, which she does, with Daniel. A few people ask if that was her boyfriend. "Not really," I say, trying to sound as if it were both complicated and nothing. I don't get back to the hotel until twelve-thirty because getting a usable take of my scene has taken until the last possible minute.

I stand for a while outside the door of her hotel suite. It is quiet inside—I don't know if he is in there or not—I don't hear his voice, but there's enough of a chance that I don't risk knocking. I just stand for a long time, hoping, I guess, she'll sense that I'm here and come out—which of course she never does.

The next morning, I can't find Rozzie at breakfast, but I do run into Daniel. He greets me with a big smile and a wave. I wonder where he has slept, but he doesn't seem self-conscious at all. "Boy, this is something, isn't it?" he says, looking around. It's still early, nothing is happening, so I assume he means the idea of this, that we're here. "I used to try out for a lot of movies, but I never made it into one."

This is such a sad admission, I don't say anything.

"I wanted to, of course. I wish I had."

"Oh, well. It's not that great." I wait for him to say something about the letter. *I showed it to her, I know what you did.* He doesn't though.

"Sure it is. Rozzie making it is the completion of my old dream. I'm nothing but happy for her." As he says this, there's something a little scary in his expression—as if he's joking, but only invisible people in his head are laughing. It's hard to tell if he's being sarcastic or not. He narrows his eyes and surveys the scene: "It's funny though, these sets. Isn't it?"

I ask him what he means.

"We're creating an alternate reality that we're leading everyone to believe is ideal."

We?

"We're perpetuating some illusion that this is attainable." He holds out the hand toward the breakfast van. "When of course it's all bullshit, right? It's all smoke and mirrors. Surfaces and facades. You ever read *Day of the Locust*?"

I shake my head.

"It's all about the people who migrate to L.A. with this one ambition to become famous. Being good doesn't matter, being an artist doesn't matter. Just fame. That's it."

I want to tell him there's more to it than that; that Rozzie is sensitive about this very issue. Does he not know her well enough to understand even this?

"And in the end, you know what happens? Sodom and Gomorrah go up in flames. God smites his city of sin. Everyone dies. Pretty much."

I stare at him, hard. "How did you know where we were? Did Rozzie call you?"

"I read about it, actually. In *Variety.*"

I tell him I have to go to the bathroom and slide out of my director's chair. We all have director's chairs with our names on them. The only one who doesn't, oddly, is the director. I knock on the door of Rozzie's trailer, and even though I get no answer, I go inside. She is sitting on the padded sofa bench staring at nothing. I can't even tell if she knows I walked in. "Roz?" I say, my heart beating. "Are you all right?"

She shakes her head slightly. "It's weird, isn't it? That he's here."

I study her face and try to tell if she knows what I did. She doesn't seem to. "I guess. Yeah, a little."

"I can't help it. He was my teacher."

"Can't help what?" My voice rises nervously.

"I don't know. Being happy to see him, even though he's obviously . . ." Her voice drifts off. "I don't know."

"Obviously what?"

"Lost, I guess. His wife left him, he quit teaching, and he sold his house." I look up at her. She explains, "The school board voted to do *Grease* and so he quit."

"Oh, my God. What's he going to do?"

"He says he wants to visit the set for a while. Maybe write a piece on it."

"What kind of piece?"

"Like for *Harper's* or something."

This sounds deluded and I can't understand why she's reporting it as if it makes sense. From understudy to drama teacher to magazine journalist? For a long time a silence hovers between us. I wait to hear her say something about my visit to his house, yet all she says is "I don't know. It's strange."

Three days after his arrival, a controversy erupts about just what sort of "piece" Daniel is writing. He's taken to carrying a notepad to the set and engaging people in what seems to me like pointless conversations, telling grips they are lighting an empty promise, saying to a production assistant that he'd like to get a word with the director. The production assistant shrugs. She has no more to do with the director than he does. She's trying to find a nest of crickets that have been singing in the last two shots.

Finally the producers knock on Rozzie's trailer door and ask if she has a minute. They want to know what magazines he writes for, what his intentions are. I drift close enough to overhear snippets of the exchange.

"It's nothing," she says. "He's never been published."

Later, I hear her say, "He needs to do *something*."

Surely all this is humiliating to admit. It would certainly be possible for her to have a boyfriend who is a real journalist, who has brown or blond hair, not gunmetal gray, and is more or less her age, yet she doesn't. For some reason, she seems to be with this man.

At last I have finished all my scenes with lines. For better or worse, I am done with my acting debut and now have only to participate in a couple of party scenes as background, which means I stand around talking to other extras about the movies they've been on. One woman claims this is her thirty-fifth movie. She started as a child, she explains, as background on *Giant* with James Dean. Oddly, she is the second person I've met who has claimed to be in this movie.

A set assistant I don't recognize taps me on the shoulder. "Seen your sister, by any chance?" he says, adjusting his walkie-talkie. Though his voice is calm, his expression is not. Keeping track of her must currently be his job. Usually it's an easy one—Rozzie's always in her trailer.

"Not in her trailer?"

"No." He shakes his head and touches the metal tucked in his ear. "Sister doesn't know," he says into the microphone. I wait. "Not in makeup, not in wardrobe, not at home base, not ten one hundred." I know this is walkie-talkie shorthand for in the bathroom. Why the steady stream of offensive language that flows over walkie-talkies should be softened by this one euphemism for the bathroom, I don't know. He looks up again. "Seen her boyfriend at all?"

I want to explain, "He's not her boyfriend. Please get this right. She has complicated feelings of obligation and duty, but he's hardly her boyfriend." But that's not the point.

Besides, what is he, if not her boyfriend?

For a while, we all do nothing. Someone will find her in the next few minutes, I assume. Rozzie is responsible about these aspects of work, and she has never, to my knowledge, been late to a set, flubbed a line, or cost any production an extra penny. Now she is first seven, then ten, then thirteen minutes late, and she is costing them money. I can feel the producers' blood pressure rise.

A half hour passes. I keep expecting her to round the corner and say, "I'm so sorry. I was getting some coffee."

After forty minutes they break us. I find Paul, the assistant director who usually deals with Rozzie, shaking his head. "It's my fault. This whole thing is my fault. Rozzie's usually so easy that I assigned a new PA to cover her, and now the dipshit has gone and lost her." Usually they never talk like this in front of us—as if they are dealing with animals or prisoners. He is flustered and anxious. It *will* be his fault if she doesn't show up in the next half hour. I try to think. The hotel?

"We tried her room and his room. We even had the concierge open the doors in case they had unplugged the phone."

"Nothing?"

"Not in your room either."

"And she knew she had this scene."

"She left makeup at two-ten. At two-twenty-two, no one could find her. Ordinarily I'd walk her, even though she's fine, she knows what she's doing, but I always walk her from makeup to the set. But, like I say, this new guy made a judgment call. She said she was fine, would be there in a minute, and he said okay."

"And no one's seen Daniel?"

"No."

My mouth goes dry. This was a big scene coming up, one she was nervous about. I wonder if she has slipped off somewhere in the wake of some kind of anxiety attack. I have worried about this when I see her mind slip away sometimes, even when she is sitting right here. But the question is, where would she go? I look around for a while, in all the places everyone has checked a hundred times. I go back to her trailer, where the PA being blamed has been stationed to sit. "I'll stay here," I say. "You don't have to."

"I can't leave," he stammers. "I'll get in trouble."

So he sits outside and I go in—to what end I'm not sure. Really, I have no more idea where Rozzie might have gone than he does.

*   *   *

Four hours later, she's still missing. I was scheduled to leave on a five o'clock flight back to school, but I go nowhere. I sit in a police station with Paul, the AD, who seems to have aged ten years in the last two hours. Since about eight o'clock, I've noticed either he or another woman named Patty is hovering around, shadowing me as Rozzie is usually shadowed through the day. Some decision must have been made that if I am not watched, I, too, might vanish. Or maybe they think I know more than I do.

The police officer asks to speak to me alone, which Paul agrees to; Paul then walks down the hall with us, points to a spot on the carpet, and says he'll wait here until I'm done. This paranoia seems beyond comprehension to me, but maybe I don't understand anything. Maybe Rozzie is in danger that I don't understand and I am, too.

Inside his office, the detective, who is balding and short, asks if I'm all right.

"I think so."

"Are you being taken care of?"

"Yes."

Then he asks if I'm scared for my sister.

"Yes. Of course."

"Do you have any idea where she might be or what might have happened?"

"No."

"But you probably know her better than any of these other people, am I right?" He waves his hand in the direction of the hallway. "Right?"

I nod. I tell him I guess this is probably true.

"So knowing her for all your life—growing up together, all of that—where do you think she might be? What would be your guess?"

"I have to assume she's with this friend of hers."

He looks down at his papers. "Daniel Wilkenson?"

"That's right."

"What's their relationship?"

"He was her old high school drama teacher. He got her started acting and cast her in her first play. I think she's always felt a sense of obligation towards him. She usually goes to visit him when she's at home—stuff like that. But recently he seems like he had a breakdown or something—his wife left him and he quit his job in the middle of the school year and showed up here without any warning or notice."

"He's been here for how long?"

"Five days, I think."

"And your sister seemed—what? Nervous to see him? Unsure? Scared?"

I can't say she seemed happy to see him. I can't tell him she hugged him until her makeup came off on his shirt. "I'm not sure. I think she *wanted* to seem happy. She feels guilty about him, I think."

"You think?"

"Yes."

He rolls his chair to the left side of his desk and sticks a pencil in an automatic sharpener. "To your knowledge, has she ever used drugs?"

"No." I think about high school—my worries, the incense in her room, the air freshener. "Maybe a little when she was younger, but not after she started working."

"Are you sure?"

"Yes. Rozzie is very serious about her work. She would never take drugs while she was working, just as she would never willingly leave a set where she was needed."

"Okay, look. If you had to take a wild stab, what would you say happened?"

"I think Daniel might have taken her somewhere, believing he was rescuing her from an idea he has that the movie business is dangerous."

"Might she have been willing?"

"I don't think so."

"Right." He nods, but he doesn't believe me. I can tell. "Okay."

Back at the production office, Miriam has arrived. Her face is pale and she seems to have developed a hand tremor. When she sees me, she grabs my wrist hard and doesn't let go. "They're saying she's been *kidnapped*. Our Rozzie has been kidnapped."

"They don't know what's happened yet."

"I'm sitting here asking them, 'Don't you people have *security?*' We're on the set of a *major* motion picture with *major* stars. The world is full of crazy people, and their security is such that their biggest star could get kidnapped in broad daylight? Right now, all I'll say is that this company better get ready to get sued for every single penny it even dreams about making in the next twenty-five years. I mean that. Every penny."

I watch her pace back and forth. The problem with her tirade is that she's inadvertently raised the point that this movie *does* have security, three full-time guards. In broad daylight, in twelve minutes, it is highly unlikely someone could have taken Rozzie if she didn't want to go. In fact, the likelihood is far greater that Rozzie got into a car and left on her own.

Another three hours and our parents are here, sitting on folding chairs inside the production office. Our father sits and studies a call sheet while our mother asks everyone who walks in what his job is. Our parents are trying to seem less nervous than they are. Though it has been eight hours and two local news camera crews are stationed outside the door, the atmosphere in this room is straining to be social. My mother even asks where people are from and follows up: *Where in Illinois?*

Over and over, we're told there's nothing else we can do besides wait and be here if Rozzie calls. The truth is, I feel better with my parents here, and I understand their method of coping far better than I understand that of Miriam, who continues to storm in and out of the office threatening to sue people. Currently, the target of her rage is the police department, which she believes is focusing the investigation on all the wrong elements (namely Rozzie's dubious relationship with Daniel, and the idea that she might have used drugs at some point). "He was her teacher. Period. End of story," she keeps saying.

When Miriam comes in for the fourth time in an hour, I excuse myself and go back to my dressing room. Paul walks me from the main trailer to the long one for secondary actors. Because they broke the crew hours ago, everything is quiet, preternaturally calm. A props guy wanders by holding a Polaroid of Rozzie, taken twelve minutes before she disappeared. We've already been told about its existence. This props man is being paid extra to stay on and talk to police about the picture and what he remembers of his exchange with Rozzie.

The makeup girls have already been questioned. I don't know what anyone else has said. We're not supposed to talk to each other about our statements. The general feeling seems to be that Rozzie was "withdrawn," seemed quieter than usual to people who had worked with her before. Even if it's true, I don't want anyone to say this. I want them to repeat the same overwrought praise she usually gets. I want them to talk about how nice she is and how she always eats fruit salad for lunch.

At the dressing room trailer, Paul says he'll wait for me on the steps. "I may sit inside for a while," I say. "I haven't really had a chance to collect myself."

"Sure," he says. "Fine."

In thirty minutes, they tell us, this will be on the news.

Every hour that passes without word makes the prognosis worse. My parents and I eat dinner at an Italian restaurant, though none of us can figure out what to order.

"What is chicken parmigiana again?" my father asks, looking up over his bifocals. This is a dish he's prepared—he's just confused.

"With bread crumbs," my mother says. "And tomato."

"Oh, that's right."

My mother's nerves are fraying. She worries that this is her fault—she never felt comfortable with this movie business and yet she never stopped it. "Mom," I say to snap her out of these thoughts, "it wasn't your decision. It's Rozzie's life. She knew you didn't like her doing movies."

"Did she? I tried to hide it."

I stare at her. "Of course she knew."

Finally, we all close our menus and look up at each other. My father asks me how Rozzie seemed this week.

"Not bad," I say. "She was happy to be working and concentrating on that."

"What did she say about this Daniel fellow?" he asks. As a rule, our father is interested in our minds, not our bodies and the men we share them with. But this is the question we can't get around.

"I don't know what their relationship was," I tell him honestly.

"I do," my mother says simply. I turn and look at her with surprise. "Or at least I did. They had a relationship while Rozzie was still his student."

"They *did?* How do you know?"

She shakes her head. "I suspected it and confronted her. It was awful. We had our worst fight ever. She said she loved him—that he was the only person on earth who understood her. Do you remember how grandiose she used to get back then?" We all nod, all cut from the opposite mold. "I made her go away to L.A. for the summer because I wanted to get her away from him. Before she left, I remember her saying, 'How would you like it if I never came back?' " My mother starts to cry. "I told her not to say such a thing, that of course we wanted her back. But she never did come back, did she? Not really."

Later, after we order and get the dinners none of us eat, my mother says she feels as if she made this happen.

"Oh, Maureen, how could you possibly think—" my father starts to say.

She's calmer now, not crying. "I think driving her away from him left the door open in a way that wouldn't have happened if I'd let it be. It would have run its course. She was smart enough, she would have seen he was a limited, sad man."

I don't know how to tell my mother it's not her fault, it's mine. I went to his house, made a pilgrimage of bad judgment, and invited a crazy person back into Rozzie's life. This is the infraction that feels so big I haven't told the police or my parents or Rozzie. I have done something so awful, there is nothing I can say.

Alone in my hotel room, I try to decide if I wasn't that surprised to hear about Rozzie and Daniel in high school because I knew all along. Maybe I knew the minute he sat beside her on the set. But if this is the love of her life, why, when he was finally free and presented himself to her, did she send him away?

The phone rings. It's the policeman I spoke with this afternoon, wanting to know if I have any of Rozzie's possessions. "No," I say. "What do you mean?"

"Like a shirt or a bathing suit? Something she was wearing recently."

"Not in my room. Those things would be in her room."

"Can I meet you in her hotel room in the morning? You can point out a few things she was wearing most recently—maybe her nightgown, some socks."

"What for?"

"We put together a scent bag for the dogs. We're not doing it yet, but the sooner we get the stuff, the better."

"Oh." I sit up. For the first time, someone is saying she might not turn up by morning—implying, it seems to me, *We might in the end be looking for a body.*

I lie there for a while, until the phone rings again. I assume it is him, or else my mother having received the same call. This whole time I haven't cried, and I know, if it's my mother, I will.

"Hello?"

"Jem?" The voice is a whisper. I feel like this is a dream, fuzzy and unreal. It's Rozzie.

"Where are you?"

"Some hospital."

I sit up and tell her she can't be, every hospital in the area has been checked.

"It's in Minneapolis."

"*Why?*" Minneapolis is maybe seven hours away.

"My eyes are screwed up. There's a specialist here."

I have no idea what to say. "Everyone here is worried you're dead."

"No. Just blind."

PART TWO

Rozzie

The day she finally leaves the hospital, she half expects a party, like the ones they have on movie sets, where everyone passes out meaningless, identical presents. Her feeling now—elation mixed with exhaustion—is so similar that, an hour before she departs, she walks up and down the hall, giving out sunglasses to the nurses, who seem, by their silence, unsure what to do with the gift. One woman kisses her on the cheek and says, "You take care, now. You're a real sweetheart."

Paula says, "*Sunglasses*. Cool. Thanks a lot."

The doctor says nothing for so long Rozzie wonders if he's left the room. Finally he says, "I've never gotten a present before."

Of course he must mean *from a patient*, but still. Neither of them knows what to say after that. It is a mistake and, she realizes, a measure of how little she understands the basic social dynamics between regular people.

Once home, the disorienting feeling lingers.

She no more knows how to be with her own family than she knew how to be with those nurses. In the five-hour car ride, they listened to a book on tape and laughed awkwardly when the protagonist had sex. When they got home, they each retreated swiftly to separate rooms, all seemingly as grateful as she was for doors to retire behind.

To other people, she knows they look like an appealing, down-to-earth family, notably unchanged by the attention her success has brought. For her, it's more complicated. Looking normal necessitates the effort of remembering what normal looks like, thinking about it all the time, covering her tracks. She thinks about a picture *Paris Match* ran years ago of her and Jemma in Italy together. They were shopping, something they rarely did together, and they looked like any two sisters—Rozzie holding a shirt against Jemma's shoulders, the two of them laughing as if something about this shirt was funny. What might it have been? Was it ugly? Obscene? What were they laughing about?

Her memory of that time in Italy is so clouded: first, by the difficult director, then by her obsession with Leonard and by the drugs he was doing and pushing her to try. The night before Jemma came, she'd been up all night resisting and then finally agreeing to smoke the heroin he kept holding out to her. She, who had only smoked pot a few times. That was how it was back then; when you went from high school plays to movies, you skipped other steps, too—like the ladder of drugs—and you willed yourself not to be scared, not to feel it too much, not to throw up in the chair where for seven hours you sat, touching the places on your face where you once had hair before the studio paid for electrolysis. It wasn't fun and it wasn't life-changing. It wasn't much of anything except a little nauseating and an easy diet trick: for seven hours, she didn't touch a single chip in the bowl beside her.

Only afterward, in the crash, did all the feelings come—a million at once, nausea, depression, horrible insecurity. For a whole day she lay in her hotel room and cried. When she remembered Jemma was coming, she jumped up and got dressed, grateful for the promise of her sister's sane presence. She nearly cried when Jemma stepped off the plane, but how could she tell her what was going on? How could she explain she was sleeping with a man five years younger than their father because he intimidated her and was the only person in six months who hadn't told her she was beautiful?

That whole visit, her obsession was protecting Jemma from the truth about her own sordid secrets. Every conversation danced around the clues; eventually she let Jemma make friends with everyone else and stopped trying to say much of anything. So then, what were they laughing about over that shirt? She'd always kept the picture because she liked the idea that maybe she'd remembered that time all wrong—maybe it was fun, *Deux belles soeurs on the town,* as the caption read.

In the hospital it was easier. With an audience of nurses and personnel they could play at being ordinary sisters, an ordinary family. Sometimes Rozzie even forgot why she ever resented her family. Now she remembers the claustrophobic, grippy feeling this house gives her and the dread she used to feel coming home to their three faces at dinner, the whole meal looking like quiet death without her.

She hates the power her family gave her years ago when she used to make adolescent rules and watch—in horror—as everyone adhered to them. She loathes herself for making the rules, loathes her parents for following them, loathes Jemma for not loathing her more.

Now here she is, living in the shadow of her worst self, with people who still know her best as that. Why did this sound fine at the hospital? It wouldn't be fine; it would be sad and awkward. She needed to get back to New York and her real life as soon as possible. There, she could work on seeing again. Harness this mystery and defy science.

Her second week at home, she goes to the Center for the Visually Impaired and signs up for a living-skills class, where, at her first session, the teacher says, "This is going to be as much about learning what you can't do as what you can. If you've been losing sight slowly, as most of us have, that means you've been faking it for a long time. You've been pretending to read menus, ordering whatever the person next to you orders."

A chuckle ripples through the room.

"You've probably been doing a lot of silly things, like eating food you don't like, and some dangerous things, too, like crossing streets when you can't see the light. Whatever vanity or pride has kept you from unfolding a white cane and using it isn't doing you any favors. Get rid of it. Throw it away. If you can't see something, you can't see it. Period. That's all there is to it. Move on."

She feels a blush creep up her body. That she is sitting in a room full of people who share her impulse toward secrecy doesn't comfort her—it makes her more self-conscious.

In the middle of his speech, though, she looks up and sees something: Jemma in the doorway, leaning in, as if she is hoping to get Rozzie's attention without disrupting the teacher. Some sort of urgency seems to be in Jemma's posture, almost a panic. Rozzie stands up and moves toward her sister in the doorway, half expecting to hear Jemma whisper, *We have to go, right away, something has happened.* Then she gets out to the hallway and the vision dissolves. Jemma isn't there at all. She stands alone for a while, trying to catch her breath.

This is the problem with unreliable sight. In the aftermath of a mistake, she feels more blind than ever.

That night, she sits in the kitchen with her mother, drinking tea. She finally wants to tell someone, *I see things sometimes. I'm not sure what it means.* For so long, she masqueraded sight—studied menus, scripts, photographs that were nothing more than a blur. Now she's doing the opposite: pretending not to see what she occasionally does. The last time this mysterious vision-clearing happened was when she visited Jemma at school. She'd gone out there intending to end the secrecy and tell Jemma about her eye problems, and then, her first three days, it was worse than ever. So bad she couldn't even step outside, and she found herself too scared to say anything at all. For three days, she sat inside feeling the contents of Jemma's room with her hands. On the third day, it inexplicably passed. She woke up from a nap to see first the purple fleece of Jemma's sweatshirt, then Jemma herself. That time there wasn't any doubt at all. They went out that night to a restaurant and she could see everything, could reach out and touch what was not her imagination—silverware, napkin, salt shaker.

It felt like a miracle. Surely it was.

This time is different. It comes and goes so quickly. For an hour afterward she mourns and wonders, is it worse, seeing just a little, every once in a while?

She tries to tell her mother: "This strange thing happened. Halfway through class, I thought Jemma had come in."

"Wasn't she waiting outside?"

"I thought something had happened and she'd come in to get me."

Her mother waits. "And?"

She doesn't say anything for a while. "It wasn't her."

"What was it?"

"I don't know." She tries to think: A memory? Sometime in high school when Jemma came to a classroom door to get her?

She wishes she was more practiced at talking to her mother. Jemma was the one who'd always had her mother's ear, who yammered on and on, telling story after story. She used to listen, sometimes from another room, amazed at how much Jemma was willing to tell their mother what boys said to her, what teachers wrote on her papers. Sometimes she felt sorry for her sister (so little was happening, all of it *could* be told to their mother), and sometimes she wondered when she started telling so little. Maybe it began with Daniel, but it seemed as if she had stopped talking to her family long before that.

"Did you like the class?" her mother asks.

"I don't know. It's strange to sit in a room full of blind people."

Her mother hesitates. "I would think it might be nice. You'd have something in common."

"Right." She wants to say, *That's what I'm scared of.* Once upon a time, Daniel used to tell her, *You have nothing in common with these people,* meaning her friends, meaning that she was different, better, extraordinary. It was that belief that had made her so, that had sent her to California able to see all her success before it happened: the meetings, the handshakes, the way much older men would steer her through a room, their fingertips pressed into the small of her back.

Later that night, she accidentally walks in on Jemma in the bathtub. "Sorry," she says when she hears the water. She starts to back out.

"It's okay. Stay. Stay."

"I just need to brush my teeth."

"Go ahead."

Rozzie uncaps her toothpaste. In class, the teacher told them to measure toothpaste by squeezing it first onto their finger. She wants to try, but she doesn't want Jemma to watch her doing something so odd, to wonder if she has missed her brush accidentally. She turns her back to her sister.

"So was tonight horrible or was it okay?"

"Something in between, I guess."

"It's funny. Halfway through, I got worried about you. I was thinking about that time I wet my pants in kindergarten and I thought, 'My God, she has no idea where the bathroom is.'"

Rozzie stops what she is doing. She hears Jemma squeeze her washcloth and spread it over her face.

"Obviously you would have asked the teacher, right? It was the stupidest thing—"

Rozzie closes her eyes and holds her breath.

"But I came looking for you."

Jemma doesn't offer any more and she doesn't ask, *Did you find the room? Did you stand in the doorway?*

That night, though, she begins to wonder how much her moments of reclaimed sight have to do with her sister. In the last week and a half, she has vividly seen three things: Jemma in the doorway of the classroom, a mug of tea Jemma had set before her, a bright yellow box of Jemma's photography paper. The latter, she reached out and touched, pulled into her lap, thrilled by the vibrancy of it, the clear suggestion of a *K* in the corner. When Jemma came in and gasped, "What are you doing?" the vision evaporated. Whatever it is, her sister has the power to cast or break a spell.

She wonders about the last time, when her vision cleared so perfectly visiting Jemma's school. She even thought: *I am meant now to look at my sister, see her more clearly,* and then Jemma was so busy, off to the darkroom, to class, to one lecture or another, and the only thing Rozzie had to look at was the purple of her sweatshirt, crossing the quad away from her. So her eye turned, found a curl of brown hair, a pair of hazel eyes flecked yellow. Men with their obvious desires and needs were easier. She doesn't even know if she loved Matthew or not; she only saw more clearly what he wanted from her.

Jemma

Home together, our old walls around us, I move soundlessly down hallways, disappear behind doors, and sit in rooms with all the lights off. If someone calls my name, I count to sixty–slowly–before I answer, for no reason other than to put space around myself, walls and air. I am here and not here.

In the presence of others, I learn what Rozzie has understood all these years: how to absent myself. I ask questions and nod through answers I stop listening to the moment they begin. I speak without any idea of what I am saying. I participate in conversations I can't remember, because I am thinking, the whole time, *I need this picture, and this.*

My mind develops a shutter release. In my head, I am snapping all the time.

Rozzie is still beautiful. Even though her eyes wander, empty, around the room, they don't look dead. They seem to be in search of other worlds. I feel like we are back in high school, only now I don't have to hide in my own room to watch her in hers. I can stand right here and hold my breath.

To actually shoot, I must dress my camera in muffling scarves and cut-up T-shirts, to silence the mechanical hum and whir. Every time I take a picture, I am sure I won't get away with this. And then I do. Over and over.

Sometimes I stand three feet away from her. She believes herself to be alone in the room so I hold my breath, move nothing but my f-stop. I snap slowly, inch my film forward; in this way I can spend twenty minutes shooting six frames. But at night, when I develop the film, I know that it's worth it. Alone in my darkroom, the images emerge in baths of chemicals and she looks beautiful, extraordinary.

I show no one and never talk about what I'm doing. Silent, invisible, I become an artist again.

Occasionally, I think she is onto me, posing, even. She will look up just as I am focusing and turn her head to the light, find an angle with more flattering shadows. In these moments, I feel my insides tremble and I wait for her to say something. And then she never does.

Rozzie

The last time she lived at home for more than a week, she was seventeen years old and she and her high school friends used to talk so much about "getting out of this town," one might have thought they were incarcerated. It was the obsession, though, and what they all had in common: this certainty that their real life and happiness lay far away. She still thought of those people sometimes, Tara, Zooey, and Leo, even though going back to school and seeing them again had been so awful that one time. They were the last people she'd had an equally balanced friendship with, the last time she'd understood how to hang out comfortably with people her own age. Since then, her friendships had changed; most lasted the length of a shoot, six weeks, or were based on proximity—her neighbors in New York, her doormen. None had much to do with having things in common because, really, what did she have in common with most people? Who else had begun adult life at seventeen?

They were all in Daniel's theater arts class, and their friendship started around the time Daniel introduced improvisation games. "You *play* at being attractive," he'd told them, staring straight at Rozzie. "You play at being a daughter, being a friend. Improvisation means taking on a role and making up a more complicated story."

Initially, they would get together for improv afternoons for an audience of no one, except, perhaps, various brothers and sisters listening in hallways. It was all soap opera, pretend fights, fake affairs. Once, she and Tara pretended to be lovers; another time, Zooey wept for hours over an imagined pregnancy. The affair with Daniel began as an improv. They all vied to be the center of the story, and she came up with the idea the day after Zooey had dominated for a whole week with her overwrought abortion bit. It unfolded in Leo's basement rec room, surrounded by wood paneling and nautical paraphernalia. She could still see the shipping wheel, the stuffed swordfish. "You guys won't believe what happened last night," she began.

The unspoken rule was that everyone stay "in the moment" and no one acknowledge a game was being played. Participants were meant to expand the story, validate it, then take it in new directions. They'd all gotten better at it over time, thinking up twists, complicating the plot. "But I love you," Leo might say while she and Tara were holding hands. But when Rozzie brought up Daniel, no one added. They all watched, dumbstruck, as if this one might just be true. Their faith fueled her. "His marriage is a sham," she said, staring at the fish, going for a flat, toneless delivery. She wondered if she was really so good or if maybe her words had some truth. She raised the stakes: "He says he doesn't love his wife, that they haven't had sex in years." She could hear his voice: *Make it matter; make it so this person's life will never be the same.*

A week later, it wasn't.

Fascinated by her deception, she tried it on the toughest audience of all. She told Daniel she'd been thinking about him. She must have known what would happen, that he'd move toward her with a swiftness that would embarrass both of them. Suddenly she was improvising with a handful of gray hair, her nose full of aftershave.

In the beginning she thought of it as a private joke, a game she was playing to pass time until they all got out of high school. She knew it distanced her from her old friends, but she didn't regret the loss. She thought this was necessary, inevitable. She'd already begun to imagine a new life. After she saw a matinee of *Sophie's Choice* with Daniel, he told her, "If you work at it, you could be that good," and she began working harder in private, away from the others: on accents, on monologues, alone in her room. To be extraordinary, she believed, she had to pull away, break her ties with ordinary people. If she worked at being part of a crowd, she would never stand apart from it.

The day after she first kissed Daniel, before she'd slept with him, Jemma asked her to pose for a photography assignment. Staring into Jemma's lens, she discovered, she could see a warped, fish-eye reflection of herself staring back. She marveled at the distortion, how she could look so unattractive when she knew—she had proof now—that she was beautiful. She wondered if Jemma might guess what had happened. Could she see the change a grown man's lips had left on her face? She waited for Jemma to say, *You seem different,* or, *What's going on?* forgetting that her sister didn't take such leaps of imagination. If Rozzie had told her, Jemma probably wouldn't have believed it: "But he's your teacher," she would say. Or: "His hair is gray," as if these two facts excluded the possibility of any others.

Back then, Jemma was so anxiously focused on the here and now—her barrettes, her socks, the eye shadow she blinked into stripes minutes after leaving the house. Jemma was sweet and well-meaning, but so different in every way from Rozzie. Jemma clamored for the shadows, the plain clothes in earth tones and styles identical to everyone else's. She longed as much to blend with others as Rozzie worked not to. Jemma would never understand how kissing a teacher could be a containable, *good* thing to do. She would see only the risk, wonder about the wife. She wouldn't see, as Rozzie did, that Daniel wasn't the sort of man who kissed his students, that by kissing her, he made her more than just a student, he made her an adult.

That was always her rationale for keeping secrets from her family. To their way of thinking, good, happy, sweet things—as Daniel had always been—would look suspicious, even worrying. She had watched her friends' faces go slack, she didn't need to watch her family's do the same.

Some days are better than others. Some days she can get up and walk, shoulders back, arms at her sides, unafraid of furniture and walls. Other days, caution creeps into her bones, and her posture reflects her fear of collision with everything unknown. By the end of these days, her neck and shoulders ache with the strain of hunching.

Her second week home, counselors begin coming from CVI, assigned to reteach her skills she's never had in the first place—sweeping, vacuuming, broiling a fish. She enjoys the minutiae of these lessons, all the tricks—the blobs of hardened glue on the stove dials, the sound of dirt hitting the dustpan. The counselors are all blind, too, which she is getting used to, even appreciating. It occurs to her she might even ask one of them about her transient sight.

She tries talking to Mary first, a woman in her forties (she guesses) who whips around the kitchen as if she's auditioning for a spot on *Martha Stewart.* "Have you ever heard of blind people who can see certain things quite clearly, but only occasionally?" she asks, trying to sound casual.

Mary stops what she's doing. "No. I don't know. I've heard of it. It's not very common. I don't like to think about it."

Think about what? she wonders. The possibility?

She drops the subject with Mary and tries again with Neil, her eccentric braille tutor, who clumps around in cowboy boots and, during the first lesson, asked if he could play country music while they worked, that it relaxed him.

He asks her what she sees.

"Odd things. Sometimes meaningless, random objects, sometimes not."

"I bet it's brain-wave projections—like hologram memories screening on the inside of your brain. You feel the object, some synapse gets triggered, you think you see it. Like projectile memory. You remember *Star Wars*—that trippy Princess Leia thing?"

Neil went blind nine years ago, thankfully before Rozzie ever appeared on-screen. None of these people ever refers to her movies.

"But sometimes it couldn't be memory—I see the right color." The day before, she had banged into a car and told Jemma, who was with her, "I bet that's some bright red Ferrari." Jemma said, "Well, it's red, anyway," which was what she'd seen, a flash of red. These can't be coincidences, but if this is her sight returning, why is there just gray the rest of the time? And why is her sister always somehow connected to whatever she is seeing? Once, when she was alone, the gray dissipated into a startlingly bright yellow sweater lying on the sofa beside her. It was so garish, Rozzie assumed it belonged to their father, who sometimes golfed in electric sherbet colors like this. She was relieved—at last, she could say these visions were arbitrary, utterly random—and then Jemma walked in the room, said, "There it is," and snatched up the sweater.

Since Neil seems interested, she goes on, "The strange part is, it almost always happens in connection with my sister."

"No kidding."

"Like it's either her stuff, or she's in the room."

He lets out a long, detonating whistle. "Spooky shit. Can you control it? Like if you really need to buy a new shirt, can you take her?"

"No."

"So what's it like?"

She thinks. "The fog rolls away, clears for a second, then it rolls back in."

"No connection to anything you're doing? Or to lighting? Could it be reflected light?"

"No."

"Weird."

She begins to think about her adolescent fascination with the occult. Maybe these are glimpses of the future or the past—another dimension of time burning a hole in the present, like watching film melt on a broken projector. Maybe she's seen a sweater Jemma would own someday. Even as she thinks this, she has to admit, it seems far-fetched. Why would she be granted powers of prophecy only to be shown flashes of clothing and mugs of tea? What sort of God works on that level?

Mostly though, she can't see much, so there is no point in dwelling too long on this. Mostly, her back aches from the strain of leaning forward, trying to see nothing; she has headaches that crawl down to her shoulders and roll through her body; sometimes her shoulder blades feel connected by a hot wire of pain. Her legs are bruised, her shins quilted in soft patches of tender skin where she has walked into coffee tables, doors, corners of chairs. Mostly, she is blind. What is a mug or a flash of Ferrari when she can't read, can't see a movie, can't find an apple at the local Stop & Shop?

Then one night, she sees something clearly: a stack of pho-tographs lying on the kitchen table. They are large, which helps her to recognize right away that they are pictures of her mother's stu-dents. First, a little blond boy wearing a bead necklace, his hands a blur, his smile huge. The next, a girl she recognizes, Regina, much older than the last time Rozzie saw her, but still balanced on her toes, her eyes rolled sideways.

One summer she worked in her mother's classroom as part of an experiment in integrating normal children periodically into the lives of these students. She was assigned to play with Regina, which, she was told, wouldn't be easy, and it wasn't. Regina wanted to play by herself, sing *Sesame Street* songs, be left alone. Rozzie was only fifteen at the time and had been so excited at the prospect of this adult assignment, getting dressed every morning, going to work with her mother, talking at night about the students they shared. But being there scared her. Some of the children bit their own hands or lay for hours under beanbag chairs. She was afraid that their eccentricities might rub off on her, that if she spent too much time in the classroom, she might begin to rock back and forth or walk on her toes. Instead of telling her mother about this, she simply announced, after a week, she wasn't going back, that she'd changed her mind and wanted to take tennis lessons instead. At the time, she thought her mother's anger was better than her mother's disapproval. But after that, she never went back, never walked into her mother's classroom again. She felt too proud, too guilty, something.

These pictures are different from the pictures of Jemma's she's seen in the past, all unposed candids shot on sets. These are carefully composed and artificially lit. The mood, conveyed in all the pictures, is surprisingly joyful, as if Jemma understands something Rozzie has not—what draws their mother to work with these children who seem so unlikely to change in any measurable way.

In the pictures it's clear they *have* changed. Puberty has come, brought Regina breasts, made her beautiful in a strange, otherworldly way. She could almost be a model, or an actress. Looking at the pictures makes Rozzie sad, as if there are things she will never understand that her sister and mother intuitively do. She can still see herself, years after that summer, waiting on a bench outside her mother's classroom, pretending to read what was even then hard to see, while Jemma went inside. Once she even looked in the window, saw Jemma in a corner, talking to their mother, delivering the message—they were going to the pool—though really she couldn't be sure what was being said. Even then she couldn't see lips moving.

She tries to engage her sister more, get her to reminisce the way they did in the hospital, but Jemma is edgy, as if she's working on an imaginary time clock. Ten minutes of breakfast chat and she will slide her chair back, drop a spoon into her bowl. "I should get working," she will say, and disappear minutes later, down the prohibitively dark, rickety staircase to the basement.

Rozzie wonders if this is how she herself used to be. Always anxious to move on, slip away. Even while Jemma takes care of Rozzie, makes her lunch, reads her mail, she hardly stays in a chair long enough to warm it. Sometimes Rozzie throws out conversational lures: "Tell me what you're working on," she'll say, and Jemma will sound vague, dismissive. "Nothing good." Or: "Just some experiment."

"Tell me," Rozzie says, and she can feel her sister hovering in the door, desperate to leave. "What's happening with the nurse series?"

"They didn't come out. It was stupid, my light meter wasn't working and I wasted a lot of film."

Is this what failure in her world feels like? A private disappointment? Wasted film? Her voice sounds so skittish, yet it seems, to Rozzie, relatively minor, not like the public flogging her own failures represent.

One afternoon, Neil leaves her with her first homework assignment, a McDonald's menu printed in braille. "Now, for me this was helpful. Maybe you eat at other places."

Rozzie hasn't been to a McDonald's since childhood; once, she shot a scene there and the props person had removed all the burgers from the buns she had to eat through eleven takes. Eventually she felt sick and they brought her a bag to spit her chewed bread and pickle into when the cameras weren't rolling.

"No, this is great," she tells Neil. "Thanks so much."

After he leaves, she keeps working on it. She wants to read ahead, shock him the next time with what she knows. She stays so concentrated, so focused on her fingertips, that when she hears a clicking sound behind her, for a minute she isn't sure what it is. Then she remembers, of course: a camera.

"Jemma?" she says.

"Yeah?"

"What are you doing?"

"Nothing."

Has Jemma just taken her picture? The idea disturbs her.

"What do you mean, nothing?"

"Nothing."

A minute later, when Rozzie calls out, Jemma isn't there.

Jemma

Working late into the night, I wonder where this will go or end. I am outside myself all the time, hardly sleeping, eating food I barely taste and don't recognize until I look down and see what's in my hand. And then I'll find cashews or a rice cake. Things I ordinarily wouldn't eat.

I sleep so little, by the afternoon I feel as if I am moving underwater. Sometimes I'm so tired my body tingles, as if I'm leaving my skin behind, traveling outside any need for it. At night I sleep in snatches filled with fitful dreams where I am in other places, back at school or in New York. The dreams play like movies, with stories I don't know the outcome of. And always I wake up before it's over. I think about Rozzie as a teenager, when she claimed she could feel herself growing, could lie in bed at night alive to the movement of her bones and muscles. At some point early on, she willed herself beautiful. Now I have seen the pitfalls on that path, and I will myself into a different transformation.

The darkroom is the only place I relax. I let down my guard, lose myself in chemicals. My prints need my hands moving over them, my wrinkled fingerpads. In the red bath of light, an irony emerges. These aren't self-portraits, but some of them have been shot at such angles, and such a distance, they might be. I have never thought of us as looking so alike—our eyes are different, our hair color—but I seem to be shooting as if we do look alike, as if I am trying to find myself.

From behind, in shadow or profile, portions of our bodies are surprisingly identical. We have the same elbows, it seems, the same ears, the same curve in our hips.

I touch these parts, study them carefully.

I wonder how I have never seen this before.

Rozzie

One night at dinner, the telephone rings.

Jemma answers it, talks for a few minutes, then comes back. She doesn't sit down. "That was just a gallery in New York," she says. "Offering me a place in their student show. They said they're sorry they held on to them for so long, but now they've decided to include me in their summer show."

For a long time, no one says anything. This seems so out of the blue. "I submitted slides a long time ago," Jemma explains. "The pictures of Mom's kids."

Now they get it. Their mother screams and scrapes back her chair. "Well done!" their father chimes.

Rozzie can't bring herself to say anything. She knows what this means. One afternoon, Matthew dragged her around SoHo pointing out the galleries he'd like to show in one day. This is a big deal. A very big deal, but suddenly her throat feels like it's filling with cotton, like she's strangling on air. She is seized by the fear that Jemma will return to New York before she does. That Jemma will take her apartment, her place, and she will be left behind forever in her childhood bedroom. She wonders if this transitory sight has something to do with Jemma taking over her life.

Of course, this is crazy. Later, lying in bed, she wonders if she is losing her mind on top of everything else.

*　　*　　*

It turns out that in a week, Jemma *will* go to New York and will—because there's no other option—stay in Rozzie's apartment. Though the gallery owner likes the photographs of the autistic kids, she wants to see Jemma's new stuff, what she's working on now. In a single day, Jemma's intensity level escalates even further and she stops eating meals with the family. She emerges from her darkroom every four hours or so, grabs an orange, some pretzels, and goes back down.

Though they barely talk, Rozzie knows what Jemma is thinking right now: *This is it. The rest of my life rides on this.* She wants to warn her—tell her not to expect too much or listen to everything she is told. There are dangers in success that can't be anticipated. But she can't.

Though Jemma is still here, she is already gone. She floats through rooms, whispering enlarger openings and exposure times under her breath. She prints and prints and prints. Rozzie can trace her sister's movement through the house by following her smell, touching towels and surfaces still damp with the chemicals where Jemma has just been.

Once Rozzie asks what Jemma is printing. She is vague: "Just some experiments."

There are other mysteries. The answering machine plays messages that don't make sense. One man says he is a photo editor and there are some problems—but if Jemma hasn't been to New York yet, hasn't brought them her photos, what are the problems? Rozzie doesn't ask. Another message comes in: "Much better, sweetheart. These are perfect."

As Jemma grows more distant, Rozzie grows less so. She sits at dinner with her parents, participates in conversation, becomes the sort of daughter she's never been before. After dinner, she stands at the sink, washing pans, with her mother beside her, drying and putting away. They talk about the calls Jemma is getting. Her mother doesn't understand either. "She's even thinking about not going back to school. She says everyone there is small-minded and provincial." Her mother sighs.

This doesn't sound like Jemma.

Rozzie begins doing more for herself. For lunch, she finds a can of tuna fish, opens it, eats it, without help from, or discussion with, anyone. Hours after the fact, Jemma calls up from the basement, "Sorry, Roz. Do you need lunch?"

She calls down. "Fine, thanks. Got it."

With no one watching her, she experiments more. She goes outside with her cane, takes a walk down the block. Alone outside, the world becomes an ocean of moving light; cars look like ghosts, flying by on Persian carpets. Trees look like giant, shadowy Ferris wheels. Once, she is gone for twenty minutes, though no one seems to notice.

She makes this discovery: away from Jemma, she sees less but does much more. Outside, her skin is alive to sensation again: she feels the wind, the sun between patches of shade. She finds the sidewalk with her cane and walks down it. Away from Jemma, she moves again; she doesn't hold still, waiting for a vision.

Rozzie's other senses didn't sharpen as her vision dimmed. She'd always had good hearing, could always tell which family member was coming down the hall by the sound of their footsteps. What has escalated in blindness is the power of her memory. On good days at home, she can walk through the whole house, caneless, and bump into nothing. She can put a glass down and know, without feeling, where the table begins. This power is not in her mind, she feels, but in her body, buried in her bones.

Her memory grows stronger the longer she is home. She can't see anyone's face or print on paper, but she can see scenes from her childhood perfectly. She can remember climbing a tree, trying to reach a bird's nest she'd seen. She can remember *exactly* what it looked like, the tiny egg within. She remembers the feeling: her certainty that the mother bird was dead and this unborn bird needed saving, this creature within the beautiful blue eggshell.

She remembers ice-skating with Jemma, sliding over the frozen pond near their house, the color of the water below. She hasn't lost the memory of colors. Once she taught herself names for them: cerulean blue, bilious green, chartreuse. Now they are all hues of gray, but in her head she can still see them, can conjure up that perfect blue eggshell.

Once she is visited by an odd memory, something she hasn't thought about in years: the time she lost her glasses over a ravine—one minute they were on her face, the next instant they were fluttering down away from her. Because her parents were there, she'd made a scene, somewhat calculated on her part. A few weeks earlier her mother had said with the price of glasses these days, they could only afford to buy new ones every other year. The point of the scene was to show her mother that living like paupers when they weren't *that* poor could emotionally scar them. She wanted her mother to feel guilty that her daughter might believe lost glasses wouldn't be replaced for two years and she'd have to go sightless in the meantime.

It actually worked—eventually she even got contacts out of the incident—but her real memory of the episode was the way Jemma sat in the car motionless for the duration of her fit. At first she loved that she was obviously scaring her sister; then later she thought: What if something had *really* been wrong? Would her sister have done the same thing–watched her through tinted Oldsmobile windows as she fell apart publicly in a dirt parking lot?

Maybe she put up walls because Jemma so obviously liked standing behind them.

The night before Jemma leaves, their mother asks her to please come to dinner. "Fine," Jemma says, scraping back her chair.

Rozzie is already there, seated, touching her food with her fork, a trick she's learned from one of her counselors.

"Now," says her mother with strained cheer, "tell us more about this show."

"It's not that big a deal," Jemma says, all evidence to the contrary. "It's only going to be up a week. It's a rotating group show of student work, so it's not like anyone's paying that much attention to me."

If this is true, why is she talking about dropping out of school?

"We still want to come," their mother says.

"You don't have to." A silence hovers for a second. "Seriously. I don't think you should."

It's obvious she doesn't want them to.

Later, when Jemma is alone in her room, Rozzie knocks on the door. "Why don't you want us to come?" She's been thinking about this all night, trying to understand it.

For a long time, Jemma says nothing. Finally, in a small voice, she says, "It's you."

"What do you mean?"

"If you come, it'll be a big deal. Everyone will pay attention to you and take your picture. I just don't want that."

For a second, Rozzie thinks she can see her sister, sitting in the chair by the window crying. "Okay," she says, standing up. "But what about Mom and Dad?"

"Then I'd feel bad about you, left here all alone."

She says the only thing she can think of, what she knows is true: "If we don't go, it won't seem real."

Rozzie

More and more, she finds herself telling the truth. It's refreshing and surprisingly easy. No one seems particularly shocked by any of her revelations. At first, she tries it as an experiment. She tells her mother about dating Leonard. Instead of worrying, her mother simply asks, "What was *his* appeal?"

"I'm not sure," she says. "I thought he was a challenge. He didn't seem to like me very much."

The more she talks to her mother, the more she wants to admit things. She remembers Jemma always playing this role. Now Jemma is the mystery, the cipher figure, and Rozzie has her mother's ear. She tells her many things, large and small: which directors she liked, which she didn't. She tells her Miriam gets on her nerves. She tells her she's had five treatments of electrolysis.

"What was that like?" her mother asks.

Rozzie thinks. "Painful," she finally says.

Talking about all this gives shape to her memories, puts them in order. Finally she begins to see what was important, what wasn't.

One night, in a whisper, she tells her mother she's had a little plastic surgery. Her heart is beating. She expects a big reaction, either laughter or tears. She's not sure which way her mother will go.

Again she's surprised. "You're *kidding*," her mother says. "Where?"

The relief is so enormous, she's the one who laughs. Suddenly, it's a mistake she made, a small matter. She feels as if she's moving back into her body, occupying it again, for the first time in years.

Jemma's second night away, Rozzie goes for her first long walk alone. She wants to practice using her senses, her hearing, her skin. She wants to take herself out into the world that, for a while, became so threatening to her.

She feels herself changing, opening up, laughing more. One night, she asks her father a question about his work and she listens—really listens—to the answer. He tells a long story about a person she vaguely recognizes, a fellow teacher, someone she has probably met but doesn't remember. For so long she had no energy for listening.

Now she does, and she's surprised. It's funny. She laughs.

She begins doing odd, unattractive things. In front of Neil, her blind tutor, she burps. They don't know each other well enough to laugh. She doesn't want to say "Excuse me," which would sound like her mother. She lets it hang in the air between them. She's almost sure it smells, too.

Even her mouth feels different, as if her taste buds are changing. For years she has lived on salads and fish. Her luxury is fruit, huge pink grapefruits she used to eat one after another, sometimes eight in a single sitting. A few years go, a dentist delivered the dire warning that her enamel was disintegrating from all the acids in the fruit. She tried to stop, but couldn't. Instead she carried a toothbrush everywhere.

Now she carves up and eats food she can't even picture. Green lasagna, spaghetti carbonara. She bites into sandwiches, breads; she tries a ginger cake her mother has made. For years, she's told people that she hates sweets. Now they're in her mouth again. It's like a buried memory, an awakening. Sometimes her body feels so awake, she wonders if there is something different running through her veins now—electricity, or green tea. She laughs at the odd places her mind is going. She decides, in all this excitement, she wants to kiss someone, feel that old supercharge again. In the old days—what she now thinks of as the numb days—sex was one of the few things she could feel. She liked doing it in uncomfortable places, on hard tables and wooden floors, where every joint registered and afterward she carried bruises for days.

Now she thinks if someone so much as brushed her collarbone, she might cry out.

The only obvious candidate is Neil, her braille tutor and the only man remotely her age she comes in contact with.

They have a joking repartee by now, a banter about his bad taste in music. She asks him one evening if he has a girlfriend.

For a long time, he says nothing.

"Well," he finally says, "not exactly." He offers no more. After a while, he coughs, shuffles some papers, and changes the subject. It's not nervousness, it's something else. She can't pinpoint it exactly, then it occurs to her: He's not interested! He's brushing her off!

She's had men not interested in a relationship before, but she's never had one who didn't want to flirt. Later she goes over it in her mind. *He doesn't know who I am,* she marvels, when she really seems to mean: *He doesn't know what I look like.*

Jemma calls from New York, her voice tight and strained. "It's going okay. I think. It's hard to tell. They like some of the new stuff, but not all of it."

Rozzie asks how New York is. Now that Jemma is there, she's been thinking about it all the time, picturing Central Park, riding on the subway. She can't wait to get back there, take her place again, negotiate her old routes around the neighborhood.

"It's fine," Jemma says. "I haven't really talked to that many people."

Though Jemma doesn't say she's lonely, Rozzie can hear it in her voice, can recognize the throat-clearing cough of talking for the first time all day, late at night on the phone. It's funny, she thinks, to feel so nostalgic for a place she spent most of the time so lonely in. Some days, she never left her apartment, never spoke to anyone at all. It's funny and not, of course.

In that stillness—that eternal, darkening quiet—she found her strength and the courage to go blind without telling anyone. Only now does she marvel at this private feat. She wants to go back there, be the person who did that, again. Only this time she'll enjoy herself, eat real food, smell things.

She begins to ready for her return. She practices separating subway tokens from her coin purse. She makes braille lists; has Neil help convert her old telephone Filofax into a braille Rolodex of numbers. Her mother reads names of actors and directors. Rozzie waits for Neil to register this, to understand, she *knows* these people. It's never occurred to her before how odd this is. That her phone book, read aloud, sounds like an episode of *Entertainment Tonight*. She wants to laugh, to poke Neil and say, *See who I know? Now do you have a girlfriend?*

He doesn't seem to register the names as belonging to famous people. He even asks how to spell a few.

*   *   *

She lets Neil go, but begins to imagine other men, faces from her past. She will miss what was for her the best part of seduction—losing herself in the steady gaze of a lover's eye. Now she will have to learn other tricks, use her voice, listen closely for clues in theirs.

With each day that passes, she grows more daring, takes longer and longer walks alone. Out of the disorienting chaos of shadows and movement, the world organizes itself. She can now stand at a street corner and know which direction a car is traveling, can hear footsteps, can tell when a dog on a leash is coming toward her.

Every accident averted is a triumph in her heart. Sometimes moving like this, down the street, feels like flying.

One night, on one of her walks she hears footsteps. She steps aside onto a soft patch of grass, but just as she does, the footsteps stop.

"You're Jemma's sister, aren't you?" a male voice says.

She nods. She's been half expecting this to happen for a while. It's not a big town, surely sooner or later she was bound to run into someone from the past. "Who are you?"

"We worked in the grocery store together. My name's Theo."

She remembers Jemma doing this job, but doesn't remember hearing this name. No matter. Here is a person, someone other than a counselor or her parents to talk to. "Are you walking my way?" she asks, stepping back onto the sidewalk.

They walk for a while together, longer and farther than she ever has before. He does most of the talking, about a business he's trying to get a loan from the bank for. "See, the problem is, I don't even have a car anymore. My car broke down, that's why I'm walking. I don't own a house. I have a nice stereo, but the bank isn't really interested in that as collateral."

Rozzie practices listening to him and the world at the same time.

It takes concentration, like learning a foreign language, translating all the time. When he asks her a question, she answers quickly. She can't talk and listen at the same time.

In front of the bank, he touches her shoulder. "This is where I peel away. But it's nice to finally meet you. I've heard a lot about you."

She wants to say she's heard about him, but she can't, so she smiles. She lifts her eyes to where his might be, and as she does, something happens. For the first time in a week, she sees—a button-down shirt, then more—a neck, curly, blond hair. She can see it all, her first face in months. And he is handsome.

That night, she calls information and gets his number. She knows how to ask men out, has done it many times before. She's not nervous. She could talk to Jemma about it—she *would*—but Jemma's left a message saying something's come up and she's staying an extra week, straight through the show. When Rozzie tried to call her own apartment back, there was no answer.

So be it, Rozzie thinks, dialing Theo's number.

She invites him over for lunch. She wants to be on familiar turf, doesn't want to be groping for a chair or knocking table corners as would inevitably happen in any restaurant. She also wants to be alone, which she only is during the day.

His response is hard to measure. He seems confused. "Is Jemma around?"

"No. She's still in New York." *Does this matter?* "Why?"

"It'd be nice to see her."

Apparently he doesn't get it quite yet, but that's okay. He will.

She is driven by this new desire inside her. She needs to feel her body again beneath another's fingers, find her edges, where she begins, where she ends. She thinks about the glimpse of his face, the smiling eyes. She wants to talk to Jemma to find out if she's right about his eyes, but Jemma's never home. For two days, there is no answer at the apartment.

It is easy for Rozzie to imagine kissing again, far harder to picture making lunch. She has never been a cook, has never been comfortable enough with food to put some on a plate and expect another person to eat it. Again her memory fails her: Has she *ever* cooked a meal for someone? Surely she has, at some point, but she can't recall anything specific, or what she might have made. Was there a chicken dish she once made for Matthew? Or did she just buy the ingredients and throw them away?

All things considered, she decides not to aim very high. Soup and bread and her new favorite dessert, stale gingersnap cookies. She puts them in her mouth and lets them melt slowly.

She asks Mary, her counselor, to take her grocery shopping. They have done this once before, and for Rozzie, it's an agony of memorization and can feeling. "Tomato paste has ridges," Mary singsongs. "Sauce doesn't."

Rozzie listens halfheartedly, knowing she doesn't need to memorize these tips, that she will phone in her orders and have them delivered when she's back in New York. But for now, she can't. She wheels the cart while Mary clears a path in front of them with her cane. It takes an hour to make it up and down the aisles, and she's exhausted by the time they get to fruits and vegetables. Mary's energy, on the other hand, is boundless. "Bad apples have a smell," she says. "Good ones don't."

Rozzie holds apple after apple up to her nose and smells no difference. After a while, she holds out her hand. "Give me something really bad."

Instead of Mary, she hears another woman's voice: "It broke our hearts to read about you, sweetheart."

She turns away, back to the apples. "I'm sorry. I thought you were someone else."

She feels a hand touch hers. "We're so sorry, sweetheart. How you doing now?"

She doesn't want to have this conversation. She wants Mary to come back and busy her with tips so this woman will understand she's not alone, she doesn't need sympathy. But Mary doesn't return. "I'm okay," she says, smiling. "Look. Here I am, shopping."

"That's right. Good for you. I saw those pictures, I said that girl's gonna be all right, you watch."

"I am. I'm all right."

"That's the spirit, sweetheart. God bless you." Thankfully, the woman pushes a noisy cart away, leaving Rozzie alone with two apples in her hands.

"Mary?" she says, and waits. Is Mary testing her? she wonders. Is she going to make her walk around asking people if they've seen another blind woman? What if she's meant to continue shopping by herself? She feels the beginning of the same panic attacks she used to get on the streets of New York, when she walked into something she should have seen: a pole, a newspaper stand, another person. Then there was always the pain and embarrassment to contend with. Now there is only the empty space where Mary has just been. For the first time in ages, she feels the sting of tears in her eyes. She can't even remember where the cart is or where the apples in her hand came from.

"*Mary?*" she tries again.

Magically, Mary materializes. "Sorry about that," she huffs. "I had to go ten bins down to find a good apple. Nice store you have here. Okay, smell."

Rozzie feels like weeping as she holds the apple under her nose. She is so overwhelmed by the whole episode, it isn't until they are waiting in line that she thinks, *What pictures?*

Waiting in line is a tricky business and Mary has given her the active role; she must stand in front of the cart and judge by shadows and voices when the line moves. For Rozzie, looking down is easiest, away from the lights, which sometimes flicker and confuse her. This time, she's off. She moves forward and hits someone's back.

"I'm sorry."

The person says nothing. She wonders if she should add, "I'm blind," or if that's obvious. She's wearing sunglasses but not holding a cane. After an awkward silence, someone—the cashier, Rozzie is almost sure because the space ahead of her feels empty now—says, "Wow, that's so weird."

"What?" Rozzie says.

"You're here and you're there. On that newspaper. And you're wearing the same shirt. It's just weird."

Though her heart races, Rozzie knows how to carry such an awkward moment off. She flattens her expression into a smile, busies her hands with groceries on the belt. "I guess I'd better get some new shirts," she says, a little too late for it to feel like the easy joke she means it to be. Her mind is busy making calculations. This shirt is new, something she's been wearing in the last two weeks, which means that a photographer has been in this town, following her on walks. That just as she was beginning to feel whole again, and safe, there is this to remind her, she is neither.

She puts the episode out of her mind. What's important right now is not perfect privacy, but her own control over her choices. She will continue to take walks, to make this lunch for Theo, to move forward into the future that will soon be of no interest to newspaper photographers or the general public.

By the time Theo arrives, the table is set, soup is made. She has cooked her first meal using the stove, reading dials with her fingers. She has even made a loaf of bread with her mother's bread machine, which, admittedly, does all the work. Still, the house is filled with delicious smells. She has put aside her grocery-store panic. She bustles around the kitchen with a sense of her own competence, accomplishing things she never did sighted. When the doorbell rings, she takes a deep breath. She is fine, she thinks, better than her old self and in the happiest of positions, a woman with a man on the other side of the door. She savors this moment of expectation, even waits until he rings again.

"Hello," she says, opening the door. "Come on in."

An hour into lunch, she feels thrown off. He knows the house, knows Jemma better than she ever realized. She's almost certain she's never heard Jemma mention his name, but his stories about her go back for years and seem to imply they're terrific friends.

"I remember that time you got your first movie," he says. "She was so excited because you needed her pictures. She kept talking about how her pictures were going to Hollywood."

That didn't sound like Jemma to her, but she remembers so little from that time. She dimly remembers Jemma sending pictures.

"I think you really inspired her. She wants to have your success, I can tell."

"Really?"

"Sure. I mean she wants to be independent and recognized and make money. I guess we all do, right? No secret there."

The more he talks, the more obvious it is that they won't be kissing anytime soon. There is no flirtation between them, no trotting out of carefully chosen intimate revelations. There is only this end-less talk of Jemma.

"You know, I wouldn't mind checking out her darkroom," he says at some point. "See what she's working on. I haven't seen her stuff in a long time."

"Okay," Rozzie says in a small voice.

What is this bleakness rising up inside her? She's never felt it before. *Good God, Jemma isn't even here and she's getting all this man's attention.*

After lunch they make their way down to the darkroom. Why not? she thinks, having given up completely on her seduction. She doesn't want to think too much about this, doesn't want to consider the possibility that with her eyesight, she has lost her sex appeal, too. She will find someone, she tells herself. In New York, when she's back at home, feeling like herself.

For now, she just has to get through this meal. She wishes she'd never asked him. Now, she'll have to tell Jemma he was here and she doesn't know how she'll put it. Whatever she says, it will sound strange and meddlesome.

When Theo finds the light string and pulls it, she squints, peers around, tries to find the autistic children she can picture in her head. She sees nothing. Instead of saying anything, Theo whistles.

"What?" Rozzie says, growing nervous in his silence. "Is it my mother's students?"

"No." Theo's voice moves around the room. He takes a long time. Apparently there are many pictures to look at.

And then, before he says anything, she knows what the pictures are of. Though she sees nothing, she knows.

Jemma

Every night I lose myself in a silent examination of her things. I never turn on the television, don't even allow myself the radio for distraction. I worry if I do, I will be heard and found out. I forget that I am allowed to be here. I have a key and permission, and even so, my heart beats as I walk past a doorman who nods.

This privacy is too much. I escape into her things, surround myself in the letters people have sent her and a few she must have written but never sent before her eyes failed her. I learn from one that Matthew behaved badly. On one of his visits, he arranged a get-together with old prep school friends and then asked her to wear something nicer before they went out. This sounds so unlike him I wonder if her presence unwittingly alters people, makes them see only surfaces. I don't know why she never told me this part—never gave us a chance to hate him together.

Sleeping so little, eating in handfuls here and there, I have lost enough weight that I slip into her clothes, amazed by what I can button and zip. It used to be I could only borrow shoes and sweaters; now everything fits. At first, I only wear them in the apartment, then I venture out, first to the hallway, then finally down to the street.

One day, I wear heels so I am exactly as tall as she is without shoes.

This is how it is to be her, I think, standing on the subway platform, swaying slightly. When the train rolls in, I close my eyes.

This is how it feels to be watched, I decide. To sense eyes on your back, turn around, and be right—find a man who lifts his eyebrows as if you know each other. I have witnessed these moments in the past and felt diminished by them, erased by the way the world's eyes train on her. Now I am inside such a moment and I see what it does, how it leaves me with no place to put my own eyes. I try the floor, the subway ads, and finally settle onto the blackened window, where I stare hard into the outline of my reflection.

Though I never pick it up, the newspaper with my pictures of Rozzie is out, sitting on kiosks and supermarket stands. I walk past them four or five times a day and haven't once looked closely enough to see which pictures they ended up using. I suppose I'm thinking if I don't look, maybe no one else will either. I keep waiting for fallout, for confrontation from one of my parents or even from her, but none comes. To sustain this good luck, I play games with myself. I hold my breath when I walk past a newspaper stand. I close my eyes when the phone rings. For three full days, I speak to no one, including strangers. I begin to think maybe nothing will come of this, maybe she will never find out and we will have nothing but extra money to show for it.

The morning of the opening, I decide ahead of time I will wear her clothes, but this will be the last of it. For one night I will dress like her, and then I will leave all this behind, quit cold turkey. I go through her closet and through the fine fabrics cut in styles I have only ever seen in magazines. No one I know wears clothes like this, and then it occurs to me—neither does she. Even as I try on item after item, I understand nothing can be learned from these things. They are costumes from movies, clothes only her characters have worn.

Piled on the floor, they begin to look ominous, like the skins of so many exotic snakes. I wonder if she has felt this, too, disoriented by her own outfits.

I begin to wonder if she is in the room with me, haunting these clothes, invisible but omniscient. I wonder if she knows all that I am trying to get away with.

I have invited none of my friends to the opening because I thought it would point out, too overtly, my family's absence. I have imagined their faces, their eyebrows knitted together for an instant, saying wordlessly, *Where is she?* And of course I'd have to say: *Look around on the walls, open your eyes, she's everywhere.* I'd want it to be a joke, but it wouldn't be funny. They'd worry that I'd lost my mind, which I have.

My insides tremble as I slip into clothes that make me unrecognizable to myself. I stare for so long into the mirror I imagine for a second breaking it with my hand, watching the blood drip onto this dress.

And then I get another idea. It occurs to me that there is a different path out of this, something that will seem crazy, but will be less so. I have disappeared from my own life, but if I act quickly, perhaps it's not too late.

Rozzie

Daniel already knows what's going on. He's seen the pictures, has read the photo credit. "It's hard to imagine what she was thinking." His tone is neutral, as if he's really been trying to guess.

"She wanted to sell pictures," Rozzie says.

"But that can't be the whole story. She's your *sister.* Maybe she didn't know they'd get used in this way."

"What? She thought the *Star* would be nice?"

"They aren't bad pictures. You look good."

"Oh, please." She sounds composed as she says this. After Theo's departure, she stormed around the house, weepy and enraged. Now a few hours have passed. There's certainly anger and a feeling of betrayal, but there's also this: a surprising sense of relief. She is no longer the only one who has hurt other people, no longer the person whose success has come at the expense of others around her. For the first time in years, she doesn't feel guilty.

She's managed to be here an hour already without mentioning that they haven't spoken since the hospital. This is the way it is with Daniel. One crisis can be isolated from every other, each drama can be attended to without alluding to a dozen obvious other ones. Like the fact that his house has almost no furniture, that his wife seems to have left him with a canvas director's chair and a few plastic glasses and nothing else. She can't see this, of course, but she's moved around the living room the whole time she's been here and has bumped into nothing.

"I never told you about this, but she came to see me once. When you were staying in her room at school."

She touches a shelf where she's sure the stereo used to be. "Why?"

"She said she was worried about you. That you were behaving strangely."

"She wasn't worried. She was mad at me. I was sleeping with a guy she liked."

"Oh. Well." He seems to puzzle over this for a while, as if trying to put it into some larger perspective. Surely it doesn't surprise him that she's slept with other men? Finally he says, "Why?"

"Why what?"

"Why did you sleep with someone your sister liked?"

"I'll admit it wasn't nice, but I was going *blind*. I wanted to feel connected to someone."

"So why not connect to her?"

"I went out there intending to tell her about my eyes, and then they got worse. It was so bad I panicked and didn't say anything."

"So instead you slept with her boyfriend?"

"He wasn't her boyfriend. He was just a friend." She hesitates. "But I knew she liked him." She couldn't explain all of it—that she had spent all her adult years being nice to strangers and Jemma was different. "Don't you think what she did is a little bit worse than what I did?"

"Maybe. But maybe not. Maybe she had her own reasons. You'll have to ask her. Get her to explain it to you."

Coming over here after Theo had left her house—making her way on bus and foot—she said to herself, *I'll never speak to Jemma again*. It was an oddly freeing sensation, as if at last she could extract herself from every difficult obligation she had to her past. "I don't want to talk to her."

"You have to, my dear. You have to give her that much."

"I don't see why."

"Well, for one thing, she's in your apartment, right?"

Daniel is right, of course. He knows her well enough to know what she's thinking—that she will use this betrayal as an excuse to run away, return to New York a month earlier than planned. In her furious confusion, she forgot that Jemma is already there. Now, the realization is so horrible and frustrating, she breaks down in tears. She wants, more than anything, to be by herself. But even this much, it seems, is impossible.

Daniel takes her in his arms, lets her cry. She has cried so little in the last two years that the sound of it takes her by surprise. Her chest heaves, her lungs close up, she feels as if she can't catch her breath. She is lost, overacting in a way she can't control. Her hands start to shake and then her body. She slips out of his arms and drops down to the ground. There are no chairs. There's nothing to catch her.

Jemma

Wearing a black cocktail dress and high heels at two o'clock in the afternoon, I walk into a hardware store and buy a screwdriver. I pull money out of a purse that matches the dress but is no bigger than an envelope. Outside, I discover the screwdriver won't fit inside the purse. On the subway, I am stared at either because I look good in this dress or because I am wearing such a dress, carrying a purse in one hand and a screwdriver in the other—it's hard for me to tell.

I arrive at the gallery four hours early to find the receptionist alone, holding a phone to her ear on what is obviously a personal call. She nods to me with one hand over the mouthpiece. I shake my head to tell her, *No, I'm fine. Go back to your call.*

Only four pictures in this show are mine, but they are placed on a well-lit wall in the center of the room and they are all of Rozzie. I brought others here, but these are the ones the gallery owners fell in love with, the ones that showed my talent in the best light, they argued. They have also brought this show a measure of extra attention, made it a curio of note in the "What to Do This Weekend" section in the *Times*. "Student photographer and sister of actress Rozzie Phillips . . . ," they read. When I saw the items, I wasn't surprised or even upset. I thought: *Oh, fine. Sure.*

Now I understand that they are incendiary. If I don't remove these pictures, this will explode the same way the house beside ours ignited one night while everyone slept. She is not even here and she is everywhere, pressing down on me, taking the air, filling the room with what feels like smoke. I pull out the screwdriver and go to work.

Rozzie

Her family has always seen Daniel as a threat, but they don't understand that she has nothing to fear from him. She hasn't slept with him in years, since high school, with one disastrous exception that Rozzie doesn't care to even think about—a Christmas vacation when she drove in a snowstorm over to his house only to discover his wife was out of town, obliging them to take advantage of the fact. But it was passionless, sad sex—they both knew it. When his wife finally left him and he came to see her in New York, she only had to remind him of this last encounter to convince him they were not star-crossed lovers kept apart by fate.

True, when he showed up on the set, he seemed different to her, edgier and more volatile, more determined to make her account for herself. Finally she came right out and told him to please stop asking her about their relationship, because she was going blind and she didn't want to think about anything else at that point. He was the first person she told.

In retrospect, maybe she had to do it that way—tell a neutral party first, then tell her family, then the world. Unveiling what had become her most private secret was enormously freeing, and for a little while, she felt as if maybe she *did* love him—but it was the same sexless, familial love it had always been. They slept chastely, both pajamaed, in the same bed. He held her in his arms and let her talk for hours about how it had been, losing her sight all alone, going to doctor after doctor. "You poor girl," he kept saying, stroking her hair, until she began to believe she *had* been brave, an example of fortitude.

For months she'd been expecting the retina to detach and for the world to go black as the doctors had described. When it finally happened, she felt proud of herself for preparing an undramatic exit. Her great fear was that it would come with such pain she'd be racked and helpless, screaming while a crowd gawked and ambulance lights pulsed onto the scene. Instead, it was simple, like blinds snapping closed instead of open. One minute in the makeup trailer she could see, and the next she couldn't—so quick and so surprising she actually said, "What happened?" thinking maybe the lights had gone out.

When Marcie said, "What do you mean, honey?" she knew nothing had, except to her. She got herself out of the trailer, and Daniel happened to be right outside. When she heard his voice, she could reach toward it and, with her hand alone, tell him, *It's happening. Right now.*

In the car she told him this was bad enough that she should probably go to Minneapolis, meaning, *Take me to the nearest hospital and I'll probably end up there,* but instead he drove her seven hours there, saying nothing to anybody and creating this whole mystery, which she had never intended at all. While they were driving, the pain began to spread from her eyes backward and felt like burning lava rolling toward the far side of her skull, eating up brain in its path, memory, thoughts, clarity. By the time they got to the hospital, she'd lost all track of time. She was scheduled for emergency surgery and lay for what felt like hours on a hospital gurney, covered by yards of sheet, surrounded by voices she kept thinking were directed at her. Having no idea where anyone was or if they were, in fact, talking to her, she tried to arrange her face in an organized way to look responsive, thoughtful, not pathetic. Daniel's voice came and went unpredictably. She assumed he was off making phone calls, telling everyone, though she didn't ask. She didn't understand until later how seriously he'd taken his role as confidant—that he'd admitted her under a false name. It was all so absurd and presumed she was at a far greater distance from her family than she was. She got angry at him, lashed out and screamed, just before going into surgery. When she got out, he was gone.

That was when she called Jemma, the only person she could think of.

Crying has helped. Away from her family, Rozzie can breathe easier, relax more, be herself: cry for a while, then stop crying, blow her nose, and carry on as if it hasn't happened, or is nothing, really, in the grand scheme of things. With her family, crying like that would have stayed with them for days. There would have been silence when she walked in the room, plaintive questions whenever she was alone with her mother: *How's everything? Are you okay?* Sharing one's heart with the people who care most means they keep caring *more,* going deeper. She doesn't want that.

Coming here makes it clear: she wants to be left alone. Daniel has his own problems, his own worries. He is happy to talk about hers for a while, but eventually they always came back to him, which is fine with her.

Over dinner, Daniel talks about issues at school, getting his old job back. "It all boils down to they couldn't find anyone else. If they had, I'd be out of a job. As it is—they're not thrilled, but they don't have a whole lot of choice." The students are pleased, he says—as if students are a collective entity with a single mind. "They're happy I'm back, I'm happy to be back. The administration wants me to be contrite and say nothing when they ask me to do *Our Town* for the fourth time in ten years."

He goes on, talks about the shows he'd like to do. After a while she stops listening; she thinks about her apartment, pictures herself sitting on her sofa, alone.

After dinner, while he cleans up in the kitchen, she wanders through the house. She wants to see if his books are all here, which they are. The history of her long relationship with Daniel, fraught as it is with obligation and guilt, with passion and fondness, has always been, at its core, a teacher-student one. The first time she ever came over to this house—a cast party for *The Children's Hour*—she wandered alone through the rooms, astounded by the number of books he owned. She remembers pulling titles off the shelves, standing in that hall and wishing she were older, that she'd already been to college, had already read all these books. She wanted to know all the things he did: every main character in every Shakespeare play, every principal speech. Her last ten years have been spent, in large part, trying to read the bookshelves in this house. She carried Penguin classics from one set to another, pushed her way through Thackeray, Flaubert, *Brothers Kara-mazov*. "Everyone should read *War and Peace* once every five years," Daniel wrote on a postcard one summer, and she ran out in search of the edition with the largest print available. Eventually she had had to give up fiction. As her eyes worsened, she stuck to plays and poetry, grateful for the islands of white space on every page, places to rest her eyes. At the same time, she loved what she was reading—loved Yeats, Eliot, Ibsen. The harder reading became, the more precious each word, the more tenaciously she stuck with it. Sometimes she'd be forced to read a poem so slowly that, to hold the whole thing in her head, she'd have it memorized by the end.

And then she'd have it. For herself, for the next time she saw Daniel, for showing off on sets, which she loved doing. Even after she couldn't see faces anymore, she could tell by the silence, the whistle of air, everyone thinking: *My God, she's smart, too.*

This was the real gift he'd given her, contrary to what everyone else might think: not faith in her looks, but in her mind.

She finds her way back to the kitchen and asks if he has a spare bedroom she can use for the night. "I want to go back to New York in the morning," she says. "And I don't want to spend all night arguing with my parents about it. I just want to go. I'll call Jemma tonight and tell her she needs to leave."

"Are you sure?"

"Yes," she says simply. "I am."

He asks no more questions. "Fine. Right up here."

She remembers the stairs, the feel of his banisters, the smell of his bedroom as he walks her past it, into a room she's never been in before. "Where are we?"

"This was supposed to be the baby's room. We had a baby the summer before I started teaching. Greta carried her full term and then she was born dead."

"I'm so sorry."

"It was a genetic problem so Greta was scared to try again. We moved out here from New York to raise a family, and we never went back. Sometimes I think we should have. We were very different in New York. Here, she never stopped feeling scared."

All this time, Rozzie has given shockingly little thought to his wife. As an unforgiving adolescent, she thought of her only as quiet and badly dressed, undeserving of Daniel's great charm. She had never understood why Daniel married her, but back then most marriages seemed beyond comprehension and unrelated to romance of any kind. Now she sees there is a web connecting her to the people around her. What she does matters. "Did she leave you because of me?"

"No. Or maybe yes, that was part of it. For some reason we couldn't recover together. We had to separate to do that."

But—*dear God,* she thinks, then asks, "How long ago did your baby die?"

"Eleven years. She'd be eleven."

How did unhappiness hang on that long?

Jemma

It doesn't take long to finish the job. Behind me, the receptionist makes frantic phone calls to people she speaks with in a raised whisper: *She's not saying why. She won't say anything.*

It's true that I've responded to none of her questions. Answering would stop me–trip me up in explanations; by not speaking, I finish the job in forty minutes. I leave while she is in the back, turning once to see the wall that was covered with Rozzie, now adorned by all children, all autistic. On my way out, my dress catches and I put a small tear in it.

That night, I pack my things to go. I know that I must return home and come clean to Rozzie, explain that I sold pictures to the newspaper in the hope that some good might come of it. I have deposited the money into her account so there need be no awkward refusals, no scenes where paper is pushed back and forth between us. I don't plan a full speech ahead of time. I can only hope that she will understand the overall gist of it–that I have been as unmoored from my bearings as she by this illness.

I don't know what she will say. I want to confess what she would quite likely rather not hear at this point. She wants to believe no one's interested in her illness, that in slipping into darkness she has found a shadow in which she can comfortably stand. Perhaps she wants to think we are equals, two sisters pursuing a rocky life in the arts. But none of this is true. My whole life has been shaped by the stretch of her light, by the shadows that fall from her reaching limbs.

If I tell her all of this, maybe she will understand why every reason I gave for selling the pictures isn't the real one, that the truth is I wanted her to stay at the bright, shining zenith of all her fame. I wanted her to hover out of reach. I am comfortable with the distance a movie screen creates.

Maybe if I tell her this, it will become less true. Maybe I will see her better and she will see me. Driving home, I picture the conversation, the tears, the accusations, the first real fight we've had in years. I feel the relief of finally getting mad. Even with Matthew I never did. It will be cathartic, a path back to sanity, and a new relationship.

Then I walk in the door at seven in the morning and know, the minute I see my father's wrinkled eyebrows—the pinched expression on his face—that what I want to happen won't. I know she is gone, disappeared again.

Rozzie

Back in New York, it only takes a few days for her to begin moving cautiously, first one block, then two, away from her apartment. She picks times with the fewest pedestrians on the street and then learns, with practice, she needn't worry about this, her cane clears a path for her. Neil once said New York is a surprisingly good place for blind people to live, and it turns out to be true: driving is not an issue, buses are everywhere. She sits behind the driver, tells him her stop. Some are chatty, some aren't, but all of them tell her when to get off.

In a week's time, the only people she speaks to are her mother on the phone and her doorman, when she leaves and comes back. Jemma is back at home, but she never picks up the phone and Rozzie never asks to speak to her. Harold, the doorman, doesn't mention her cane, which she keeps folded in her hand until she's out on the street. Maybe he doesn't notice or is being kind. Or maybe this is the door-man code of etiquette: one speaks of weather or mail and nothing else.

After a while she starts making calls, letting people know she is back. She sets goals for herself and establishes rules: She must make four phone calls a day and take two outings. She must get dressed and put on lipstick. Even as she decides the rules, though, she bends them. She counts telephoning her mother as one of her calls.

Her second week back, she stands on the street corner in front of Lincoln Center, waiting to cross, and a man comes up behind and taps her on the shoulder. When she turns around, he takes her into his arms, whispers into her neck how good it is to see her, how good she looks.

For a long time, she cannot think who this is. Finally she realizes it's Leonard, whom she hasn't seen in five years, since the day she left Italy. Flabbergasted, she says nothing. She remembers what he looked like, remembers feeling so destroyed by his rejection that she once sat in a hotel room hyperventilating into a brown paper bag. She remembers all this, but she can't remember *him*. What was he like? What drew her so powerfully to him? She has no idea.

There are whole portions of her life like this—where she can recall tertiary, unimportant details and can't remember accurately what really happened or why. She almost wishes she was drinking or taking drugs, to explain the gaps in her memory, but after that one time in Italy, she never did again.

Leonard crosses the street with her, tucking one hand into her elbow, a mistake sighted people always make, and asks if she wants to have a drink with him. Inside a restaurant, he tells her about the last two movies he's worked on, titles she doesn't even recognize. His stories take on a momentum of their own. He mentions names she has never heard of, then the point of the story seems to be how famous this person has become. "So everybody's buzz buzz buzz about Ben Ligni. I'm saying, 'Little Ben Ligni, I knew him when he had pimples.' Seriously. Do you remember him with those pimples?"

She doesn't. She has no idea what he's talking about. "Sort of," she says, not wanting him to clarify because she can guess—he had a small part in their movie, a walk-on or an Under-5, and is now soaring past them all, to Sundance, to Cannes. This is the same story actors tell each other over and over. Sooner or later, they all become scorekeepers of the younger crowd.

The amazing part of the encounter is that he tells her, over and over, how good she looks, but he never once mentions either her eyes or his marriage. Are both of these topics too awkward to allude to? The last time she saw him, they spoke of almost nothing except his wife. This time, when they say good-bye, Rozzie wonders only why she once believed so fervently he was the love of her life.

She quickly discovers Leonard isn't the only one. Some friends want to talk only of her blindness, some seem to think mentioning it would be rude. She begins going to dinner parties and is told, again and again, how well she looks. To remind people she *isn't* fine, she crafts a few stories, funny anecdotes about wearing dresses inside out. "As if I wasn't a bad enough dresser *already*," she tells a dinner group of eight.

She goes on, makes things up, tells the group about washing her hair with Palmolive and brushing her teeth with depilatory cream. Slowly, she is becoming an actress again, taking on a role: funny, brave blind girl.

After one dinner party, she gets more invitations, calls from people she cannot remember. Sometimes, she will have a whole conversation with a voice she can't place until long after she's hung up, and then she'll recall, *Oh, right, the hairdresser.*

For weeks, it's thrilling. She is the center of every gathering, the well-adjusted, disabled inspiration. She can hear the conversations unfold after she leaves, everyone talking about her.

Her friends who are actors or writers are all generally caught up, like Leonard, in talk of the business and pending projects. Strangely, blind and not working, she has more to say to them than she did when they all had jobs in common. Some evenings she goes home, her mouth dry, her throat sore from talking. But gradually, her stories grow less funny. She tries to make a point. "It's *okay*," she tells Suzanne, a woman who once played her sister. "I swear I'm okay. It's weird. I'm happier now than I was before."

She wants to explain how this feels—to sever oneself from all ambition, to want nothing. Without jokes, though, she fears sounding a little Buddhist and extreme. She keeps talking. "We all started so young. Did any of us know what we wanted? We were what? Seventeen? Eighteen?"

Sometimes the silence following one of these speeches is thick and uncomfortable.

Some people, she knows, assume she's lost her mind along with her sight, but Suzanne is different. Two years ago, Suzanne was twenty and the movie she made with Rozzie was her first. She was fresh from Texas, still speaking with an accent when the cameras weren't rolling. Since then, she's made three movies. She's lost the accent and her hand in Rozzie's feels clammy. "Wow," she says, her voice a little caught. "That's great. You've really found some peace. All I can do is yoga, yoga, yoga."

Rozzie knows she doesn't always get her point across, but sometimes she must, because a few people grab her hand and press her fingers. "You've made me think," they whisper. Once she sits at a dinner next to a man who says, "You're cut free, hallelujah," and begins to sing "Let My People Go." Though he is obviously joking, it feels this way, as if she's been cut free from tethers that hold these others.

The problem is that conversation sooner or later returns to its old touchstones: which movies are bad, which plays are overrated, who's getting what work where. Rozzie hasn't seen a movie in months and hasn't read a review in longer. One of the main joys of going blind has been going blind to these details. She doesn't want to concern herself with them, but being with these people reminds her of everything she must work to ignore.

Gradually, after a month or so, the phone calls dribble away, and she finds this, too, is a relief. A break from long evenings of playing Helen Keller.

She begins spending time alone, going to concerts, taking walks around the city, listening for hours to books on tape. Finally, she calls Miriam. "What about voice work?" she suggests. She's been thinking lately about an accent game she used to play, in which she would sit at a restaurant beside a table of foreigners and, in the time it took to eat a meal, learn their accent. She could do it, too; even hard ones such as Czech and Dutch. Lately she's been thinking, *What I'm really good at is voices.*

"But—" Miriam is obviously unsure. "What about scripts? How will you read them?" Miriam speaks slowly, as if Rozzie might not have thought about this.

"My computer will read them. I'll memorize everything the night before."

"You can't do that."

"Miriam. I *did* do that. For years. Just get me one job. I'll show them I can do it. I'll blow people away. I promise."

When she hangs up, her heart is pounding. Here is the real truth. She doesn't really want nothing. Emptiness is hard and not working is harder.

For a week nothing happens. Miriam gets her no readings, no appointments, doesn't even call back. Rozzie sits alone in her apartment listening to the radio, studying the voices, the way they roll in and out of sentences. She tries to imitate them, speaks out loud to her empty apartment. She plays games with herself, dials to static, imitates that, finds a Spanish station and repeats as much as she can phonetically remember.

A restlessness grows that is not unhappiness exactly, but there's less conviction in her voice when she tells well-wishers on the street about the new peace she feels.

It's true she's relieved to be out of the movie-star loop. The acting she's done in movies has little to do with what she imagined years ago when she pictured becoming an actress in New York. In her heart she still has that dream, the fantasy that always included a struggle she never actually endured. She dreamed about taking classes, waiting tables, about the years it would take before she'd finally be recognized in a blaze of mature talent. Back then, she imagined it would happen when she was twenty-eight. She is only twenty-five now, but feels immeasurably older.

It catches her breath to think of that old vision of herself, standing on a stage, as Hedda Gabler or Lady Macbeth, bringing beautiful language to life, speaking the lines that Daniel wove through all of his lectures. She didn't realize that these plays were hardly ever done anymore. Nor did she realize that taking her first job meant she would never speak a beautiful line of poetry for an audience again.

This move into darkness is a move back to poetry, to the world where words once traveled on wings.

She finds a braille copy of Shakespeare's collected works, though her braille is still rudimentary. Working her way through even the plays she knows well and loves is slow going, but as she reads, alone in her apartment, with all the lights off, her mouth forms the words. At first she reads quietly, modulating emotion out of her voice. Then she lets go, gives herself permission to act fully, all the parts. Her apartment comes alive with character and conflict. She laughs at her own jokes, pauses to reflect in soliloquy passages. When she gets to Feste's song, she sings.

She carries her reading outside with her, occasionally recites a line or two aloud, seated in Central Park. So be it, she thinks, here is Free Shakespeare without the crowds.

She sees nothing, has no idea if anyone watches her or not. But between line readings, she believes she hears the sound of walkers stopping, pausing for a moment. And for the first time in her life, she feels like a true and real actress, how Meryl Streep in her best roles must have felt, as if she were not herself at all, but a character speaking the lines of her heart.

One night, walking home, cane in one hand, fat Shakespeare volume in the other, she thinks of Jemma. She imagines her sister was in the park, watching her performance, applauding in spite of the mild embarrassment Jemma would no doubt feel. She has no idea where this idea comes from. She hasn't spoken to Jemma in almost six weeks. Since arriving in New York, she's had no vision, no temporary reprieves from all this grayness. She's assumed the explanation is being here in the city, or else that enough time has passed for her retinas to finally settle into permanent detachment. This is her real life, how it will be for the rest of it anyway, and her eyes seem to have understood this fact and stopped trying so hard. She hasn't once thought of her sister's absence in conjunction with this.

Then for some reason, she thinks about the first play she was ever in. No performance matched that first, in her own estimation, that extraordinary submergence of self into other. She took on those problems, felt Karen's heartbreak, as truly as if it had been her own. Leaving it behind was one of the hardest things she's ever done. Maybe that was why she got so upset when Jemma didn't see it. This character was her new self, her emerging self, and she needed to have it seen and understood by those around her.

She realizes she has never quite forgiven her sister for missing that performance—for so obviously feigning some illness to *avoid* seeing where Rozzie was headed, the future that lay before her—and she looks back on that time as a turning point. Ever after, she has put a distance between herself and her sister. A peculiar distance that necessitated proximity. She invited Jemma to all her sets and spoke only minimally, superficially, when she got there. What was she trying to tell Jemma with all her silence and secrets? *It doesn't matter what you think, I don't care?*

It comes to her, quite suddenly, that the opposite must be true. How strange that she has felt, all this time, judged by her sister. That night, for the first time, she feels the weight of her sister's absence from her life. In cutting herself off from Jemma, she is cutting herself off from part of herself, from the doubt that Jemma perhaps never voiced but always represented. But why? she wonders, almost aloud. For the most part, Jemma has done nothing but love her disproportionately all their lives. Perhaps it all comes back to the ephemeral nature of celebrity—that being lofted too high gives power to those that hold you, makes you dependent on the air currents and their whims.

And in whose eyes did she first look and see herself reflected as larger and more glamorous than in the life she led? She wonders if acting was ever her own idea or if it was born of the vision she saw in her sister's eyes.

She decides the next morning to call home. When she asks about her sister, her mother's voice shifts: "It's a little unclear. She's supposed to be back at school by now, but I'm not sure she's there. The telephone number she gave us doesn't work."

"Have you heard from her?"

"Not for a week."

"Wait a second. It's been a week since you've heard from her and you haven't told me?"

Jemma

It is the strangest sensation, to look up and see her suddenly, though of course I am here, in her city. It isn't impossible, only improbable. I lift my hand, start to call out, then stop. She seems to have some sort of purpose. She sits down on a bench, folds her cane, drops it into a satchel from which she retrieves a large leather-bound book. I am too far away to read the title, but it has the heft of a Bible.

She has on her sunglasses, though it's a bright, sunny day and everyone does. She looks no different from anyone else until she opens the book and begins to read without lowering her face. Though I've taken pictures of her working on her braille, I've never watched her read for any length of time. Now I have no choice. I am here without my camera and she is before me.

I watch her fingers move, all in a row, inching across the lines. I had thought she was still a beginner, reading menus and children's books, but clearly she has advanced. Has she, in two months, been working only on this? Or maybe she's not reading at all, just putting on a show? Though I have been photographing her for months now, I haven't been watching her. Not in the old way that I used to, where I could sense her motivations and shifts in her mood. This time I have no idea what she's thinking, or about to do.

Her lips begin to move.

She is four benches away. I hear nothing, but people around her stop and listen.

She is putting on some sort of show, gathering an audience of people like me who have time on a weekday to sit in the park watching whatever happens around them. A couple sits down across from her, smiling and nodding. They know who she is, I can tell by their eyebrows, and the way their smiles stay on their faces. This is, for them, a rare New York moment, a story they will tell for weeks to come. At first it makes me happy to watch them watching her, and then I worry. Their story could so easily turn mean: *You remember that girl, the actress who was missing and then turned out to be blind? You want to hear the freakiest thing?* I want to go over and protect her—sit beside her and stop the reading by telling her I'm here. Move them away with my eyes, with a look that says, *You can stop staring now.*

And then I remember I'm not supposed to be here at all.

Rozzie

She starts making calls. Her mother, unwilling to believe she might have two children turn up missing within six months, says she's not worried, that she's sure Jemma is safe back at school, too busy to call. Rozzie knows, in her bones, that Jemma isn't there.

She calls the school, is connected to the registrar's office and a woman who tells her that she can't say for another two weeks who has registered for courses and who hasn't. She calls the art department, speaks to a secretary who is new and sounds all of eighteen years old. "I don't know her, so I can't tell you if I've seen her or not."

"Could you ask around and I'll call back?"

Rozzie does and no one has seen her. Her heart gallops ahead. *I'm right,* she thinks, momentarily pleased to have her intuition confirmed. *Jemma is in trouble and only I know it.* She leaves a message with the woman and hangs up. She must concentrate on this, push these ephemeral powers further, to find where Jemma might have gone. She keeps thinking Jemma might be somewhere in the city, but that makes no sense. If she were here, where would she stay, if not with her?

She calls Jemma's old friends around town. No one has heard from her, but Rozzie doesn't let on that she is particularly worried. She makes it seem a matter of a delayed phone hookup, not a big deal. She asks what they thought of her show and is shocked to hear none of them had heard about it. These were Jemma's best friends a year ago, people she once spent all her time with. Why wouldn't she have seen them when she was here or invited them to her show?

The next morning, she decides to make her way to the gallery, find out exactly what happened before the opening. This is the farthest she's traveled from her apartment yet, and the most unfamiliar terrain. She hardly knows SoHo at all, and twice she must ask directions. Finally a man says he can walk her there.

Inside she asks to speak to Stella, the name she remembers Jemma mentioning. The woman at the front desk must recognize Rozzie or take her for a potential buyer. "Of course, right away," she says, and walks off.

A moment later, she hears a British accent. "Ms. Phillips, come into my office."

"I'm sorry to be bothering you right now, but there's a bit of a mystery about my sister. I'm sure she'll turn up in a few days, but for now no one knows where she is and we're wondering if she might have gotten in touch with you."

"No, no. I don't think she would have tried."

"Why not?"

"I don't think she understood the ramifications of pulling pictures when a show is in place. It did everyone a disservice. Most of all her."

"Do you know why she did it?"

The woman seems unsure what to say. "We assumed you asked her to."

"No."

For a minute they sit in silence as Rozzie absorbs this.

Finally the woman says, "They're remarkable pictures. They deserve a showing."

Until now Rozzie hasn't thought of them this way, has never considered that Jemma might have had an artful design in addition to her paparazzo motivation. She has assumed they were all snap-and-run shots, her with her braille books, her counselors, her white cane. Sad, vulnerable images that had nothing to do with what she was feeling.

"I didn't know she was taking them." Rozzie's voice is small; she hardly recognizes it. "We've never really talked about them."

"Hmm." Stella seems to consider this. "It's interesting that you didn't know. That may be why they're good. There's an unguarded quality to them. We didn't know if that was real or staged."

Rozzie feels suddenly exhausted and saddened, sitting in this chair, across from this woman. She doesn't want to hear about these pictures or how she appears to other people. She is grateful Jemma pulled them out of the show, thankful the face she no longer knows is not being viewed by people she hasn't met.

"Thank you," she says to the woman. "I should probably go."

When she gets home, she makes the call she's been avoiding all this time—to Matthew, who she knows will still be angry, will want to accuse her of using him to put distance between herself and her sister. And he'll be right, she knows that. But it's also possible that he may know something. She dials anyway and speaks quickly. There is an edge to her voice, a frantic quality that must communicate (she's not even sure what she's saying), *Please, let's not go over it all, just tell me if you know where she is.* Because she gets to the end of her speech and can hardly believe it.

He's talked to Maya. He does know.

And he tells her.

Jemma

Maya, who is crazy in her own way, understands my new fragile state. When I show up on her doorstep and say, shaky-voiced, I have driven here instead of driving back to school, she closes her eyes and nods sympathetically.

"Sure," she says. "I understand."

She, too, isn't returning to school, but for the far better reason that her summer internship has become a legitimate job offer.

I tell her a little of what's going on. That I'm not functioning well, that I can't sleep, that I seem to eat without tasting anything I've put in my mouth.

"Sure." She nods, unsurprised. "Been there. Done that."

She is the first person I've really talked to, and the relief is huge. In speaking, I realize I am cracking a door, letting light into what has, for weeks, been an all-black interior. Maya doesn't question what I am doing here, doesn't point out that at school we were never *that* close. What I have suspected is true. She knows the manifestations of craziness, how you move in extreme and unpredictable ways, how confusion can be so great you start a road trip with one destination and alter it entirely after a single green-and-white sign that says New York City, Route 2. How it can, in the moment, seem to be not a highway sign, but an instruction.

For three weeks, I lived at home awaiting the start of school again, then on the drive there, I knew I couldn't return. I have come to New York to avoid school and also to get away from my parents and the weight of worry I see in their faces; to be around Maya, who has learned how to be both frightened of the world and functional at the same time. Every morning she goes to work at a food magazine where she sprays shellac onto chickens and organizes grapes in artful ways to be photographed. I have been here for three days, and I have watched her be efficient and compartmentalize her emotions. At work she is neutral in the face of other people's anxiety, steely to criticism. The day I spend with her there, I watch and imagine how no one would ever know she goes home at night and drinks two glasses of white wine, crying steadily.

One night, after I've been here a week, the phone rings and it is Rozzie, for me. I haven't prepared what I want to say, how to explain all this in a way that will make sense. It is easier to be around Maya, who doesn't know me well enough to expect certain things. With Maya I have managed to sound all right. I tell her small bits of the truth—that it was hard being home, that I'm worried about my work and what I'll do with my life, and she nods as if none of this is surprising or unusual. She listens, even lets me cry, then after a while goes to bed, saying she has to be up early.

I sleep on a futon that during the day serves as a step stool to reach a stereo placed on an illogically high shelf. "I don't really get these people," she says as she unrolls it, meaning the people she sublets from. In New York it is possible to have this sort of privacy, to be misunderstood by someone who is living among your things, or sitting right here.

On the phone, I promise to go see Rozzie, though the moment I hang up, I want to call her back and say I can't, I'm not ready.

Maya shrugs at my panic. "You're here in the city. She's here, too. Right?" She pours herself another glass of wine. "Just go. Sooner or later you're going to run into her anyway." Maya doesn't know that I've already seen her, reading in the park. She stares at me, sees my hands shake. "Or don't go. You want to know what difference it'll make? None. Life goes on. That's the whole thing. Life just goes on."

I do go. I change my clothes, wash my face, walk outside into a night that is surprisingly warm. When I get there, I am grateful that she looks well and doesn't seem angry. I expect her to yell at me about the newspaper, but she doesn't. Instead, she pours me a cup of tea and opens a box of gingersnap cookies.

"Here." She holds out the box. "Have one. They're my new favorite thing."

It feels as if it's been years since I've seen her put a cookie in her mouth, but she does it now easily, snapping it in half with her teeth.

For a long time we talk of nothing. She asks where Maya lives, what her apartment is like. I describe Maya's block, and her job. Maybe we can pass the whole visit this way, I think—like distant relatives, having a yearly cup of tea. I think about Maya's words: *It makes no difference. Life just goes on.*

Then she asks if I intended to call her.

"Of course. At some point. I hadn't thought about it that much."

"Do you mind telling me what made you come to New York?"

I start to cry. I can't help it. "What happened with Matthew?" I say, as if this is the heart of all our problems, the reason for my tears, which I know it isn't.

"What do you mean?"

"Why did you come out to the school where I was trying to start a life and"—I think for a minute—"take over?"

For a long time, she doesn't speak. "I didn't mean to."

"I couldn't even stay there. You were everywhere. I didn't even exist anymore."

"That's not true."

"It *is*."

Rozzie speaks quietly. "That's how you *felt*. That's not how it was. I'm sorry if you felt that way."

"Did you love him?"

She folds her lips together. "I wouldn't have let it happen if I didn't think that was a possibility."

"And what happened?"

I wait for her to tell me the story I already know: that he was superficial, starstruck like everyone else. Instead she says, "I don't know. I guess it was my fault."

I hear the sadness in her voice. I know that she doesn't want to have this conversation at all. "It's not Matthew," I sob. "Matthew doesn't matter." I wish it were easier to tell her what I've really been thinking: that I'm supposed to be the person who knows the real her, apart from her celebrity, but in my head, she's always been a celebrity. I've lived for the electric thrill of her attention, the spotlight feel of her eyes on me alone. During the time she vanished from the world and the policeman assumed, being her sister, I might know where she was, I wanted to tell him, of all people, the truth: *No. I've just been watching her like everyone else. For a longer time, maybe, but no different.*

She asks very softly, "Did you love him?" in a kind voice that suggests I could have, it was possible, even if he didn't reciprocate.

"I think maybe I just wanted to love someone."

"You should."

And then I really cry. "I don't know what to do with myself. I feel like I've failed at everything I've done." I could delineate it all, but it's obvious, she doesn't need the particulars: college, romance, photography.

She nods and lets this sit in the air for a while. "I don't see it that way," she finally says. "You're a photographer. You should be taking pictures."

"It's *hard*—" I am sobbing now.

"Of course it's hard. It *should* be hard. That's why most people don't do this stuff." She takes another cookie. "You don't have to take pictures of me. You *shouldn't* take pictures of me. I'm not the reason you're good." Her voice changes, softens as if she's just thought of something new. "Thank you, by the way, for taking those pictures of me out of your show. I appreciate it."

I stop crying and look up. "How did you know?"

"I went to the gallery. I told them I was looking for you."

"What did they say?"

"Not much. They said you're good. They said you should keep going. They just said they wanted you to expand your subject matter a little. Get away from the portraits of movie people."

"Really? You talked to Stella? That's what Stella said?"

"More or less."

It's probably not true, and it isn't as if this solves my problems, but for a minute or two it makes me feel better. Rozzie was *there* at the gallery, the place where I set my future on fire. She talked with them, smoothed the ground I tore up with my screwdriver and my craziness. I picture their faces when she walked in: the surprise, the pleasure. They had her in their show, they lost her, and there she was again: my sister. My beautiful, blind, movie-star sister.

Rozzie

Sitting across from Jemma, in the same shapeless, gray landscape she's been living in for months, she realizes how much she was expecting to see when Jemma came. Now that Jemma is here and they are laboring for conversation, she throws out a question, moves her head, her eyes, around, searching muslin haze for streaks of clarity, and finding nothing, she can hardly contain her disappointment.

It's a surprise, really, to feel such intense desire after months of placid acceptance. Her eyes sting from trying so hard. Finally she must close them, in fear that she might begin to cry senselessly as they talk about Maya, some friend of Jemma's she's almost sure she's never met. Even if she has, she doesn't care about this girl.

The disappointment is so huge she begins to wonder what else she was expecting. With Jemma in the room, she feels her posture shift, her voice alter, imperceptible to anyone but herself. All these years it has never occurred to her how profoundly she changes in her sister's presence. Now that she's aware of it, she can't bear the affectation, and the effort it takes. Her back starts to ache, sitting like this, so upright, so tall. Why does slumping back on this sofa, putting her feet up on the coffee table she knows to be there, feel as inappropriate as standing up and taking her clothes off?

She already knows that when Jemma leaves, she will crawl into bed and weep, as she hasn't done since that night at Daniel's. Suddenly it seems as if only her sister—first the loss of her, now the return—awakens these feelings. The surprise of this thought makes her wonder if she can even wait until Jemma leaves to cry.

It's as if no one else—no man, no friend, not even their parents—matters as much. And she just doesn't understand—will never understand—why she feels so phony with her sister. She worries for an instant that she's been talking this whole time, spinning the same tale she's been telling at dinner parties, about being fine, better than fine. A deep breath reminds her no, she's been quiet mostly, asking questions.

She's said a few things, she doesn't know what. She'll get through this visit, make it to the end, and this bad phase will pass, as the others have before.

She keeps breathing, closes her eyes, and focuses within.

She will never understand this.

PART THREE

Jemma

I only stay in New York a week, long enough to know that I don't belong here. I don't go back to school, either, because my instincts also tell me it's not a good idea. I go back to the only place I can think of, home, and do something I don't plan ahead of time. I call Theo and ask if he would like to have dinner with me. At the restaurant, with menus between us, we talk about what happened with Rozzie and what I did.

"Maybe you wanted her to keep being famous," he says.

He has a point. For so long I have seen myself in relation to the spotlight focused on her. I have learned how to stand to the side of that light, how to find its edges and move with it. I tell him more— all about the gallery and the crazy way I switched the pictures and left.

When I get to the end of the story, he laughs. "And what happened?"

"I have no idea. I didn't go back and I didn't go home that night. I never heard from them. Isn't that strange? They either took me out completely or put up the old pictures of you, but I don't think they would have had time to do that."

He thinks about the story, laughs, and shakes his head. "They must think you're crazy."

"I'm sure they do."

"You're not, though." His eyes hold mine. "It was a good thing to do. I think you were right."

After dinner he asks if I'd like to come back to his apartment, see where he lives these days. I assume this means he's not living with Stacey, though we haven't mentioned this yet. The surprise is that he lives with his brother. After all these years of talking about my sister, I never knew he had a sibling. I feel bad when he tells me, and he seems to guess what I'm thinking. "I don't talk about him much," he says. "He's kind of odd." I ask what he does.

"Nothing right now. He's on disability because he hurt his back. He used to work as a manager at Taco Bell."

I can see it's hard for him to talk about. Instead of saying any more, we drive in silence into an apartment complex not too far from our old supermarket. A dozen identical doors are in a horseshoe around a central parking lot. Outside one, a very pregnant woman sits on a lawn chair.

"Hey, Marie," he calls as we walk toward the door. "How's it going?"

"Tired of being a beach ball, thanks."

"I bet," Theo says, and they both laugh.

"Who's this?" Marie smiles my way as Theo fishes for his keys.

"This is an old friend of mine." He smiles down at the lock. "Named Jemma."

"Hi, Jemma," she says, and I can't be sure, but it seems as if her eyebrows go up just a fraction, as if maybe she's heard my name. Maybe I'm imagining this, though.

Paul is the physical opposite of Theo—large and doughy, where Theo is lanky, muscular without effort. Paul is also a head taller, though he stoops as if his posture is a perpetual apology for his size. "Listen to this," he bellows when we first walk in. "Mom wants me to buy Uncle Walter's old Chrysler. Ha! That's a laugh." When he sees me, he laughs, as if to demonstrate. "Uncle Walter's Chrysler is about as old as I am, never mind how old that is." He doesn't look me in the eye, but looks at my shoulders, my knees, as he describes the car.

Though I can see why he embarrasses Theo, it's hard not to like him, his obvious anxiety in a girl's presence, his pant leg caught up in his sock.

Alone in Theo's room, I ask what Paul does with his time. "Nothing much. He draws comics. He can collect disability for six more months, so I think that's his plan."

The irony, of course, is that he looks fine and Theo doesn't, but there's no need to point this out. I can see we both have siblings we can't easily explain.

"Why do you live together?"

"My mother asked me to."

We're talking about one thing, but we're in a bedroom and the door is closed. Our eyes find each other's, our bodies move together. His good hand is on my elbow, guiding me over to the side of the bed. Soon we are kissing and I haven't even asked what happened with Stacey. Was this the apartment they were going to share? Instead of asking, I move my hands up under his shirt. He is tan, his skin still warm as if the sun has been baked into it. Being touched by him is strange at first; one hand operates much differently from the other. His good hand opens wide, taking everything in; his bad hand stays curled up, protective, but he doesn't hide it. He touches me with the back of his fingers, circles my breast with his knuckles. This unselfconsciousness is part of his beauty, his strength. It's what I need to learn from him.

Jemma

I need to find a job. The money I made and saved on the movie sets has run out, and I can't expect my parents to pay for the film and paper I need to keep going. They are already being kind enough, letting me live at home and asking no questions about my plans.

I go into my old camera store, where I was once told the owner likes to hire guys. This time I ask to speak to the owner and am surprised to find it is an older woman. Her name is Margaret.

"I'm a photographer," I tell her. "And I need a job."

She wipes at nothing on the counter. "Okay. Come on back. Let's talk."

She asks me where I've been studying, what I've been doing. I tell her everything, that I've been to school, have had some professional success, but am not ready yet to make my living at it. I need time, away from the scrutiny of teachers and fellow students, to find my niche, that I've decided for now to stay in this small town and shoot here.

"You don't have to live in New York," she tells me. "A lot of people don't. Look at Sally Mann. Look at Mary Ellen Mark."

My heart lifts. "That's right."

It turns out she's a photographer, too, and works in a darkroom set up on the second floor of her store.

"This was my way to stay independent," she says, nodding toward the store.

Soon, we aren't talking about jobs anymore, we're talking about photography, the journey she's taken. "Here, let me show you my setup," she says, and I follow her up a dark set of stairs to a converted attic. On one side is a large studio, on the other a darkroom. "I used to do portraits. Thank God I'm through with that." She takes me into her darkroom, turns on the light, and I can't believe it: I know her work.

"You were in *Aperture* last year."

I can't get over the fact that I've noticed this woman's work enough to remember her name and that I never knew she lived here. I study a few of her prints and see this *is* our town she's shooting. She seems to read my mind. "I don't do all my shooting here. I travel a lot. But I like to do some. We've got an interesting mix of people here."

She must sense my admiration because she goes to show me more. She unlocks her print filing cabinet and opens the drawers. There's a wonderful range and depth to her work—portraits, land-scapes, still lifes. "This is the work I'm getting some attention for," she says before opening the last drawer, the one at the bottom. I know she is storing them down here for protection—if anything spills, if a pipe breaks, these will be the last affected.

At first I'm disappointed. She pulls out a series of young girls in nature—swimming topless in our lake, building sand castles. It's not that they aren't good—they are—but everyone is getting attention for this subject these days, the final cusp of innocence, the first gleaning of sexuality. So many people have done it thoughtfully and dis-turbingly now that I've sworn it off entirely. When I'm shooting and a prepubescent girl comes into my viewfinder, I put down my camera and turn away. Young girls do not need to carry this weight, be looked at this way.

Margaret pulls her versions out of the drawer, spreads them on the table. "These two were in *Photography*."

She is obviously proud of them and the success that has probably felt hard-won. I look closer at the one that was in *Aperture* and suddenly my heart stops. It is of my neighbor Wendy, though she looks to be fourteen or fifteen. She's standing in the woods at the far end of our street, just outside a spill of light, so that she seems to be part of the shadows beneath the trees, wearing a top I remember we were all wearing one summer, a bandanna tied tight around our flat breasts. She stares into the camera but looks surprised, as if she's been caught doing something she shouldn't be. The tension in the picture comes from the shadows around and behind her—the mystery of where she's coming from or going toward.

"Everyone calls this the girl meeting the boy in the woods. Even though there's no boy there." Margaret laughs as if this is a joke, a trick she's intentionally played on the viewer. But even she doesn't realize what she has. Only I know why this picture is so eerie and haunting, and I marvel at the peculiarity of how the past overlaps with the present. Perhaps I have avoided taking pictures of young girls because it is hard for me to remember how I used to be: a sister who once stood, waiting forever, in shadows. But here is another one, and in seeing her, I can hate my old self less. It is touching, an act of such pure love it defies any words.

She is visiting the place she believes her dead sister still lives.

Margaret offers me a job, three days a week behind the counter, two days a week printing for her. This suggestion seems to take even her by surprise, and she quickly adds, "Let's see how our styles mesh."

I take it to mean she's as excited to have found me as I am to have found her.

I float home and call Theo because there is no one else to share my good news with. He's happy for me and seems to understand this will mean a break in my bleakness and self-absorption. He suggests we get together that night for a celebration.

Because no one else is home, I call Rozzie, who miraculously is.

"You want to hear something bizarre?" I tell her the whole story, of meeting the woman, slightly knowing her work, but never knowing she lived in our town, and then I tell Rozzie about the pictures Margaret is most famous for. Halfway through, it occurs to me that Rozzie may not even remember the story or the time that Wendy came to our house. Maybe it made no impression on her. Sometimes it seems our memories are like this, as if we lived two different childhoods.

Then she surprises me. "She was visiting her sister," she says simply.

"Right. She must have been. Or she thought she was."

"Wow," Rozzie says, and nothing more.

I remember how it felt in the hospital—as if we were spinster sisters, married to one another. Now it's as if we were strangers on a blind date, tiptoeing carefully through our conversations, cautiously picking what we say.

Rozzie

She meets Timothy on a blind date, her first.

"I'm more than qualified for this kind of thing," she tells him over the phone. She is joking, though he seems not to get it.

"Why?"

"I'm blind." Oddly, she's never said this before, never had to.

"Oh, right. Suzanne told me."

Suzanne is their mutual friend. "He's funny," she'd told Rozzie. "And outside this whole business."

That is the main draw, of course: the prospect of an evening spent not talking about movies. Really, what she wants is an evening where she doesn't talk at all. Ever since Jemma was here, she's found herself slipping back into her old social habits: withdrawal and silence. When she does go over to other people's apartments, she is a quiet, polite guest. She follows the conversation, laughs at what seem to be the jokes, compliments the food, and goes home. For now, she's decided this is easier.

She doesn't want to have an impact, affect people the way she's affected Jemma all these years, without wanting or meaning to. It's a weight, a responsibility she's not up for. She wants to go back to the old days when she moved through parties and crowds of people nearly unaware of what was going on around her. She took in no names, smiled at everyone, drank seltzer with lime, and remembered nothing the next day.

Surely more was going on back then. No doubt she was talking, flirting, maybe even forging what felt, on the other side, like a new friendship. The morning after some parties, Miriam would call and tell her she'd been wonderful, that such and such producer loved her, thought her so intelligent. And even after Miriam had described the man, what he looked like, what he had been wearing, she wouldn't remember him or a single thing she'd said. Now she wonders if this obtuseness wasn't responsible for her success. She must have appeared to want so little.

She'd like to go back to living in that old fog, where jobs and people appeared out of the mist, grabbed her hand, and claimed her.

She meets Timothy in a Japanese restaurant uptown near Columbia. It's her first outing like this, walking alone into a restaurant, asking the hostess to escort her to the bar. It is still sunny outside and bright, so walking into this place feels like walking into a cave. Everything is black. She can make out no shadows, no movement. Her eyes can take twenty minutes to adjust, she knows. When she gets to the bar, she closes them to speed the process along. She wills herself not to be frightened of this dark, not to contemplate a time when this might be all she sees.

"Asleep already? I haven't even started talking about my work yet." His voice is low, with the thinnest trace of a Texas accent, the same one Suzanne used to have when they first met.

She smiles, keeps her eyes closed. "They adjust a little faster this way."

Halfway through dinner, she realizes he's got all the same conversational tricks she does. Every question she asks, he answers, then asks her. He tells a long story about his brother, then turns around and says, "What about you? Do you have any siblings?"

"Yes. A sister." She leaves it at that, focuses on her chopsticks and sushi.

"And?"

"And what?"

"You love her? You hate her? What?"

"Oh. Umm—" She has never talked about Jemma with a man. She has no prepared answer, nothing easy to say. "She's a photographer. And we've always been close, in a way. When I was having a hard time with my eyes, I leaned on her a lot, but I don't think she ever realized how much. I think she's always felt I never loved her enough." What is she even saying? "I think my success was great for her in a way and hard on her, too. It made her believe she didn't know me anymore, but really she did. There wasn't any more to know."

Now that she's started talking about this, she wants to go further, tell him what happened with the pictures, tell him that her sister broke her heart—but to her surprise another impulse accompanies that one. Already, she likes this man well enough to imagine them meeting and she wants him to like Jemma. She wants him to understand that even when they are hardly speaking, she loves Jemma. She always has.

After dinner he walks her home, twenty blocks down Broadway. She starts out with her cane, but after she hits a No Parking sign, he offers his elbow and she takes it.

He keeps asking questions, surprising ones that make her think. He asks sweetly if her blindness will affect her work. She laughs a little. "Oh, probably," she says, but then she tells him what she hasn't told anyone yet: she may have a job. That afternoon Miriam called with a prospect, narrating a documentary. "It's just a meeting right now, but they know the situation and they're willing to meet with me." In her voice, she hears the hope this has given her, the way one phone call can warm her whole feeling about the future. She already knows she will have to sell herself, convince them she'll be worth the extra effort she'll require. She hasn't wanted to say anything for fear of jinxing the prospect.

They are at her apartment. He takes her hand, folds it into his. "I'll keep my fingers crossed," he says.

Jemma

Three months into my job with Margaret, she asks to see some of my work.

I think for a long time about what to show her. The more time I spend with her, the more I love hearing what she has to say about photography, but she is a steely, discerning critic. She talks a great deal about other people's work, can analyze a single photograph in surprising ways. "This composition is sentimental," she will say of a landscape. "It gives us no choice on how to view it. It demands that we see it the same way the photographer does."

Sometimes her analysis extends past the picture to the photographer. "He's just so hung up on skin, skin, skin," she says of someone being profiled this month in *Aperture*. "He's all about surfaces. There's no depth. No *feeling*."

I am eager to hear what she will say about my photographs, and anxious. I bring in a little bit of everything—some of my old stuff, actors on movie sets, some of my mother's students, some of Rozzie. I even bring in some of my new things. I know I need feedback; I tell myself I want to hear what she has to say.

She flips through it all slowly, thoughtfully. "Interesting," she says of one. And then: "*Very* interesting."

The longer she takes, the more nervous I become. I'm not ready to hear her tell me I'm hung up on skin or beauty.

Finally she speaks: "These seem to be all about isolation and the walls people build around themselves. It's interesting to have this set of autistic kids in the center, framed on both ends by celebrities and actresses. The actresses have learned how to put up certain masks, so their isolation doesn't strike us until we see how you've set up the pictures. In every one the central figure is turned away from the focal object of the picture. Here there's a candle that *we* look at but she doesn't." Margaret is talking about a picture of Rozzie sitting at dinner, behind a candle in sharp focus. She doesn't mention the obvious reason Rozzie doesn't look at the candle—that she can't *see* it.

"With the autistic kids, the isolation is more obvious and thus the connection is easier. We understand who they are, looking at these pictures. The hardest to grasp are the ones who have theoretically made their lives the most public."

In the last year I have grown so apprehensive of overthinking my work the way I did at school that, at some point, I stopped analyzing it altogether. I didn't go back to school because I hated the self-consciousness I felt working there, the need to examine and explain everything I did. My work is more interesting, I believe, when I don't think it out ahead of time, when I shoot intuitively, instinctively, the things I am looking at.

But sooner or later, I need to reflect on what I am producing. I know she is right, that my work is about loneliness and isolation. I don't shoot moments of connections between people, I shoot the moments when connection is missed. Lately, I have been taking mothers and babies at the local park. In a setting rife with lovely moments, I find the fractured, painful ones: a baby crying in the foreground while a mother looks away, a little boy holding a flower to his mother's back.

I suppose I am trying to say it's not the mother's fault, that there is love here, too, in the mistakes we make.

*　　*　　*

Just recently, Rozzie has been calling home more. She talks at great length to our mother, more than I remember her talking in the past. I listen to my mother's end of the conversation, often little more than exclamations or questions: "Goodness. Why?" or "Oh, my, what did she say?"

From what I gather, Rozzie's life is going well. She has worked on two jobs since I've seen her—one a documentary, another a public service announcement. Neither has been about blindness, which must be what she prefers right now. We have only talked a few times, but once she admitted that the producers on the second project thought of her after seeing my pictures in the *Star.* "So I guess I should thank you even though I don't feel like it," she said.

In these conversations, we are careful with each other. When the other person makes a joke, we laugh quickly, perhaps too heartily, as if these are long-standing, easy riffs between us. She doesn't tell me the stories she tells our mother, but I get the highlights: She's met a man she likes, they've been on three dates. He's a chemist, well-known in his field.

"A *chemist?*" I say, disbelieving.

"He teaches at Columbia." If they go out around school, she tells me, he's the famous one; students constantly interrupt their meals to talk to him. She obviously enjoys the novelty of this. I picture her sitting back in her chair, smiling warmly as a scene she has no part in unfolds.

I wish I understood more about her life. I wish I could ask if she ever has truly dark days, where she weeps for her fate or feels sorry for herself. If she does, she doesn't tell me, part of our long pattern of being certain things to each other.

I am upbeat and so is she.

Maybe this is fine.

Surely there are worse things than being cheerful and polite with one another. In this distance, an unexpected warmth grows up between us. We both get nostalgic, sometimes for memories the other one doesn't share. "He reminds me of that guy Warren, who used to live up the street. Or his voice does anyway," she says of a director she has recently met for another voice project.

I remember no Warren.

"Sure you do. The guy with that nasal-register voice."

No, I don't.

She can't believe it. *"On our block,"* she says as if I am forgetting a family member's name. Her irritation also has a ring of pride to it. For years, she remembered virtually nothing of our past; now it's all coming back to her.

Sometimes I think maybe I am here to help her reclaim it.

We talk about Wendy—about that one conversation we both remember well. "I actually thought, this is what happens if your sister dies: you go crazy," Rozzie says.

"Really?" This sounds so unlike her, so irrational. It sounds more like—well, me.

"What else could I think?" she says. "Here was an older sister whose younger sister had died."

Rozzie

She throws herself into being with Timothy, negotiates harrowing subway journeys to meet him at Columbia for lunch or coffee, quick rendezvous that last less time than she wants them to. For hours afterward, she will walk around campus thinking about their conversation, enjoying the luxury of a stroll without intersections. Once, she walks for so long, she runs into him again at the end of his day. She blushes at the emptiness of her own schedule, claims in a stammer to have been at the library, looking something up. He slips a reassuring arm around her. "It's good to see you again," he says.

It makes her anxious, her determination to have this work out. She imagines the ways they might disappoint each other. In the past, it has always happened so suddenly—in a single conversation or one cab ride uptown—the guillotine realization: *This man isn't smart* or *I hate his hands.* She has never understood how feelings can be so strong one minute and absent the next. She's never stayed with any man long enough to know what love feels like over time. For reference, she has only this old fondness for Daniel that is comforting and pleasant, but not enough to sustain long conversations when they're together. It grows so quickly awkward, guilt creeping into the pauses.

One afternoon, traveling to meet Timothy, she realizes with a start, maybe the problem all along has been her own uncertainty with conversation. It has always felt like such an effort: listening, listening, holding up her end. Years ago, she used to say what she liked best about being with Jemma was not having to say anything at all. She still remembers some of their best times together: the wordless walks up Broadway from the Village to midtown, miles without a single word between them. Would Jemma remember these walks the same way, with such a nostalgic tug, as if the closest she had ever come to love was the hours she had spent not talking to her sister? For Rozzie, there was a serenity she didn't otherwise know—walking in public unafraid of strangers, or her eyes giving up. She could study the mosaic of gum blots on the sidewalk, her own shoes moving around the designs. The more time she spends with Timothy, the more comfortable they grow, and the more she thinks about those old times with Jemma.

Jemma

One morning, Margaret tells me she has a proposal.

"You're free to say no," she says. "It's up to you. But I do a show every year upstairs at the local library. It's not a very big deal—we get almost no attention, but I was thinking this year of including some-one else."

She pauses. I feel my face flush.

"We could do a joint show. I think our work might be interesting juxtaposed."

"Sure. Okay." It's hard for me to say any more. I don't know how to express gratitude well.

The show is scheduled six weeks away, but when I tell Rozzie, she says she wants to come home for it and bring her new boyfriend: "Would that be all right?"

"Of course," I say.

Margaret leaves the choice of which pictures to include up to me, except to say this much. "Go with what you're most interested in having people see right now." She puts the emphasis on *you,* which I take to mean, *Don't think about others or how they'll react.*

I go back to the pictures of my mother's students, one portrait of a girl we've known the longest, Regina, who is now sixteen and quite a beauty. She has changed over the years, become quite verbal, though her language is hard to understand because she reverses all her pronouns. *You* means "I" and *yours* means "mine." This mistake is common among autistic children and it used to confuse me. Now I understand it better: *You* is what they're called by everyone else. For all their isolation, they still talk about themselves in the language other people have given them. I can understand this, see how easy it is to make this mistake.

I decide to go with an idea that springs from Margaret's feed-back: all photographs with only a single figure in the frame—studies in isolation. Once I've made the rule, I make one exception: the baby crying in the park, sitting atop a sandbox dune, her mother's back in blurred movement behind her. It's a hard picture to look at for long—the baby's face is contorted in the agony of abandonment, but she wears the emotion the rest of the subjects convey without crying.

The more I shuffle pictures, the more I see another possible idea, a gradual aging of the subject. I can begin with the baby and move through the youngest of my mother's students, up to preadoles-cence. I can even use my old, first pictures of Rozzie with the pea-cock feather and our grandmother's shawl. When I print up a new version of this picture, I'm amazed at how good it is and what I never realized I had. A beautiful girl who wears no makeup, but seems already to understand the power of her naked good looks. She stares into the camera with more raw sexuality than I ever remember at the time, terrifyingly young and beautiful at the same time.

By including this picture, Rozzie's face becomes a thread through the show, but it isn't the main thing, because I end on myself, one of the portraits of me running toward the chair. I don't know how others will read this, but for me it makes sense; it means the story of my life ends with me, looking at my own back, my own lines.

* * *

Rozzie arrives on Friday with Timothy in a rental car. She looks different from the last time I saw her, more clearly and obviously blind. I watch from the window as she steps out of the car and stands beside her closed passenger door. Though she knows this path well—this is *her* house, after all, not his—she waits for him to come around and lead her home. My heart falls at this servile gesture.

For the rest of the night, there are echoes of this. In one story, she talks about Timothy going downtown to run an errand for her; in another, she talks about Timothy picking out the clothes she is wearing.

Wait a minute, I want to say. *He's picked out your outfit?*

I know I'm only irritated because I cannot quiet the storm of insecurity raging in my chest. Timothy seems like a nice man, no doubt smart, kind to her, and attentive. But I don't want to be thinking about him or her. With the prospect of this show, I want to think only about myself, have every conversation be about my work and me. I want someone to go through my entire oeuvre, piece by piece, and find new adjectives to compliment it all.

Instead, the night is spent asking Rozzie questions about her life in New York, listening to answers that stun all of us: "I've been cooking a lot for Timothy. Sometimes I make his lunch and he takes it to school."

Even our mother's jaw drops at this: "You do?"

His head bobs like a bespectacled marionette's. "Delicious ones."

Later, back at Theo's apartment, in his room, lying in a T-shirt next to his warm body, I go over all this, how different she seems, how disturbingly transformed.

"Why don't you give her a break," Theo whispers into the back of my neck. "She's legally blind and living in New York. Of course she's going to sound dependent on him. She has to be. She has to find someone she can ask to help her."

"It's not that. It's fine that he's here. I'm happy for her. I *am*." I try to decide what I'm really upset about. "It's just that at any given event or gathering, even if it's just the two of us, the contents of her life are always more compelling than the contents of mine. I have a show—or half a show, anyway—and we still spend most of the night discussing her life."

Theo thinks about this and nods. "It's true, we did."

"Doesn't that seem ironic maybe? Or even wrong?" I don't know if this is what I'm mad about. I wish I could put my finger on it.

"A lot of the time, you're the one asking her the questions, making her do all the talking."

And of course, he's right. My own impulses mystify me.

Rozzie

Packing for the trip, Rozzie was giddy at the prospect of three uninterrupted days with Timothy; alone in the car, he would have no classes, no lab to get back to, no meetings to attend. As she laid in her shirts and a dress for the party, she spun out the stories in her head that she wanted to tell him, imagined all the places she would show him, landmarks of the childhood she wanted him to know.

Now that she's here, it's harder than she thought. Though she sees less now than she did four months ago, she feels their eyes on her, the weight of their eternal expectation. They like Timothy fine—that's not the problem. It's—what is it? They want more from her. Or Jemma does.

After dinner their first night home, she and Timothy go for a walk. For a long time, they say nothing. Finally, he breaks a stick. "Your family's interesting," he says.

Oh, God, she thinks, *here it comes.* He's going to say something either mean or else so true she'll feel unmoored by it, lost somewhere between him and them.

Before he can say anything, she offers this: "There's something I haven't told you. A few months ago my sister took pictures of me without my knowledge and sold them to a newspaper. I assume in some twisted way she thought she was doing it for me because she gave me the money she made from it. I took the check, but we've never once talked about it." This sounds so odd, suddenly.

"What did you use the money for?"

"My computer."

He knows the machine well, has marveled at the things it can do for her—read her mail, a book aloud; it can even read a script slowly enough for her to memorize lines. "So it did help you."

"Yes. I suppose."

"So maybe it wasn't so awful."

She tries to explain. "In my business, my image is as much a commodity as your research is in yours. I don't like it, but I have to be very careful who takes my picture and where it appears. Especially given the situation with my eyes."

"Okay."

"So that's that." She wonders what he is thinking.

For a long time, they don't say anything.

Finally he bumps his shoulder into hers. "I don't know if this applies or not, but when I was in eighth grade, my older brother joined a jazz band that turned out to be really good and played weekends around the city at weddings and parties. He started wearing these great suits with baggy pants and hanging out with older guys. A year earlier he'd been a complete dork, then there was this transformation in the span of a few months. I thought maybe he was going to drop out of school and start taking drugs or something. I didn't know, but I got so freaked out, one night I poured vegetable oil into his trumpet, which gums up the keys and ruins it."

She waits for him to explain why he has told this story. "It's hard being a younger sibling. You have to watch your god change. Or goddess." He pats her hand. "Maybe she didn't want anything to change."

"What happened with your brother?"

"Nothing. He got the trumpet cleaned and fixed. He kept playing. Eventually, I got into martial arts and I stopped caring so much. I became—you know—what I am now: an incredibly cool judo guy."

She laughs. For so many years she has felt unlike other people—her experience shared by so few others, all of whom were too edgy and unsure of themselves to be friends for long. Inevitably work or something came between them. It is a truth seldom spoken, but fill a room with successful actors and actresses and find a group of people with surprisingly few friends. Only her family softened the feeling of loneliness that used to creep over her.

It finally occurs to her what she wants from Timothy is something akin to what she's had with her family: a durable tie, inevitability. She and her family have survived the silences, have weathered the distance secrets created. The obligatory phone calls, made week after week, speaking so often of nothing that mattered, became a ribbon of voices that saved her from the darkness. To her great surprise, she suddenly realizes these are the relationships she feels most proud of. Forgiveness has worked quietly, in the shadows of this family. That they are all here is a measure of the love they never express.

Jemma

The next morning I go back home to eat breakfast with my family. Rozzie comes into the kitchen and, as soon as she figures out we're alone together, comes closer. She seems to have something she's been waiting to ask me. "Are there going to be any pictures of me?"

"A few. Not that many." I hesitate. "I've picked ones where you're hardly recognizable. One is a silhouette. Another is the back of your head, and one is from years ago." I hesitate here. "That first one I ever took." My voice strains to be casual.

She stares at a spot beside my elbow. "Weren't you in the tenth grade when you took that?"

"Yeah, but it's a good picture. Or it's an interesting one. It fits in with the others I've included."

Here she surprises me. "How so?" Her tone is simple; she doesn't mean how do *I* fit in, she means the picture.

I take a deep breath and I tell her. "It's all pictures with only one person in the frame. As it happens, most of them are girls or women, and there's a progression of ages, so it's almost a coming of age. How girls discover their bodies, their looks, themselves. That picture works because you look young, but it's the first time I remember you looking really beautiful. There's a quality of discovery to it." I hesitate for a moment. "I know you were critical of those pictures, but you really do look beautiful. I promise."

She closes her eyes and nods. "It's fine."

I assume the conversation is over, which is okay. I'm grateful for what she's given me—an opening to talk about my work, permission to use her face, which I know, in a perfect world, she'd rather I didn't. This is her gift to me.

Then she says, "Could I go early, with you, and try to look at them?"

She is standing in the doorway, her back to me.

This is so unexpected I'm not sure what to say. For some reason, I think of the first play she was ever in, which I refused to go to. I wonder if she has all along been more generous than I.

"Sure. We could go right now, if you want."

She nods and steps back into the room. "Okay."

We don't talk in the car ride over. In the parking lot, she gets out and stands by her door as I watched her do in our driveway with Timothy. I assume this means it is not a gesture of new-girlfriend supplication; that she sees so little, she's decided it's safer this way, to wait and be led. So then why are we coming to look at these pictures?

I lead her inside, speak to the director of special events at the library, who tells us it's fine, she'll walk us upstairs and open the door for us.

I love this space—blond wood floors, white walls, high ceilings with skylight windows. On a sunny day, as this is, light fills the room and bounces off the walls. All of the photographs are black-and-white; though Margaret's are by the door, mine are larger, more noticeable at first. When Rozzie walks in, she moves across the room straight toward the first one of mine, the baby crying, and I wonder if this is the reason I've been printing so large, wielding portfolios I can hardly manage onto subways, covering whole walls with a single print—all to give Rozzie something she might just be able to see.

And she can.

There's no question. She is right in front of it, my sad, sad baby, crying for an eternity, and Rozzie is leaning in to it, studying the huge, pudgy feet. When she turns around, there are tears in her eyes.

"It's a baby, right?" she whispers. "Right?"

"Yes."

I cross the room and stand next to her. She starts laughing and crying at the same time. "It makes no sense. Sometimes I can see things. Little flashes. Bits of things."

She turns, moves toward the next picture, a student portrait. She shakes her head, whispers, "Too dark"—not a criticism, but a fact for her, and moves on. She gets to the one of her in high school and spins around, smiling now unmistakably. "Hey, you're right. This one isn't too bad."

She keeps going quickly, explains it won't last long, that she has to see as much as she can while she has the chance. She doesn't make it all the way to the end and the picture of my back. About five pictures from it, she turns around and walks away. "That's it. Let me just rest for a second on this bench."

She sits for a while with her eyes closed, drawing deep breaths through her nose. Apparently this has taken it out of her. Finally she opens her eyes. "They're good. Very good. I like them."

I nod and thank her.

"It's very unpredictable, this seeing thing. I wish I understood it better."

"Have you told the doctors?"

"I told one. He said he didn't know what it meant."

"Do other people have it?"

"I've never met anyone, but I've read about it. Supposedly it's not that uncommon. I don't like it much, actually. It throws me off. But in this case, it's nice." She folds her lips together as if she'd rather not talk about it anymore.

That's that, apparently. She doesn't want to dwell on this or marvel in the wonder of it. She even asks me not to tell anyone. I wonder if there's more to it that she's not saying, but I don't press. It's enough, I know, that we've come this far—that she's used whatever sight she has to see what I'm doing, to look at me. I take her hand and squeeze it. "Thanks for wanting to come here."

She nods and smiles as if I'm being funny or sentimental. "Well, sure. We came all this way."

Her last night in town she asks if I'd like to take a walk. Except for going to see my pictures, we haven't done anything alone the whole three days she's been home. We've gone out with our men and allowed them to carry the bulk of the conversation. I have mostly stepped back, allowed Timothy to do the things she needs done.

This time she brings her cane, but she doesn't unfold it.

Instead, outside the front door, she tucks her hand in my elbow. She turns her face to the sun and says, "I like Theo." She seems to be leading to something, but says no more.

"I'm glad. So do I."

"What's wrong with him exactly? Why does he limp?"

This is such an old issue, I've almost forgotten about it. "He had cerebral palsy. But it was mild. It doesn't seem like that much of an issue anymore."

"So it's not going to get worse?"

"No. I don't think so. It hasn't in all these years."

"That's good."

We continue for a while. "Why? What made you ask about that?"

"I guess I was wondering if you'd be taking care of him at some point."

"No. I don't think it's like that."

It's a funny conversation—her worried about something that hasn't crossed my mind.

"Do you think you'll marry him?"

"I'm not ready to get married yet."

"Hmm . . ." She thinks about this for a while. "I am," she finally says.

"Why?"

"I'm not sure. I just want that. I want someone who stays in my life for better or worse. I like that idea."

"That's nice." I squeeze her hand with my arm. This is as sentimental as we can be with each other, as close as we can come to saying what we have been. I think about the mystery she has always been to me and wonder if I added to it, for my own purposes—if I needed her to elude me so I always have something elusive just ahead. Surely it wasn't easy to play this role. It required staying in motion, perpetually performing to a ubiquitous audience, to air charged with expectation. Maybe she's an actress because I made her be one. Or maybe that, too, is an exaggeration of my power.

I can't say for sure.

But here we are now, out walking the street we grew up on, going nowhere specifically, just into the sun, which is all around us. "Lead on," she says, and for a long time we walk, saying nothing.

ACKNOWLEDGMENTS

Of the many books that were of help to me, *Planet of the Blind* by Stephen Kuusisto and *Sight Unseen* by Georgina Kleege were especially useful in detailing so beautifully how the "legally blind" see. I am also indebted to *The Art of Seeing* by Aldous Huxley, a book I found both fascinating and obviously notable for its catchy title.

Many thanks to dear friends and early readers of this book who gave insightful comments and also kept me going when confidence wavered: Christina Adam, Bay Anapol, Stacey D'Erasmo, Gordon Kato, Diane Wood Brown. And to my lovely writing group: William Diehl, Rachel Haas, Robin Lewis, Ben James, and especially Jeannie Birdsall, who added her gifts not only as a discerning reader and fellow writer, but as a photographer, as well. I feel immeasurably lucky to have found Eric Simonoff as an agent and Gillian Blake as an editor, both of whom do their jobs with great skill and good cheer.

A special thanks to Elizabeth Haas, whose friendship has sustained me in writing and life; to my grandmother, who bought me my first computer; to my sister, who believed I should be a writer long before I entertained such a dream for myself. It's hard to find words to thank my mother for all she has given me, except to say I'm certain this book would not exist without her extraordinary faith in it. And last, thank you to Mike, Ethan, and Charlie, the boys I love even more than writing.